T 44084
12.00

>>> FILE DUMP <<<

FILE DIRECTORY

>>> FILE DUMP <<<

REPORT TO FIELD OPERATIVES

ÆON TRINITY TRANSMISSION [NEPTUNE DIVISION]

Extraterrestrial Office, Deputy Office Director Giorgios Alekandros Gamemenos

Fellow Æon Members —

The recently exposed Huang-Marr conspiracy — involving rogue psions pursuing immoral research — shook society's faith in the psi orders. Ironically, it took an alien attack on our Solar System to help restore humanity's confidence in psions.

Although human forces dispatched the savage Chromatics with authority, the aliens' first venture to Earth came as a complete surprise. Rather than address this concern, though, the United Nations — and, admittedly, the Æon Trinity — maintained attention on rooting out corrupt psions. We became overconfident, assuming that the threat posed by the "demon lizards" had been dealt with.

A few intrepid individuals did not let the Chromatic issue lie, however. They pursued the strongest lead humanity had on the aliens — the Crab Nebula, where Chromatics had battled colonists at the Karroo colony for half a decade. A captured alien revealed that the Chromatics had discovered the secret of interstellar travel from enslaved Upeo wa Macho — humanity's vanished teleporters.

It appeared that the aliens located and captured their Upeo prisoners based on information given to them by beings they called "gods of light." Æon intel-analysis teams are split on how to interpret this information. Some suggest that an elite "priesthood" acts as the Chromatic government — and thus *all* orders come "from the gods." Others believe these "gods" are the mysterious alien Doyen. Little is known of these secretive beings as they are not prone to intervention. However, based on previous research, the Doyen are generally thought to be kindly disposed toward humanity.

Whatever the Chromatics' source of information, it allowed them to force the Upeo to transport the aliens across the stars. Humanity barely learned of the second, more massive, Chromatic invasion in time. Mankind — psion and neutral — worked together to defend the race from the alien attack. The horror of Huang-Marr lingers with us, but the psi orders proved that such corruption is the exception to the rule. Psions are still dedicated to humanity's defense.

This brings us again to the Chromatics. It is of vital importance that we rescue our long-lost Upeo comrades. The teleporters' abilities represent a key strategic advantage that must be returned to our hands, certainly. But we cannot in good conscience leave humans in alien hands.

Toward that end, the United Nations with Æon Trinity and psi order support, is preparing a massive assault and extraction mission that will leave for the Chromatic homeworld (dubbed "Chrome-Prime") in just over two weeks' time. It will encompass a ruthless elimination of the infrastructure necessary to maintain the Chromatic presence in space and the recovery of any and all teleporters on the planet.

Your team is assigned to the task of scouting a medical site on Chrome-Prime where injured Upeo are treated, and rescuing any humans you find. As part of our efforts to aid the UN endeavor, one of our Triton research teams is currently interrogating a Chromatic prisoner dubbed "Vermilion." These interviews shall hopefully gather data salient to this mission. You will receive transportation from bay R-106 at Yutu Yinchon Spaceport to the interview facility in the Haoa Flint lunar base, scheduled for departure on April 22, 8:30 AM Lunar Standard Time. Investigator Emily Gaboriau is on hand at Haoa Flint to provide you with further details.

Best of luck,
Gamemenos
Extraterrestrial Office, 21:54:13 4.20.2121

Hope Sacrifice Unity

Illegal Medical Experiments Exposed, Psions Implicated

Members of Æsculapians, Orgotek Participated in "Biorg" Project

INTERNATIONAL CENTER, OLYMPUS, LUNA — The Æon Trinity announced in a press conference yesterday that a team of investigators uncovered and brought to justice the perpetrators of a criminal series of medical experiments involving the theft, modification, and regrafting of human organs. These illegal tests intended to create a more formidable human warrior.

Angel Rigault, representing Æon, claimed that the "Huang-Marr Bio-organism Interface Project" was orchestrated by a small group of psions operating independently within the Æsculapian and Orgotek orders. He further claimed that all the conspirators were captured, and all data pertaining to the illicit experiments had been relayed to the United Nations for scrutiny.

The conspiracy first came to public attention several months ago, when a supposed Aberrant was blamed for many missing persons in Olympus' Downside. Æon investigators later revealed that the Huang-Marr researchers were, in fact, responsible for kidnapping individuals with genetic material appropriate for their work and using them as parts. Victims were apparently selected based on Æsculapian clinic records. The so-called "biorg" created in these experiments received experimental bioware reportedly modified to utilize taint radiation. In fact, investigators unearthed an Aberrant who was helping the human conspirators. The biorg test subject, apparently driven insane from the implants, murdered at least one individual before being brought down at the Montressor Clinic.

According to Mr. Rigault, the last of the Huang-Marr conspirators were either killed or captured during the recent Chromatic raid on an Earth orbital station. The UN recently appointed a special committee to investigate these claims, and to determine the extent of other possible corruption within the psi orders.

UN Initiates Full Psion Investigation

Concerns About Malfeasance High

In the wake of the scandals that have rocked several of the psi orders, the UN announced the creation of an investigatory committee with the task of uncovering the extent of the Huang-Marr conspiracy, and if other conspiracies still exist within the psion community.

The committee's initial investigation took place behind closed doors. Sufficient evidence was found to warrant full-scale hearings, which entail depositions from Æon associates involved in the exposure of the Huang-Marr conspirators, and explore whether several unnamed high-ranking psions from the Æsculapian and Orgotek orders were also involved. Other scheduled witnesses include experts on Aberrants and Chromatics.

The chair of the committee is Vice-Director Philip Bacciocci, of the UN's Department of Psion Relations. In recent years Bacciocci has been noted for his hard-line stance against what he calls, "the unbalancing intrusion of psions into issues of world government, out of proportion to the percentage of the population that they comprise." The other committee members have taken a variety of stances on psion issues, with Council on Human Rights Abuses Director Felicia McMullen in furthest contrast to Bacciocci. Nevertheless, sources within the Æon Trinity have expressed concern that the committee may be a facade for a "witch hunt" designed to weaken the psi orders, to the UN's gain.

HAOA FLINT STATION>>>ÆON ARCHIVE

SURVEY: HAOA FLINT STATION

SAFRA AUSBURN, ENGINEER REPORT, 3.7.2116

Overall, the facility will suit our needs, although the United Nations left it in poor shape. Its military forces are a bit paranoid about psychometry and they removed everything that might hold a psi trace, down to bare metal. We're going to have to bring in everything — not just desks and chairs, but even some fairly large bits of infrastructure. The specs are geared toward privacy, so I recommend using a radial plan with a heavy-security paradigm.

Interisio Lunar Contractors would be our best bet for this. They're industrial-commercial, and they've worked with Æon before. They've got the requisite sources for the security gear we'll need, too — including the Class-4 steel doors and Class-3 steel walls, ceilings and floors indicated in the specs. We should handle the computer internally, though.

STATION MAINTENANCE REPORT

1.23.2120

Today marks the completion of Haoa Flint's first six months of service as a privately contracted, Æon-administrated station. The jump-ship administration offices have been relocated successfully to Mare Ingenii and we have tenants in five of the eight sections with no measurable strain on the facilities.

Unfortunately, the same can not be said of my maintenance staff. The security procedures in place make access to the separate sections slow at best. The various sections are reluctant to let in station technicians, citing security concerns. This makes routine maintenance impossible, leading to an increase in failures. My people are let inside once something breaks, of course, but we invariably get blamed for letting it break in the first place.

STATION MAINTENANCE REPORT

1.27.2121

At the request of Emily Gaboriau in Section 3, two D-cells have been refitted. D1 has been reinforced and D4 has been refitted from cell to quarters. Further, the partitions on either side of C2 (facing into C1 and C3, respectively) have been fitted with one-way glass. This permits viewing from C2 into either adjacent chamber. Also, tables and chairs in C1 and C3 have been bolted down.

Gaboriau asked if the one-way glass was opaque to frequencies from 10^{13} to 10^{16} Hz. When informed that it was not, she requested that it be replaced or upgraded to block those frequencies.

>>> End closure report <<<

The Future of Medicine

Æsculapian Purges Continue
— Waltara Griffin, © 2120 *Opwire* chipzine

With the Huang-Marr conspiracy exposed, the leadership of the Æsculapian Order is trying to restore its prior image as a group of selfless healers. The revelation that elements within the order were engaged in positively Frankensteinian experimentation on humans has shaken public confidence in the once-respected vitakinetics.

The "Basel Elite," as they are called, comprise Proxy Matthieu Zweidler, Dr. Karl Mullenhoff, Pierce Monahan and much of the Æsculapian's top administrators. They are actively engaged in an attempt to eliminate those elements of the order that display a public image not in keeping with their own largely technocratic leanings.

The famous Port-au-Prince branch of the order, noted for its encouragement of healing practices that are at odds with "accepted" European medical tradition, is subject to an investigation (and winnowing) unlike any previously encountered in its already-controversial history. Sources within the Port-au-Prince office indicate that over 20 vitakinetics there are on suspension in the order, and are forbidden to practice their abilities further. Whether these edicts will be honored remains to be seen.

There is some concern in the medical community that the purges will also include those very researchers who have made the most radical breakthroughs in vitakinesis and the medical sciences. Research and experimentation, seen as the focus of the Huang-Marr conspirators, have suffered in the backlash. The Basel Elite is strongly encouraging a return to tried-and-true methods. Medical experimentation, in and of itself, has come to be seen as dangerous and unethical. Those with long memories will recall that biotechnological research (quite a different practice from modern biotech) suffered similarly in the previous century, as the public claimed such experimentation resulted in Aberrant mutation.

In this writer's opinion, the valid concerns about ethical behavior among the vitakinetics should not and can not be allowed to halt medical research. Despite the dramatic improvements in humanity's individual and collective physical health over the past decades, there are still a thousand areas where further exploration is necessary. Even the highly controversial field of human augmentation must continue to receive attention.

The human race today faces threats unmatched in its history. It is not only prudent to improve ourselves to meet them, it is necessary. The psions can not stand alone; the non-latent human must have the ability to compete on his own terms with foes like the Aberrants and Chromatics. While hardtech is constantly improving the lethality of the average soldier, intrinsic faculties and powers will always triumph over equivalent, but external, tools.

This writer urges the Basel Elite to reconsider their hard-line attitude, and to once again embrace experimentation in their order. While the means of the Huang-Marr organization were unethical and criminal, their goals were noble. Their research may someday prove to be the keystone of humanity's defense.

20 Questions with Susan N'gamba

— Cori Heisler, *The Painful Truth* © 2120 MMI

Susan N'gamba is a key figure in recent human-psion-alien relations. She has an impressive military record with the UAN, and served as a liaison with the Upeo wa Macho Order. As the mayor of Karroo Colony, she was instrumental in gathering the information that prepared humanity for the recent Chromatic invasion. In the course of that event, Ms. N'gamba revealed that she was a teleporter herself. As one of the first Upeo to return to Earth, she is currently representing the order in the UN psion hearings.

PT: Good morning, Mayor N'gamba, and thank you for joining us.

SN: Thank you for having me, Cori. By the way, it's not "mayor" anymore. I've resigned as mayor of Karroo Colony.

PT: What led you to that decision?

SN: I knew that my *de facto* position as speaker for the Upeo made it necessary that I remain in Earth-space. Notse Eyadema, my former executive assistant, is serving as mayor *pro tem* pending elections. He's doing a fine job, so I imagine the post will become permanent.

PT: You say "*de facto*." I gather you didn't expect to end up as the representative of the teleporters?

SN: Not at all. I didn't even realize it had happened until 10 minutes after I'd teleported into the General Assembly. Suddenly, I was "The First of the Returning Upeo." I'd been almost too wrapped up in the Chromatic threat to see the obvious. Of course, I'm fully prepared to step down once Proxy Atwan returns.

PT: That raises a huge question about your proxy and your order. We'll get to that in a bit, though. First, let's talk about you.

SN: [laughs] My favorite topic.

PT: You're being called the savior of humanity for bringing the warning of the Chromatic invasion to the UN. Do you feel you've earned that accolade?

SN: [laughs] I'm almost modest enough to deny it, but I'm not too proud to admit I had help. I was just part of a team at every step. Apparently, somebody decided I'm the most hologenic.

PT: That's certainly what the people who schedule my interviews think—hard to get more hologenic than a teleporter with a distinguished military and government record! So how did you learn of the planned invasion?

SN: I was in the right place at the right time. An Æon team came to Karroo and captured one of the Chromatics that lurk in the Crab Nebula. It was the first time that we had the right combination of people and

tools to get information out of one of those aliens.

PT: And you brought the info to the UN.

SN: I… [hesitates] I knew that humanity would be caught unprepared. I knew that the only jump ship on hand wasn't ready to return to Earth in time. I had to break my cover.

PT: Why were you and the Upeo in hiding in the first place?

SN: That's a complex question…. In the simplest terms, Proxy Atwan decided that we teleporters were in danger of becoming "slaves" to the other orders, serving as a taxi service. She ordered us to leave, and go into hiding.

PT: Do you think that was a wise decision?

SN: The proxy had access to far more information than I did, or do now.

PT: Hmm… That's not much of an answer, but I get the feeling that's all I'm going to get. All right; what prompted you personally to reveal yourself?

SN: I weighed the cost to humanity versus my duty to the Upeo. It wasn't an easy choice.

PT: And how did the Æon Trinity and the orders react to your reappearance?

SN: Oh, they were very pleased to have a teleporter again — almost too pleased. Negotiations regarding the Upeo's future position are under way.

PT: What do you think that position should be?

SN: The Upeo are perfectly able to follow the dictates of their consciences regarding their duty to humanity. We will not be caged.

PT: Do you really think the powers-that-be would "cage" you?

SN: I'd hate to try to predict their actions. I'm not a clear, after all.

PT: Let's hope it never comes to that, anyway. On a different tack, what role did you play during the actual Chromatic invasion?

SN: Well, it was obvious that human safety was best served by destroying the Chromie mother ships as quickly as possible. Unfortunately, there were captured teleporters on those ships.

The team I was with was given *carte blanche* to try to save as many as we could, but we knew that the fleet couldn't afford to worry about our safety.

PT: How successful were you?

SN: We managed to rescue only one teleporter from a single mother ship. Less than I'd hoped for, but even so, we were lucky.

PT: How many teleporters remain in Chromatic captivity?

SN: Unknown. Too many. We've got to rescue them.

PT: That's why the United Nations is spearheading the organization of an invasion fleet, correct?

SN: I'm not at liberty to discuss that, actually.

PT: Of course not. Still, it's impossible to keep a fleet that size secret, especially one camped out right on Luna's doorstep. And considering the UN and the psi orders stepped up military efforts in the wake of the Chromatic attack, it doesn't

take a genius to figure out what's happening.

SN: Is that another question, Cori?

PT: [laughs] No; good point. That's a topic for another show. All right, what do you regard as being in your personal future?

SN: I'm going to continue to represent my fellow teleporters as long as my services are needed, and protect humanity from all threats.

PT: How's that go? "Foreign or domestic?"

SN: [laughs] Yes, indeed.

PT: Given your stature, have you considered becoming the new Upeo Proxy if Bolade Atwan doesn't return?

SN: There's more to being proxy than stature.

PT: Regarding all the events of the last few months, is there anything you wish you'd done differently?

SN: I can't change what's happened. Now is the time to focus on the future.

PT: Any last thoughts?

SN: Oh, "freedom," "hope," "unity." Stuff like that.

Olympus Screamer

"Lift a rock on the Rock and we're there"

HOT TOPICS — HOT TOPICS — HOT TOPICS

touch " ▶ " for stories

Headline
▶ Aberrant attacks on rise!
> ▶ What do they mean, "more systematic?"

Exposé
▶ UN psion investigations continue, blame here, blame there, blame everywhere.
> ▶ Survey: Can psions be trusted?

Earthwatch
▶ "Pyrocides" continue in Rio. Is an escaped Chromie to blame?
> ▶ Kostbaar's new Chromie-inspired fashions. Cutting edge, or sick 'n twisted?

Interview
▶ Swab that vacuum: In the space navy with Phoenix Squadron.
> ▶ Fleet buildup continues. We gonna bust some heads?

Rampant Innuendo
▶ Cori's been a bad girl. Rumor rocks our competitor's career.

Shameless Self-aggrandizement
> ▶ Meet our lawyers! Mean, aren't they?

REGULAR FEATURES — REGULAR FEATURES
▶ Off With Our Heads: Word from the Honcho-in-Chief
▶ Kill no Trees: Back to France
▶ Visual Bytes: Reviewed, *Hook Hammond*, *Bova-Beasts*
▶ Back to Front: Psions Investigated and the Newer Economy

▶ SELECTION CONFIRMED: RIO "PYROCIDES"

A series of shocking murders in Rio de Janeiro's Paris Square district has left the city huddled and hiding. As of this week, 17 citizens from all demographics have been found dead, all charred to the bone. Police forensics experts state that the injuries are almost certainly caused by pyrokinetic abilities. They further claim that the frequencies and techniques apparently used do not match known pyrokinetic methods.

Witness reports are few, but match in several details. The perpetrator is described as hunched and dark, with unusual spots of glowing color. Several witnesses have mentioned a loping or leaping gait. Most believe that the murderer is non-human, and rumors of an escaped Chromatic have spread widely.

The Brazilian government, Norça and Æon Trinity have ignored inquiries asking if any Chromatic captives from the recent invasion are incarcerated in Rio. Local authorities are sweeping the area, but report no conclusive results.

"ALIEN ON THE LOOSE" >>>ISAIAH MON VICH

REPORT: YELTSINGRAD

>>> **Warning:** Other headers suppressed. This is an unsecured document. To protect their identities, operative names have been replaced and referential pronouns conformed to male. <<<

As of this date, we have seven operatives placed in or near the Floor, the President's entertainment compound. Operative Philaster is an assistant security secretary in charge of the Floor's third baccarat room. Operative Pharamond remains in the entertainment division, working mainly as a life model off of which the holodancers are based. Operative Dion has no official position in the President's organization, but he is recognized as a regular gambler. Operatives Cleremont and Thrasiline's small medical services booth is still in operation, and has changed location to the first ring outside the Floor. Operatives Arethusa and Euphrasia are currently posing as persons of no discernible occupation, primarily moving in the outer circles of the Pit.

And as of yet, Philaster and Pharamond have not been successful in penetrating the last lines of security surrounding the President. Pharamond believes that certain members of the entertainment division do perform for the President personally, but he cannot confirm this. He notes that those he suspects as being the President's personal performers seem to be more content, but also more exhausted and sickly than the regular Floor performers.

Philaster's role is not proving to be the breakthrough we expected. The details now available to him on security procedures are no more extensive than those we had obtained through simple observation. In particular, he has not been told any details regarding the psionic security in place. We have obtained no further clues on the identity of the First Secretary, but we have increased our confidence ratings to 90% on gender (male), to 73% on race (Asian), and to 71% on origin (Australia). Philaster has not come within 100 meters of the President.

Through his regular visits to the Floor, Dion has engaged just over half of the known members of the President's staff in conversation. >>> excerpts attached <<< Data analysis shows that 92% are content with their positions and 74% are strongly loyal to the President. None would provide details of the President's background, and voice-stress indicator's suggest less than 5% have

such details. No more than 8% of the staff interviewed have actually had face-to-face contact with the President.

CONVERSATION IN THE PIT

— **Excerpt: Audiofile, operative Dion and Secretary Donald Phindle (one of the President's staff members)**

Phindle: Thanks for the drink, cutie. Can you stay and talk for a bit? I could use the company.

Dion: Is this 20 a tip?

Phindle: Yeh.

Dion: Then I can stay and talk, pal. Tell me about yourself.

Phindle: Oh, I came up the well from the 'States. I didn't always live by the rules and the FSA bosses don't care for that sort of thing, yeh? That's why I came here. The Boss Lady knows exactly when to stop making rules and start letting people do their own thing.

Dion: I couldn't agree more. The Floor does right by me. Which reminds me, I've got a bet on with a friend that I'll never meet someone who's met the Prez themselves.

Phindle: You'll gamble on anything, won't you?

Dion: You been watching me, cutie?

Phindle: The President doesn't pay people to be stupid, my pal. And no, I've never met her.

Dion: So tell me more about what rules you broke. I love dangerous men.

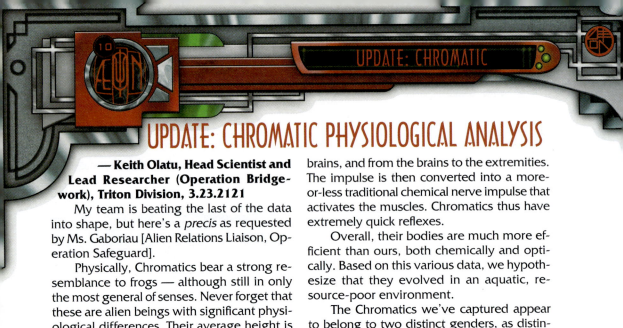

UPDATE: CHROMATIC PHYSIOLOGICAL ANALYSIS

— Keith Olatu, Head Scientist and Lead Researcher (Operation Bridgework), Triton Division, 3.23.2121

My team is beating the last of the data into shape, but here's a *precis* as requested by Ms. Gaboriau [Alien Relations Liaison, Operation Safeguard].

Physically, Chromatics bear a strong resemblance to frogs — although still in only the most general of senses. Never forget that these are alien beings with significant physiological differences. Their average height is 175 centimeters, weight 80+ kilos. The arms are well developed, and terminate in three-fingered hands with opposable thumbs.

They possess two pairs of eyes, and photon-sensitive organs all over their bodies, particularly in the head region. Furthermore, they can emit light over a wide range of frequencies. These sensing and projection abilities are controlled by the upper brain, located in the head. Higher thought is controlled by a larger secondary brain, which is halfway down the torso.

Their basic chemistry is similar to our own, including structures akin to DNA, amino acids, *et cetera*. They absorb oxygen and some nutrients through their skin, in either air or water. They consume food much as we do; their mouth is a vertical opening roughly between their arms. They show a preference for meat, and after some acclimation our captives consumed beef and other animal products with no pronounced ill effects. They do seem to show signs of vitamin deficiencies that we are unable to satisfy, however.

In addition to absorbing light from their environment and processing it into chemical energy through a process not unlike photosynthesis, the Chromatic nervous system appears to be partially optical. Their nervous system is composed of a central trunk of tubes lined with bioluminescent patches and light-sensitive spots, and branches of more conventional nerves. This allows for the lightspeed transmission of nerve impulses between the brains, and from the brains to the extremities. The impulse is then converted into a more-or-less traditional chemical nerve impulse that activates the muscles. Chromatics thus have extremely quick reflexes.

Overall, their bodies are much more efficient than ours, both chemically and optically. Based on this various data, we hypothesize that they evolved in an aquatic, resource-poor environment.

The Chromatics we've captured appear to belong to two distinct genders, as distinguished by the genitalia along the insides of the legs. The details of their reproductive process are unknown, but they seem to be egg layers. This is very tentative; there may even be a third gender involved in the process.

They are, on average, not as intelligent as a typical human. This and various linguistic indicators suggest a primitive society that is difficult to reconcile with its obvious technological level. Going into the tech and the language would take too long here; look for that in the main report. (And no, we still haven't figured out why or how the toadie ships are based on our designs, but it's clear they are. We've got plenty of theories, though.)

All the Chromatics we've studied have been extremely powerful photokinetic specialists in addition to their innate, biological light-manipulating abilities. All rate at least 80% on the Orgotek photokinetic test, and they are capable of astounding holographic tricks. Some also have the abilities of pyrokinesis and electromanipulation, but they rate much lower in those fields. A few evidenced some damn surprising attempts to escape using holographic trickery. Just to be safe, we're keeping them all in damping harnesses now.

I should point out that all of our subjects are apparently the equivalent of soldiers, and thus, may not represent the Chromatic norm. Though our questioning indicates that they come from a large society of similar beings, it is possible that they are lying, and are (for example) genetically engineered warriors

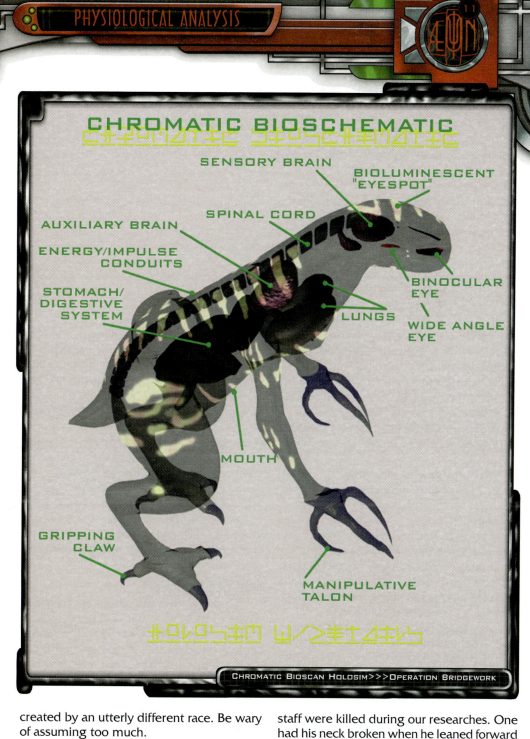

CHROMATIC BIOSCHEMATIC

SENSORY BRAIN

BIOLUMINESCENT "EYESPOT"

SPINAL CORD

AUXILIARY BRAIN

ENERGY/IMPULSE CONDUITS

STOMACH/ DIGESTIVE SYSTEM

BINOCULAR EYE

LUNGS

WIDE ANGLE EYE

MOUTH

GRIPPING CLAW

MANIPULATIVE TALON

Chromatic Bioscan Holosim >>> Operation Bridgework

created by an utterly different race. Be wary of assuming too much.

While I'm giving warnings, please exercise extreme caution around Chromatic prisoners. Even without their psi powers, Chromatics are formidable fighters. Two of my staff were killed during our researches. One had his neck broken when he leaned forward a fraction too far. Chromatic reflexes are so fast, he never knew what hit him.

Good luck.

Keith Olatu

CHROMATIC HOMEWORLD, DESIGNATE: "CHROME-PRIME"

Filename: Chrome-Prime Data and Theories
Filetype: Polytype data, volatile
Filesubtype: Precis
Division: Triton, Xenoscience Department
Encryption: DSE
Lastfilemod: 4:50:27 4.10.2121

>>> Warning: This is a volatile document. File may change without notice. Do not modify without locking corecopy. <<<

>>> Warning: This is an agent-generated precis. Due to the limits of satisfactory intelligence, SI-generated summaries are not guaranteed to be contextually intact. <<<

>>> Warning: Level 3 clearance required for access. <<<

This file is an attempt to collate data gathered from our studies of the Chromatic aliens in custody (including biological and linguistic indicators) into a coherent picture of the Chromatic homeworld. The backbone of this text, however, is formed from a series of interviews with Clarence Greaves, a member of the Upeo wa Macho recently rescued from Chromatic captivity.

Excerpt: Greaves interview, 10.14.2120/2 [audiofile conversion]

Most of the little bastards' civilization is underground, I think. Their system of caves and tunnels is vast, and I got the impression that was how they *all* lived. I saw only a few actual in-use living quarters — if you call what those fucks do "living." We were kept at one point in what I guess was a disused "home," some kind of smoothed-out cave.

They live deep, close to water of some kind, either standing or running. The lizards don't go near the surface for days at a time, and I think they only go up because they have to, for the war. Demonic fucks.

Excerpt: Greaves interview, 10.17.2120/1 [audiofile conversion]

Breezes from above were always dry. Breezes from below were always wet. I guess the surface of the planet just dried out. I never saw where the water ended up, but there might be underground lakes.

Excerpt: Greaves interview, 10.20.2120/2 [audiofile conversion]

The surface looks like Mars. Maybe a little more yellow in the sand, and the sky is a deeper red. It's dry. Skin-cracking dry, zero-percent humidity, yeh? The only life I saw on the surface was these weird spherical, black plants. And toadies, of course. The limber little shits were everywhere. Their sun is orange-white. Hot; damn hot.

Excerpt: Greaves interview, 10.20.2120/3 [audiofile conversion]

I only saw the planet from space once. It looked wrinkly, and was red in spots, yellow in others. I didn't see any oceans, polar caps, or moons.

BIOLOGICAL INDICATORS

Chromatic skin can absorb nutrients and oxygen equally well in air and water, indicating present or ancestral amphibious behavior. Large bodies of water are, thus, implied, probably of at least ocean size. The skin is also abrasion-resistant, which may be an evolutionary adaptation or an engineered genetic enhancement. If the former, it indicates frequent contact with rough (rocky?) surfaces.

The Chromatic ability to absorb and emit light is more problematic. It may indicate an environment where light is in short supply, and is hoarded and controlled, or it may in-

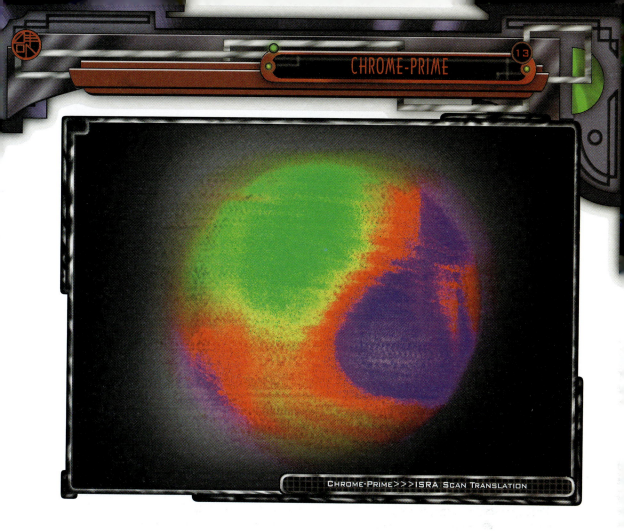

CHROME-PRIME>>>ISRA SCAN TRANSLATION

dicate that light is plentiful, and was, thus, a plentiful source of energy for those evolutionary mutations that learned how to control it. Chromatics have proven very sensitive to low temperatures, and are most comfortable in the 50-60° C range. Their visual sensitivity is equally acute across nearly their entire range of perceivable frequencies. This gives us few clues from which to determine their home sun's type.

LINGUISTIC INDICATORS

The Chromatic language — primarily a combination of different light-generated glyphs, accentuated by occasional barks and possibly also gestures — is extremely rich in the description of light. It is assumed that evolution provided the species with photokinesis before the language came into being. Recent research has discovered a broad subvocabulary describing water, both as a beverage and as an environment, including specialized terms for currents, etc.

The Chromatic word for "sun" (as distinct from "star") is "bright one who is above, of a specific white-orange color." The precise frequency of the color indicates their sun is probably an F9 or G0 star, similar to our sun but slightly larger and hotter. The internal structure of this word suggests it was created relatively recently.

CHROMATIC LANGUAGE
OPEN REPORT TO PROJECT BRIDGEWORK STAFF
— Emily Gaboriau, Alien Relations Liaison, Operation Safeguard, Triton Division, 4.17.2121

We've made major progress on the Chromatic language, and I thought I'd share some tidbits with you. Fascinating stuff, but we're having trouble making a coherent picture out of it. Let me know if you have any insights.

Without a doubt, Chromatics use light forms as their primary language. However, in the area of sound, we've identified 10 distinct vocalizations. They translate roughly to "we're being attacked," "come here and help me kill this," "I've found food," "I wish to mate with you," "get away from my stuff," "I recognize your authority," "danger," "I'm injured," "anger," and "come here so I can talk to you."

We've also identified what appears to be a form of gestured communication. We don't know any of the details, as the subject refuses to discuss it. Further, it's possible that the gestures are simply body language, as with humans, or even part of a mathematics system.

Our studies have borne more fruit in the Chromatek' primary mode of light-based communication, especially now that we're using one of Orgotek's new translation devices. The software we had before made serious errors nearly 30% of the time.

Our linguistic guy dubbed Chromie grammar "simultaneous agglutinative," a type unknown on Earth. Since the aliens can emit multiple light constructs at once, they create their compound words by "saying" two different words simultaneously. There's apparently a complicated hierarchy among the method of communication so that you know which word is modifying the other. Thus, they can distinguish between "high raft" (a noun meaning "spaceship") and "raft high" (an adjective possibly meaning "sea level").

Because of this, we've managed to nail down another 200 or so compound words, but we've only discovered a few dozen more basic nouns. We've even eliminated some that your team thought were basic, but were actually unrecognized compounds. Their basic grammar is, indeed, very simple. I disagree with your theory that lightspeed communication has slowed linguistic evolution. The near-complete absence of tense, case, conjugation, declension, or anything more complex than "this happen to him in the past" has pretty much convinced me that we are, in fact, looking at a young, Bronze Age language.

This is supported by the savagery and lack of intellectual complexity evident in Chromatic Subject V, our primary subject. He's made repeated, unprovoked attacks on my people, and seems to be borderline sociopathic in his inability to deal rationally with the situation. We have discovered that he's more tractable when the interviewer is actually in the same room with him, so (despite the obvious safety issues) that's how we're dealing with him.

(By the by, we're now reasonably certain that individual Chromatics are named for events of some kind, but color-names have stuck among my researchers. Hence, thanks to being Subject V — the 22nd Chromatic captive — the crew came up with "Vermilion.")

I'll send you our improved "Chromie-English" dictionary soon. Once again, thanks for all the help. Emily

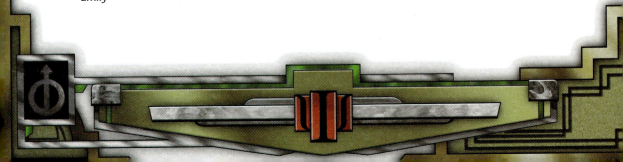

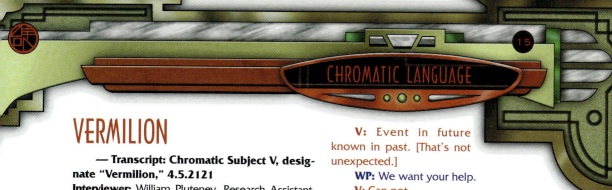

VERMILION

— **Transcript: Chromatic Subject V, designate "Vermilion," 4.5.2121**

Interviewer: William Pluteney, Research Assistant, Alien Relations (Operation Safeguard), Triton Division

Note: Interview facilitated by newly reprogrammed translation software (dubbed "Chromie 3.0") running on an Iris Obsidian.

Note: "____" indicates an unknown word. Text in brackets is an attempt at idiomatic translation.

WP: Chromie 3.0 running, interview begins. Good morning, Vermilion.

V: Light growing in future-near? [Is it dawn?]

WP: Yes. We might take you to see it. Would you like that?

V: ____. Animal. Light not here? Take self to cold-dark? Kill! [Bastard. You'd dump me into space. I'll kill you first.]

WP: No. We don't want to lose you. We need to ask you more questions.

V: You lose self/me in past. Ask. [You're so inept, it's like you've already lost me. / You've already made the mistake that will lead to your losing me. Ask your questions.]

WP: The Chromatics have captured human teleporters.

V: Question in past. Yes. [You've asked me this before. Yes, we have.]

WP: How?

V: High-far-beasts are prey. [Humans are our prey.]

WP: Yes, but how did you catch them?

V: Yes? Black war, then. Agreed! Find in past/found vanishing beasts where we knew they were. [Isn't war awful? / This will be an evil war. We knew where to find the teleporters.]

WP: Where were they?

V: There and there and there. Near to homes, and far away in cold-dark above. [In various places, both near our home system and in space.]

WP: How did you find them?

V: [silence]

WP: Did you use psi abilities to find them?

V: ____. Beast. [You're an idiot.]

WP: Hmm. We want to get our teleporters back.

V: Event in future known in past. [That's not unexpected.]

WP: We want your help.

V: Can not. ____.

WP: Yes, you will.

V: You know future? No, you do not know. You prey. [An animal like you can't make me.]

WP: We will find a way to make you.

V: Can not! Self is not weak! Black war with high-far beasts! Not help! [We're at war, and I won't talk.]

WP: Perhaps we can make a deal?

V: What? You say that in past, you say this in present. [You're unreliable.]

WP: Would you like better quarters? Brighter lights, better food?

V: Quarters better in present, worse in past. Lights in present bad. [I've had worse. The lights are already too bright/the wrong color.]

WP: Perhaps we could be kinder to the other prisoners.

V: In present, in future? [You'd just put it off.]

WP: No, we'd do it as soon as we got the information we needed out of you.

V: You can not. Can you? Distance far. All prisoners, prisoners here, there, better quarters? [You can't/wouldn't do that, I think. You're too far from being decent. You'd just do it with a couple prisoners, the ones I'd know about.]

WP: If we trust each other, maybe we can make some progress.

V: Progress? To what? —No! [No deals; our goals are incompatible.]

WP: I'm sure we can find room to negotiate.

V: Talk this, talk that? Exchange? No! High-far-beasts! War! [No deals!]

WP: Calm down, Vermilion. We're just talking.

V: No! Talk, talk! Not blue! [Too much talk!]

WP: What—

Note: At this point, Vermilion shoved the table with his legs, shearing the bolts holding it to the floor. Mr. Pluteney was struck hard enough to rupture several internal organs and break two ribs. Vermilion was subdued and returned to his cell. Mr. Pluteney is currently recovering.

>>> file break <<<

>>>EYES ONLY ▸ OPERATION CARAVEL ▸ EYES ONLY<<<

CLASS-A TARGETS

Capital ships in orbit
Orbital stations of grade 3 and above
Positively identified missile bases on surface
Communication nexuses of grade 6 and above

CLASS-B TARGETS

Secondary ships in orbit
All stations facilities
All satellites
All positively identified military installations on surface

CLASS-C TARGETS

All other ships in orbit
Materiel depots on surface of grade 4 and above

CLASS-N TARGETS

Any vessels not in orbital space
Any stations not in orbital space

CLASS-X TARGETS

Positively identified civilian concentrations on surface
Possible Upeo wa Macho locations

TARGET EXIGENCIES — OPERATION CARAVEL

Operation Caravel's purpose is to reduce or eliminate the Chromatic threat to Earth, and to rescue the Upeo wa Macho teleporters in captivity. Those areas where we suspect Upeo are being held have been declared Class X, and are not to be fired upon under any circumstances. Civilian centers are also Class X; this is not about xenocide.

Intelligence reports that the Chromatic presence in space is purely military. All non-natural objects in orbit and near space are valid targets. Intelligence also believes, with a lesser degree of certainty, that the actual Chromatic civilization is predominantly subsurface. It is possible that all surface targets may be valid military targets.

Targets shall be eliminated in order of class from A to C, proceeding to the next class only when 90% certainty of class elimination has been reached. Class N, as usual, consists of targets that will have to be hunted down. Do not proceed to Class N until all prior classes have reached 95% certainty.

During the orbital battle, the E-19 Stealth drop ships will insert the rescue teams, assisted by those few free Upeo who have revealed their existence and been authorized for active duty. The three primary rescue sites comprise a field post/prison, a hospital, and a facility for the construction of psion damping harnesses. The secondary rescue sites include four structures where Upeo were temporarily housed during their captivity, and a staging area for surface-to-orbit teleports.

The L-B Military Equipment Lifters and the reinforced infantry platoons they carry have the primary mission of inserting demolition teams to destroy certain high-value targets (launch facilities, biotech plants). They will also be used if necessary to back up the rescue missions. Once orbital space is secured, they may be used for intelligence-gathering missions, but this is regarded as a very low-priority goal. Most sites that would contain useful records or high-ranking Chromatics are likely to have been obliterated by this stage.

>>> file break <<<

>>> file break <<<

FOR STORYTELLER EYES ONLY!

This section covers Storytelling information for running the first episode in **Alien Encounter**, a new adventure series set in the Trinity Universe. Players should restrict their reading of material to the full-color setting section, letting the secrets below unfold during game play.

What Is This?

Colors of Sacrifice is the first adventure in the ongoing **Alien Encounter** series. It follows up the events covered in the previous **Darkness Revealed** series, but it's not necessary for characters to first go through that adventure trilogy before diving into this book.

The **Alien Encounter** series, which begins with **Invasion** and concludes with **Deception**, throws the characters headfirst into the events that will determine the future course of human-alien relations and alter forever the balance of power in the galaxy. Characters taking part in this adventure have access to information that can easily sway the destiny of mankind, and change humanity's perspective on the history of the past two centuries.

Invasion covers the events of a war between two races, but is intended to focus tightly on the actions of the players' characters. While the plot as written does point in certain directions, you, the Storyteller, should regard this book as a resource to be mined for whatever best enriches the series you run. This is worth mentioning, especially if you've previously run the **Darkness Revealed** series, since unlike that trilogy, **Invasion**'s two episodes are tightly connected. In fact, *Colors of Sacrifice* is designed to end in a cliffhanger that leads inexorably into the second episode, *Vermilion Falling*. Nevertheless, within these covers is a wealth of information on the events and inhabitants of the Trinity Universe, and any number of plots can be woven from the threads provided.

Each episode is split into two parts: full-color setting and black-and-white rules information. Players should read the setting material during appropriate points in the episode as the Storyteller sees fit. Those pages help set the stage for the scenario, providing initial leads

and helpful clues for the characters to follow. The rules sections provide details for you to run the episodes, as well as general source material useful during the adventure and in other games that take place in the same setting.

The setting section, in part, describes the events of the previous **Darkness Revealed** series. If you played that previous adventure, there may have been changes to continuity between what happened in your series and what's described in this book. Be sure to inform your players of any necessary changes made to ensure continuity.

The Plot

The the following brief plot synopsis describes the events of *Colors of Sacrifice*. Later sections cover the details more fully. **Again, if you're not the Storyteller, stop reading now! The Æon Trinity is watching you.**

Overview

In the wake of the recent Chromatic attacks on our Solar System (as detailed in the **Darkness Revealed** series), the United Nations has decided to mount a massive assault on the Chromatic homeworld with the intent of finally ending the alien threat. A secondary goal of the mission is to rescue the Upeo wa Macho teleporters who were captured by the Chromatics and forced to transport alien warships to human space. As *Colors of Sacrifice* begins, the characters discover that they have the assignment of scouting a facility on the Chromatic homeworld, Chrome-Prime, and rescuing any Upeo they find.

To this end, the characters are authorized to interrogate a Chromatic prisoner (dubbed "Vermilion") who was captured during the aliens' recent invasion. He is currently in the hands of the Æon Trinity's Operation Safeguard team. This group of scientists has determined that Vermilion is a high-ranking figure in Chromatic society, and could be a source of vital information if handled properly.

They are correct, but not in the way they think. The Chromatic *jihad* against humanity was caused by misinformation given to the aliens by certain members of another race, mysterious beings known as the Doyen. This deception is the only true motive the Chromatics have to destroy humanity. Vermilion comes to realize this over the course of **Invasion**. It is up to the characters to learn that their Chromatic captive is more than a crazed bug-eyed monster, and to start seeing him as a valiant warrior fighting for the wrong reasons.

The first meeting with Vermilion takes place in Haoa Flint Station, near Mare Ingenii on Luna. This region is a hotbed of intelligence activity and inter-order rivalry. In an environment of close-mouthed suspicion, the characters must interrogate the alien to discover the most likely site that the remaining Upeo (numbering possibly as many as 20) are being held on the Chromatic homeworld. This involves some intense sessions as sworn enemies of vastly different species struggle to learn from one another without giving up any advantages.

The characters are making good progress when complications occur (of course). Luis Ulloa, an overzealous and misguided Norça, has covert mercenaries kidnap Vermilion. The characters are the only ones with the means to rescue the alien. Acting quickly, they pursue the kidnappers to the criminal den known as the Pit. The characters track their quarry through this hive of scum and villainy, finally confronting the kidnappers in the Chain Hotel and recovering Vermilion.

After returning to Haoa Flint, the characters must quickly meet up with the invasion fleet staged on the far side of the Moon. The team and its charge are joined by Clarence Greaves, a member of the Upeo order rescued from a Chromatic mother ship during the aliens' assault (possibly rescued by the characters themselves if they went through the events of **Darkness Revealed**). They're all to take part in the rescue mission, Greaves to assist with his teleportation skills and Vermilion for his knowledge of the area (and the hope that hostile forces might give pause if they see the humans have a Chromatic captive).

The invasion fleet (a truly impressive array of craft from various governments and the psi orders) jumps to Chrome-Prime via psi coordinates from Greaves himself. The transit goes off without a hitch and the invasion commences immediately. The problems begin when the characters reach their designated site, a Chromatic hospital of sorts. The Upeo were supposed to be there, but the characters find nothing but Chromatics, ready for conflict. It's an ambush!

Greaves tries to teleport them out, but there's some sort of damper functioning — quite possibly the same thing that trapped the Upeo here on their first venture to Chrome-Prime. The team must flee across the surface of the planet with Greaves and Vermilion, pursued by armed and angry Chromatics.

The episode ends with the characters in mortal danger, deep inside hostile territory. The second episode of this book, *Vermilion Falling*, resolves both the characters' situation and sets the future course of human-Chromatic relations.

Theme

The theme of *Colors of Sacrifice* is discovery, with a side of betrayal. The prime goal for the characters is to learn from Vermilion (and he from them). At first, they should merely be seeking tactical data for their mission. In fact, that is secondary to a much more important issue — coming to realize that Vermilion is part of a civilized culture. The Chromatics are not simply savage brutes. As events progress, the characters should be drawn into learning about Vermilion as an individual, and the Chromatics as a people. This sets things up for the shocking revelations of the second episode, *Vermilion Falling*.

The other theme, betrayal, is an ever-present undercurrent in the Trinity Universe. Other orders have their own exigencies regarding Vermilion and the Chromatics, and the characters will only uncover a fraction of the plots surrounding them. Worse, the center of their plans — Vermilion — must similarly come to trust the characters as they must trust him. However, this hasn't yet occurred by the end of the first episode, resulting in the characters heading right into an ambush.

Mood

The mood is tense. At Haoa Flint Station, physical conflicts between Vermilion and his interrogators and intellectual battles among the Project Safeguard staff combine to form a stew of anxiety and frayed nerves. Vermilion is a confused, violent individual who is trying desperately to come to terms with the fact that the religious teachings to which he's dedicated his life may be based on falsehood. This strain and tension can be felt by all who interact with him (though they usually come away with the impression of murderous rage kept barely in check). Every encounter with the alien builds tempers to a frazzled pitch, even spilling over into issues unrelated to Vermilion.

To compound the problem, the interviews don't always go well. Vital information is needed and Vermilion is not terribly cooperative. The

Chromatics have a key tactical and logistical advantage as long as they hold the teleporters — a detail not lost on the Chromatic hero.

Speculation on the true nature of Chromatic society is rampant and heated. Key decisions must be made based on incomplete data, tentative hypotheses and outright guesses. Everyone involved feels very strongly about some aspect of the operation, and simple discussions often turn into shouting matches.

The Pit, the center of criminal activity on the Moon, cannot help but be tense as well. Borderline paranoia is not just a personality disorder here; it's a way of life. The area is, in theory, tightly controlled by the mysterious President, but she allows a great deal of activity to occur without interference. The Norça-sponsored kidnappers who flee here with Vermilion are without option or recourse — but so are the characters who pursue them.

Once the story moves to Chrome-Prime and the events of the actual invasion, things grow even *more* tense. A jump into hostile territory — to take on the enemy on his own homeworld! — is not conducive to relaxation. Additionally, the characters are teleporting directly to an alien site with little immediate backup. When the ambush is sprung, every imaginable disaster seems to have come true. This episode should end with the characters believing they may not escape Chrome-Prime alive. And, in fact, there's every possibility that they won't!

Setting

Haoa Flint Station

The facility where Vermilion is being kept is a small structure just outside Mare Ingenii on Luna's far side. The site is owned by the Æon Trinity, but portions are rented out to private agencies.

Vermilion and other Chromatics captured during the recent alien invasion were originally sent to Montressor Clinic for study (as detailed in **Ascent into Light** and **Trinity Field Report: Alien Races**, respectively). After investigations into psion malfeasance began, the United Nations directed the aliens to be transferred. Most of the Chromatics were simple warriors with little to contribute beyond genetic information. They were quietly relocated to the Lebedev Crater Penal Colony on Luna (see **Luna Rising**), and are extracted from time to time to take part in further biology, language and culture tests.

Vermilion was the only Chromatic hero to be captured alive; researchers quickly learned that he possessed a great deal of possibly worthwhile information. As a result, he was taken to Haoa Flint Station to undergo more intensive study.

Design

The station is designed roughly like a three-layer cake; each successive layer gets smaller. The top layer contains communication and sensor gear as well as defensive armaments. The middle layer (at ground level) has docking and storage facilities. The bottom layer is where the characters spend most of their time. It's set underground and divided into eight radial "cake slices" around a central utility core. Normal Earth gravity is maintained throughout.

The commgear on the top level is the best available; Flint can send and receive signals from anywhere in the System (even bouncing to Earth from Lunar-orbiting satellites). Most normal comm traffic goes through the land line to Olympus, however. The defensive weapons emplacements are similarly state-of-the-art.

Haoa Flint's docking bay on the second level can hold up to four craft at a time, and Flint has three more external docking ports. As a matter of policy, Flint does not allow any ships to dock inside except in an emergency and externally docked ships are kept to a minimum.

The central core contains life-support gear and a fusion reactor, along with such shared facilities as the cafeteria, gymnasium, supply center, medical bay, elevators and stairways. Each slice surrounding it is given over to a different project. The characters are able to tell from simple lunchtime gossip that, aside from Æon's own UN-backed project, a selection of different psi orders and private concerns are represented here. It is very difficult to find out what each group is working on, however. Everyone on the station believes in keeping their mouths shut, and minding their own business. As a result, small talk tends to revolve around sports and entertainment.

Consider Haoa Flint's lowest level like a clock face when viewed from above — only with eight divisions instead of the normal 12. Operation Safeguard occupies Section 3. Section 2 is a Neptune Division administration unit coordinating fleet supply logistics for the impending invasion; Section 4 is empty (though, of the Safeguard staff, only Gaboriau knows this). Section 5 is devoted to Æon-specific staff who maintain the station (Neptune maintenance crews and food-preparation staff, Proteus security and communications personnel). You can fill the other "slices" with any projects you think are interesting if you want to involve the characters in subplots other than their mission. Otherwise, don't worry about what's happening in the rest of the station.

The walls are solid and soundproofed between sections and between each section and the core. There are few doors between each as well, and security is rigorous. People are not allowed to travel from one section to another without a good reason. Travel between the core and one's "home" region is unrestricted, but logged via constant video surveillance.

Each section has four rings of rooms separated by narrow corridors, lettered from the inside out. In the Safeguard section, D Ring contains Vermilion's cell, two empty cells and a cell converted into quarters for one of the biotechs, Sunil Payaparaji. (He studies Chromatic technology, but has little involvement in this episode.) C Ring contains two rooms fitted for interrogation with a monitoring room set between them. B Ring has the standard quarters, and is where the characters bunk down. A Ring contains the offices and quarters for Emily Gaboriau and William Pluteney, the characters' contacts during their stay with Safeguard.

History

Haoa Flint (named for an obscure hero of the Aberrant War) was constructed by the UN in the late 2080s as the headquarters for CINCSPACLUN — Commander in Chief, Space Command, Lunar. The site was deliberately located on Luna's far side to make it a more difficult target for Earth-based threats. It was constructed on a relatively limited budget; at the time, there was no obvious threat to worry about save direct missile strike (avoided by the location) or the hypothetical return of the Aberrants (hopefully avoided by the Ultimatum).

In 2104, the Aberrants returned, and the 25-year old Haoa Flint was determined completely unsuitable as a modern command post. The UN, including SPACLUN, operated out of Olympus, but hung on to the old station until the Æon Trinity bought it in 2116.

Haoa Flint was a gutted shell, but this made the installation of heavy security that much easier. For its first several years the site served, in utmost secrecy, as part of the *Mazat* jump-ship plan-

ning offices, handling a great deal of the adminis-trative details. Æon saw no reason to relocate these offices even after The Colony destroyed much of the original jump-ship construction station in 2119. Once Orgotek donated to Æon its recently revealed secret site in Mare Ingenii, the offices relocated there.

With Haoa Flint empty once again, the Trinity promoted it as a secure facility available for contract. Flint is far enough from Olympus to provide privacy, but close enough so as not to be entirely isolated. Its internal security is formidable and a number of prisoners — human, Aberrant and alien — have been kept here. A few private concerns have rented out portions, but the psi orders option the majority of space.

An Interior Look

The station is gloomy at best, cramped and not designed for comfort. It's of a good size overall, but there are other groups working on projects unrelated to the Vermilion investigation, and space is tight. Further, the actual architecture of the station tends toward narrow corridors and low-ceiling rooms with inadequate lighting.

Those in the station are mostly intelligence experts doing data-analysis of one form or another. They are uniformly unhappy to be at Flint due to the close confines, and unable to discuss their work due to security reasons. This makes for poor cafeteria conversation at best. Over half of the hundred or so people stationed there are psions, representing all of the active psi orders. There is significant inter-order rivalry, tending toward outright rudeness and bitter office politics at times.

The Pit

The Pit, formerly known as Yeltsingrad, is where Las Vegas went to die. A bubbling center of gambling, sex, drugs, smuggling and tightly controlled violence, it's home to the worst humanity has to offer. Murder is rare here only because dead people don't spend money. Its texture varies widely from plush, extravagant casinos to the most decrepit, barely livable relics of its origins as a Russian base. The Pit is governed by the mysterious President, a meta-crime lord who gets a cut of everything that passes through the gates.

History: Yeltsingrad

The Pit was originally Yeltsingrad, a Russian mining-operation constructed in the 2040s. Even at the time, it was a minimalist, stripped-down base. The few luxuries (such as the Yeltsingrad Museum of the Arts) were less there for the residents to enjoy than as symbols of national pride.

Yeltsingrad emulated traditional Russian urban design (e.g., Moscow), being laid down in "rings" around the city's central core. The core itself was the only portion visible on the surface (and received the bulk of resources devoted to constructing the station). It originally contained the best living quarters, administrative offices, main life-support, hydroponic gardens and such structures as the art museum. Everything about the core was designed to be impressive on camera, with surprisingly large boulevards, green gardens and striking Revisionist Revolutionary architecture.

The first ring outside the core was the "bootstrap" facility for the mining operation, containing the minimum necessary to get digging underway. It included quarters for the miners, maintenance depots for the drilling vehicles and a bare minimum of ore processing machinery. This ring, while still functional and reasonably well designed, was far less photogenic than the core and still incomplete when Russia declared Yeltsingrad "finished" in 2045.

As the drills worked their way outward, more rings were created in the tunnels they left. These were filled with heavy processing plants, more life-support equipment, more quarters — even an occasional library or other structure in ultimately failed attempts to alleviate the impression that Yeltsingrad was nothing but a mining town.

Yeltsingrad effectively stopped dead in 2049 when the Aberrant War began. Russia's resources were diverted to the war, and for months the inhabitants had no idea when or if needed supplies would come. The Space Brigade came first, taking over Olympus and the surrounding settlements. The invading Aberrants, looking to establish a safe haven for their kind, ordered all humans to Olympus and took Yeltsingrad for their own. A collection of humans whom the Space Brigade brought from Earth during the course of the war was allowed to live in Yeltsingrad during the Aberrant occupation. The captive humans in Olympus came to call these Aberrant sympathizers the "Space Cadets" and Yeltsingrad earned the name "the Pit."

The Aberrants left in 2061, and the Earth nations returned. A survey team explored the Pit, reporting it basically functional but stripped nearly bare. Most of the core remained intact, some of the structures in the outer rings were gone, but there was no indication what had taken their place. Unexpected holes in walls and gaps in floors made it clear that there was substantial re-engineering, but the Brigade took everything with them when they left.

Although the Space Brigade had connected the Pit to Olympus via the Yeltsingrad Corridor, the complex remained distinctly separate from the rest of Lunar colonization trends. The sprawling, poorly equipped site was often written off as not worth refurbishing. National and private colonization efforts preferred to start fresh with state-of-the-art techniques.

Yeltsingrad languished in obscurity, home to a few despairing honest workers who slaved away to keep the city livable, and growing numbers of criminals and madmen who found the Pit was the perfect bolt hole. Power went to the strong, and life was cheap. A black market formed with astonishing speed. The criminal subculture soon grew into the dominant culture; Russia was in no position to enforce its claim on the colony and by the time other governments on Luna were in place, the Pit had become a power in its own right. It wasn't simply a case of thousands of criminals hiding out,

as innocent colonists still maintained small footholds in Yeltsingrad.

Instead of trying to deal with the mess that the Pit had become, Lunar society turned its head and closed its doors. The Pit was on its own, and thrived accordingly. For over 30 years the Pit seethed. The physical infrastructure was constantly within a hair of breaking down, the society was a patchwork of mob alliances and treachery. The Olympean government made occasional half-hearted efforts to restore law, all of which ultimately failed. A rough sort of structure asserted itself as powerful mob bosses entrenched themselves in Crime City.

The President

The President appeared mysteriously in 2096. With the aid of a few dozen skilled locals, she began a systematic takeover of the Pit. Those syndicate heads that didn't bow to the President's authority (most, since she was a complete cipher at the time) were targets of assassination. The underlings were then given the same choice — death, or giving a cut of the action to the Boss Lady. A few of the North American syndicates and the Russian Mafia knuckled under. The rest struggled against a surprisingly determined foe and ultimately retreated to Olympus' Downside. She controlled the Pit within the space of four years.

The President is secretive to the point of clinical paranoia. Despite heroic efforts, no one has successfully determined her identity. She always appears in public cowled, masked and gloved. Psions have determined that she is neutral, but have been unable to mind read her. Her voice sounds natural, but it doesn't always sound the same, and analysis indicates it is electronically altered. There is no indicator of the President's age, hair color, eye color, racial background — even her gender is suspect. Only her height and build are known, at least in general terms. It has been suggested that the President is actually a group of people, but intelligence experts discount the possibility. The President's "Cabinet" — her closest advisors — may know more, but aren't talking. Many of them have adopted similarly secretive personas, in fact.

The President's most obvious quirk is her apparent interest in United States presidents. She particularly celebrates the more publicly criminal of them, such as Harding, Nixon and Clinton. She says that the office "was used for shameless personal gain more frequently and flamboyantly than any similar position since the Roman emperors."

Taint in the Pit

So far as anyone knows, Aberrants occupied the Pit continuously for nearly a decade. By all expectations, it should have been noticeably irradiated with taint. This was not the case, however. The first human inspection team detected only the faintest traces of taint, well below accepted danger levels (which were understandably low to begin with). Despite the paradoxical nature of this discovery, no further investigations were made. There was too much on Luna that needed fixing to worry about this minor mystery.

There have been no known problems in Yeltsingrad relating to taint. A few Aberrants are suspected to pass through the Pit regularly, but there seems to be no permanent presence, and no after-affects from the occupation.

The paranoid, of course, suspect that the Pit is the site of a complex Aberrant experiment involving "cloaked" taint. They suggest that the President is actually an Aberrant who exploits this "invisible taint," and feeds on the suffering like a vampire. They worry that the Pit is home to a new breed of Aberrant that secretly corrupts humans from within. These suspicions remain simply that, but it doesn't stop people from speculating.

The Floor and her personal mansion use red, white, and blue frequently in the decor, and portraits of presidents decorate the walls. Much of her organization's nomenclature is based on the old US government — inner advisors the "Cabinet," her major domo the "First Secretary," the "Secs" slang for "Secret Service." Her masks are usually featureless, but sometimes (particularly for special occasions) they're modeled on a president. Catch phrases such as "four score and seven years ago" or "read my lips" pepper her conversations. This mild obsession sometimes gives the Floor the air of a theme park, but she's the boss.

Life in the Pit

The President announced her "Bill of Rights" on January 1, 2100. Unauthorized murder is illegal, as is any attempt to cause permanent harm (authorization must be given by the Boss Lady). Damage to the infrastructure of the Pit is illegal, including endangering the community in any way. Lastly, the President has a 5% "tax" on every transaction — her cut. In theory, everything else is permitted. (The practice is sometimes different, though most take their chances and hope they don't rile the President's ire.)

In one sense, everyone in the Pit works for the Boss Lady. Those who actually consider themselves her employees number over 10,000. Of those, roughly 1,000 are her security staff of Secs — highly trained, heavily armed individuals who keep the peace and enforce the President's laws. They also do not, technically, have the authority to execute lawbreakers. (Some do anyway, and are sometimes punished for it.) Laws are often enforced harshly in the Pit, but with a surprising consistency. See **Luna Rising** (page 108) for more details.

Of the thousands not directly involved in enforcement, most work on the Floor, the casino that now occupies Yeltsingrad's core (see below for more details). The remaining residents indulge in numerous endeavors, both criminal and legal, including doctors, bookies, diplomats, drug dealers, librarians, prostitutes, merchants and smugglers. The President gets a piece of all these activities — even those that extend beyond Yeltsingrad proper. In the Pit, her power is absolute and in Olympus it is equal to that of the syndicates. The Boss Lady's influence extends even further, in fact, even if it's only a representative or two in the major Lunar and Earthside cities.

Pit Geography

The Pit extends out from the central core in six complete rings and two incomplete ones. The six main rings were all created by the Russians during Yeltsingrad's initial operation. The outermost rings are relatively recent constructions, having been dug out since 2080. The neighborhoods get progressively more decrepit, violent and dark as one gets further out, and even the ring right next to the core is actively unpleasant.

Life support, while functional, receives only basic maintenance, so the air smells like the inside of someone's lungs. The lighting is adequate, except where the tubes haven't been replaced — or where someone is selling something, in which case dimness helps hide the merchandise's flaws. The floor and walls are simply not washed; water is valuable. Water in the Pit is not used for drinking; straight out of the tap it's brown and carries a faint smell of rot. It could be sterilized and filtered, but it's cheaper to drink pre-packaged beverages and a lot safer.

Most food in the Pit (whether in restaurants on the Floor or at a cart in the third ring) is grown locally, tending toward vegetables, algae and tank-grown soy. The President discourages the sale of unsafe food, but there are no guarantees as to flavor, texture or nutritional content. Meat is scarce, very expensive, and is usually from smaller animals such as rats and dogs.

The Floor focuses on goods and services related to entertainment, but one can buy nearly anything elsewhere in Yeltsingrad. A sizable percentage of everything stolen outside Earth's gravity-well passes through the Pit. Craft components, consumer electronics and biotech are readily available. Perhaps the only things difficult to find are items with little use off Earth, like umbrellas and skis.

The sex industry in the Pit is large and desperately energetic. Interested parties may indulge in the entire range of human sexual behavior (from the merely kinky to the actively perverse) or simply watch. The President even permits "snuff sex" (where the victim is killed during the act), so long as the victim volunteers. The prostitutes are usually clean (unless you want them dirty), but only a rare few are guaranteed to be healthy. Those get regular checkups in Olympus and post their clean bills of health in their chambers. They are priced accordingly.

Both private and social drug experiences can be arranged as well. Opium dens are surprisingly popular, as are the distinctly opposite PCP "romper rooms." (Deaths that occur in the latter are considered suicides.) Selling instantly lethal drugs is frowned on, but the President seems to allow some leeway here (drugs *are* dangerous). You won't get much sympathy if you buy cheap; after all, you get what you pay for.

Several assassins and mercenaries available for hire make their homes in Yeltsingrad. A few pirate crews also call regularly, but Lunar space is generally too hot for them. In addition, a surprising number of people with relatively ordinary professions (geared toward the illicit) can be found; if you need a plumber to do something shady, you can find one here.

The Pit also contains many thousands just trying to get by. They wash drug-dealers' clothes, tend to mercenaries' wounds, care for prostitutes' children and, otherwise, provide the necessary infrastructure for a Lunar city of 100,000 people. Some even make very good livings at it. A lot of money passes through the Pit, and at the prices most of these criminals charge, they can afford to be generous to the help.

Culture

Pit culture respects self-reliance, but like any space-faring society, it places an emphasis on cooperation. This is part of why the President's Bill of Rights is respected; the woman you randomly kill today may be the woman who would've fixed the life-support system tomorrow. Complete strangers band together in an instant to protect their communities.

Even so, those strangers aren't above screwing one another over for a percentage. The Pit is a society one step away from total anarchy. Privacy on personal issues is taken very seriously, and an off-hand comment can be taken as grievous insult. Business is conducted cleanly and with few digressions. People are extremely slow to make friends; truly close relationships are usually familial.

Murder is usually a no-no, but theft is commonplace. Rape and beating the hell out of someone don't usually fall under the Bill of Right's "permanent injury" dictates. Terror is acceptable. There is no such thing as "property ownership," so you only own a piece of corridor so long as you can hold it. Arson is a crime (you might endanger the air supply), but ripping someone's home to shreds is allowed.

In short: The Pit is not a nice place.

The Floor

This is the heart of the Pit in more ways than one. While the Floor technically encompasses Yeltsingrad's entire core, it usually only refers to the casino that surrounds the President's personal mansion. The mansion, originally the Yeltsingrad Museum of the Arts, is rarely seen by anyone but her cabinet and personal staff. Reports say that many works of art in museums on Earth are actually a part of the President's collection, symptomatic of the mansion's reputation as a place of staggering luxury. Security — physical, electronic, psionic — is tight in the extreme, so much of this remains rumor. (It is quite unlikely any character will ever get into the mansion without actually, *sincerely*, joining the President's staff and working through the ranks.)

The casino itself is one of the largest in known space (though, admittedly, not as opulent as many). It caters to nearly every form of gambling known to mankind — craps, poker, blackjack, baccarat, roulette, cockfights, boxing, holocombat, armed duels. Aside from these activities, one can find all manner of physical and chemical diversions. And if you can't find it on the Floor, you can usually find it elsewhere in the Pit.

The Floor ranges up to 10 levels in places. The two lowest are used for support facilities: dressing rooms, kitchens, locker rooms, medical facilities, maintenance. The main floor, a meld of two floors creating a large seven-meter-tall space, occupies the next level up. It's packed with gambling tables, slot machines and bars covering thousands of square meters. The decor is heavy on red and gold, with red-white-and-blue bunting draped anywhere appropriate. The Floor's main entrance leads directly here.

Most of the games could be automated, but the President prefers the human element. Aside from dealers and floor bosses, numerous waitstaff, barkeeps and prostitutes roam about, as well as roving pairs of Secs. All are surprisingly pleasant — in a predatory, intelligent way. (The President channels her stupid employees into roles where talking isn't required.)

There's an arena sunk into the center of the main level, surrounded by seating for several hundred. It typically holds ongoing dancing spectacles, although there are occasional martial- or erotic-arts demonstrations. Arena combat occurs once each day; simulated VARG combat is popular, but there are also physical matches. Extreme boxing and wrestling matches are put on several times a week. Gladiatorial-style death matches happen monthly, varying in style with each event.

The next level up contains suites with one-way plexi windows that observe the main floor. Some of these are simply private offices for various Floor supervisors. Others are available for private meetings, sexual trysts or simply to lay low for a bit. The next two levels are used for more private gambling. (There is a rumor, spread by the President's people, that the proxies meet here once a year for a high-stakes poker game.) Gamblers can bet on "animal combat" on this level as well. A kennel and veterinarian's office are located to one side to support this activity.

The remaining levels are a mix of hotel, brothel and apartment complex. A large number of suites of varying quality are available for hourly, daily, monthly and yearly rates. Like everything else on the Floor, rates start at "expensive" and go up from there. Apart from specific lodging accommodations, these levels also have a selection of ballrooms, theaters, shops, conference rooms, gyms, spas, and other esoteric facilities.

In the rest of the Pit, depravity of any sort takes place and hostility is a way of life. On the Floor, it all seems to melt away. It's surprisingly polite and civilized, but with an undertone of desperate tension; the mood is not unlike a city occupied by enemy forces. The President wants your money and it's bad business to harm paying customers. However, the Boss Lady's running the show and wants everything a certain way. Unruly sorts have a habit of vanishing quickly and quietly.

Weapons are permitted on the Floor (it is the Pit, after all), but the use of one provokes a rapid, heavily armed response from the Secs and the defensive weaponry hidden in the walls — anti-personnel lasers, gas ducts, and (for true emergencies) shaped charges designed to drop the entire observation level. The scanning gear at the Floor's standard entrances has an effective 8 Dice Pool (Engineering) to detect concealed weaponry. The Secs keep tabs on those who look like trouble, but don't make any moves unless the need arises.

The President employs a few freelance psions for similar purposes. There are a few clairsentients known to be on staff who hang out on the main floor or on the observation level. They're paid to report any use of psi, and to try to pinpoint the user. A Sec then politely and firmly stops by and tells the user to cut the crap or get the hell out. If the psi use is overtly offensive, the Secs treat it like someone using a weapon — shoot first, worry about bystanders later.

Chain Hotel

This "theme" hotel, located between the second and third rings out from the Floor, is a den of carefully metered and priced kinky sex. Organized around the concept of bondage, the Chain Hotel offers unusual sexual escapades for hire. While many of the employees work there for the thrill, as many are simply in it for the money. The atmosphere see-saws wildly from gasping arousal to quiet desperation. Visually, the entire complex is done up in shiny black and chrome, full of odd textures and symbols of dominance.

Upeo Medical Site, Chrome-Prime

The Chromatics built this structure after the Witnesses relayed the coming of the Bodiless Ones. It originally served as a warehouse for the vast quantities of materiel being produced for the war effort. Unfortunately, several portions of the floor collapsed into the underground tunnel system, and the building was mostly abandoned.

When the Chromatic invasion was being planned, the alien leaders (the heads of various dynasties) knew that, even though it was black war, some of their people might be captured. It's possible that the humans would learn about the captured teleporters before the captives could achieve some form of redemption in committing suicide. This didn't worry the leaders much, since in black war you assume that any captives are effectively dead — so why should the humans care about the Upeo?

The Witnesses said so, that's why. The word came down that there was every possibility that these dangerous beasts would try to rescue their Upeo thralls. Strange as this sounded to the Chromatic leaders, they knew that the Witnesses spoke with the wisdom of the gods, and planned accordingly. The Chromatics picked a few sites that would be good ambush points, and quietly moved the Upeo there.

The object of the characters' mission is ostensibly a medical center for injured Upeo. Like the other sites, it was cursory and temporary; the Chromatic leaders had no real intention of making permanent installations. However, when Vermilion and his fellow warriors left Chrome-Prime, the sites were still in operation as centers of Upeo presence on Chrome-Prime.

The medical site is chosen over the others (training areas and testing facilities) because security is presumably more lax. Clarence Greaves, the rescued Upeo, confirms that the testing facility in which he was kept was under heavy guard at all times. Vermilion says with all honesty that the Upeo can be found here. He suspects that the sites were turned into deathtraps after he left, but (as he didn't actually witness this), he's not lying when he doesn't bring it up. This may seem like semantics, but the Chromatics are very, very serious about not lying. They're not above manipulating what they say, though.

In person, the facility is dusty, falling apart and full of traps. It resembles a Babylonian ziggurat, constructed mostly of stone and reinforced with roughly smelted iron. It seems to fit more in the category of ancient ruins and collapsed temples, but some looking around reveals new supports and additions. Like the Chromatics themselves, it is a study in contrasts.

Running Colors of Sacrifice

Introducing the Characters

This episode assumes that the characters are beholden in some way to the Æon Trinity, with plenty of ties to the previous **Darkness Revealed** adventure series as well. If either of these assumptions is true, it makes perfect sense that the characters would be assigned to the mission of rescuing the Upeo. It's still easy to draw the characters in if they didn't take part in **Darkness Revealed**: Æon simply assigns them to the rescue mission. If the characters aren't immediately associated with the Trinity, however, things get a little more tricky.

Characters As Independent Operatives

The simplest rationale is that the Æon Trinity and/or the United Nations seek out the characters and try to recruit them. The characters may be well known, with skills well suited to the mission. Alternatively, they may have Allies, Contacts, Followers or Mentors involved in the planned invasion who draw the characters into it as well. Their Allegiance might come into play — their orders or their governments may have assigned them as part of the invasion force, and they're subsequently transferred to this special assignment.

Characters hired freelance are offered ¥100,000 per person for the mission. (This can be bumped up to ¥250,000 with skilled bargaining — just make sure to roleplay it.) The characters receive one-quarter of this amount up front. Further, they can request special equipment. Use your best judgment here; Æon and the UN aren't stupid. If you think a character is just trying to get some free gear, you needn't accommodate him.

Of course, if the characters are already part of the invasion force, they get their orders with no negotiation (or extra money). Hey, no one said life was fair.

New Characters

If you're dealing with newly created characters, you may want to encourage the players to include previous field experience in the characters' history. Otherwise, you could run a couple introductory sessions that give the characters an opportunity to prove their mettle. Assume that an Æon or UN member saw their talent and figured they'd be perfect for the mission.

Non-combat Characters

In this situation, it's not immediately obvious why the characters are chosen for the assignment. If the team isn't combat oriented, then bring the characters in to interview Vermilion and provide appropriate research support for the mission. The actual rescue team (based on typical military soldier templates, **Trinity** page 306) "sits in" on the interviews, benefiting from the characters' people skills.

During the kidnapping, the combat team defends Vermilion and suffers casualties in the process. The mission can't be carried out by the couple of survivors, and there's no time to bring in new personnel. It requires people already familiar with Vermilion (and the information gleaned to date). The characters are the only choice, and are summarily "drafted" (with encouragement that seems uncomfortably like veiled threats, if necessary) to rescue Vermilion and join the mission to Chrome-Prime. The remaining military personnel are on-hand to provide armed support for the characters.

Behind the Scenes

With regards to the events of this episode, the human powers of the Trinity Universe are largely of one mind. They all want humanity to survive, and they all recognize the Chromatics as a threat. Nearly everyone, normal and psion alike, is doing his best to expedite the fleet's mission.

The Æon Trinity

This mission is a prime example of the purpose to which the Æon Trinity is dedicated: the protection and service of humanity. Although Æon isn't in charge of the invasion (that's the United Nations' job), it provides support in any way that it can — drawing in personnel and resources that will benefit the mission. The ships of the fleet and the warriors aboard them are virtually iconic symbols of the Trinity's core beliefs. With regards to interrogating Vermilion, Æon believes it has the best possible team to do a difficult job under immense time pressures.

The United Nations

Although the United Nations of the 20th century is primarily a civilian body with little influence in military affairs, the 22nd-century UN is a different beast entirely. The Aberrant War was key to engendering a stronger military presence within the UN — many nations were forced to work together to combat Aberrants, and the UN was the best tool by which to do so. The details of this aren't relevant here, but will be covered in other releases. For now, it's sufficient that the UN is the most effective authority to coordinate an international military effort of this magnitude.

Despite myriad and valid concerns about the integrity of the psion community, the UN member nations are fully behind the invasion. It's been a year since the first hints of the Huang-Marr conspiracy were revealed. During that time, the psi orders have continued to dedicate themselves to humanity's defense — most notably in repelling two Chromatic invasions of human space.

It's become apparent to cooler heads within the UN General Assembly that the orders are like any other organization — unfortunately prone to corruption. The United Nations must pursue any evidence of illegal and immoral acts by anyone, neutral or psion. It must also utilize every resource in defending humanity against hostile intent, and psions are especially well suited to this. At present, the Chromatics are much more dangerous than a handful of rogue psions are.

The Orders

The psi orders are also firmly behind the invasion. The scandals exposed in the past year involving corrupt psions have cast a pall over the Gifted community. The vast majority of psions is committed to helping humanity, and was shocked by the reports. Whatever the individual psion's take on the specific events being investigated by the United Nations, they all know that one bad psion makes every Gifted look bad in neutrals' eyes.

As a result, the psi orders are not blind to the fact that the invasion of Chrome-Prime gives psions an opportunity to show their talents in the best possible light. The orders aren't beyond turning it to their own political advantage, distracting Joe Hologram from the orders' dirty laundry.

The Norça and Luis Ulloa

The Norça are as fiercely dedicated to defending humanity as are the other orders. That's not their only dedication, though. Among other pursuits, Proxy del Fuego long ago initiated a research program dedicated to gathering as much data on all life forms as possible — including aliens. The Norça keep this effort relatively low-key, compiling information quietly and efficiently.

Due to these efforts, some elements within the order feel that they should have been placed directly in charge of studying Chromatics. Their only peripheral involvement is made all the more galling by seeing the flamboyant Orgotek and bumbling Æsculapian personnel given prime access. Even the Ministry has muscled its way in for the purpose of encouraging communications with the captives. Luis Ulloa, a non-psion member of the Norça, has taken these feelings of resentment to heart.

Ulloa is stationed in Haoa Flint as one of the computer security personnel. He plans to kidnap Vermilion, having known the alien was on the station from the moment the Chromatic arrived. The Norça spy believes that there is a good deal that his order can learn from Vermilion, particularly if the shifters can replicate the optical Chromatic nervous system. As a side note, Ulloa is concerned about the supposed Chromatic murders in his hometown of Rio as noted on page 8, and hopes that grilling Vermilion will give him leads. (The murderer is *not* actually a Chromatic.

This is all just a self-rationalization, though. The true motivating force behind Ulloa's plans is the desire for glory. He hopes that this daring ploy will enable Ulloa, a marginal latent, to experience the Prometheus Effect. He dreams of blossoming with noetic power and playing the prodigal to del Fuego. Vermilion provides the perfect prop with which to accomplish all this.

Norça as a whole have no idea what Ulloa's up to, and he will take any blame to protect the order, viewing himself as a martyr to the cause.

The Mercenaries

Ulloa has hired a mercenary team, led by Joan Milovanovic, to kidnap Vermilion. They are battle-seasoned professionals, and they "stay bought." Dedicated to the end, these mercenaries keep to their contract even when the plan starts to fall apart around them. They may surrender when it becomes the only option, but they don't willingly betray their employer. They are not the most skilled mercenaries in the Solar System, but they are as honest and reliable as they come.

The Proxies

There is a serious, private concern felt among the proxies and their trusted aides: A Doyen was apparently on the side of the Chromatics. The proxies were under the impression that the alien Doyen were relatively benevolent and pretty much hands-off regarding human affairs — major reasons why the race's existence was kept secret from humanity at large. The proxies knew from the moment they first learned of the Doyen, years before the Qin first contact, that the Doyen knew of and were enemies of Aberrants. However, it seemed that the Doyen bore no ill-will toward humanity as a whole. Recent events call this into question.

The Chromatics hate Aberrants, and consider humans to be just as tainted. The proxies are worried that the Chromatics may have somehow persuaded some Doyen — or possibly even the whole race — to see things the Chromatics' way. Alternatively, some (or even all) of the Doyen may have encouraged the Chromatics to make war on humanity. But then why reveal themselves to the proxies in the first place?

The bottom line is that the proxies have only conjecture and supposition to go by. The invasion of Chrome-Prime is necessary to ferret out the truth about the Chromatics' mysterious mentors.

The Chromatics

Understanding Chromatic motives requires at least a basic familiarity with their cultural views on war. The development of Chromatic culture was heavily influenced by the struggle for resources. This occurred both between Chromatic tribes and between Chromatics and another native life form that the Chromatics call "Howlers." howlers are about as intelligent as *Homo habilis*, and both larger and better armored than the average Chromatic. Howler light-creating abilities are rather primitive, but some are active photokinetics. Until recently, the conflict with the howlers was serious enough that the Chromatic race was in danger of extinction.

Approximately two millennia ago, Chromatic culture created a distinction between two forms of conflict: "war with animals" or "black war," and "war with equals" or "blue war." Black war is easy for humans to understand: It is all-out war, without thought of quarter or surrender, and is fought without restraint. Black war is only used when genocide is the goal. (Chromatic conflicts with the howlers are always black.)

Blue war is a much less human concept. It is not "limited" war; atrocities are perfectly possible under blue war. Instead, it is best described as "negotiated conflict." For example, if a given Chromatic tribe announces to its foe that it will start poisoning the enemy's water supplies, the opposing tribe has three choices. It can surrender, it can announce that it will begin poisoning water supplies as well, or it can call for negotiation to establish a mutually acceptable level of conflict. Approximately 80% of Chromatic tribal conflicts over the past few centuries were carried out under agreed upon blue war terms. The remainder involved at least one tribe that did not accept the blue-war/black-war ideology. Those resisting tribes were subjected to black war by default, and are now extinct or assimilated.

The Chromatics believe that humans are little more than dangerous beasts to be exterminated. It's worth noting that Chromatics don't consider "beasts" in the same light as humans do. To the aliens, a "beast" is something cunning, dangerous and not to be trusted. But that doesn't mean that a beast is not a thinking creature. Chromatics don't really consider the issue of sentience as such. To them, all beings think; some are simply smarter than others.

Since the Chromatics view humans as beasts, they never even considered the idea of blue war. Chromatics practice black war against humanity. The aliens don't try to negotiate, and they do not expect any diplomatic overtures in return. As a result, the captured Chromatics were treated very oddly, from their perspective. Mostly the humans demand information and insist on cooperation. Chromatics become intractable, regarding such ultimatums as a black-war situation. There is no inference of negotiation, of "superior thought" if you will — although that's not even a clear interpretation of what's required to enact blue war.

Sometimes, however, humans ask for advice, or cajole, or make offers of better treatment in return for help. Such treatment feels like blue war, which surprises the Chromatics. After all, what do beasts know of such civilized matters? Sometimes it actually results in a helpful Chromatic. More often (particularly when the human interrogators try the "good-cop/bad-cop" routine) it results in a confused, paranoid Chromatic who isn't sure what to believe.

Vermilion

Vermilion, in particular, is confused. He has maintained his grip on his emotions and his sanity. (He's one of their best, after all.) Still, he doesn't know what

Thralls

A Chromatic captured by the enemy under black war becomes a "thrall," a prisoner and slave without an identity of his own. This is considered one of the most horrible disgraces a warrior can suffer, and most prisoners promptly commit suicide. Those who don't are branded cowards and non-persons. They receive no respect from their captors and are considered the lowest form of life by their former allies.

The status of a Chromatic captured under blue war depends on the terms that have been negotiated, but it's almost a given that there will be some form of prisoner exchange. A blue war prisoner has not been disgraced since (by definition) blue war is fought between equals, and being overcome by an equal is no dishonor, merely bad luck.

The Chromatics currently in human custody feel that they are thralls. Combined with their hatred and fear of humans, this creates an ongoing, almost overwhelming sense of rage and shame.

to think of humans. He's particularly dumbfounded by the restraining harness, as Chromatics are controlling the human teleporters in much the same way! It appears to him that humans have somehow found out about the Chromatics' treatment of the Upeo, and are following that as a standard for treatment of POWs. This is clearly blue-war behavior.

This shook Vermilion from most of his shame and despair. He's been trying to pump his interrogators for information on how they view the conflict, but (since humans don't know about blue war versus black war) he's getting mixed signals.

For you, the Storyteller, the goal of Vermilion's relationship with the characters is to realize that humans are equals, not beasts — and, thus, that his "gods of light" have not been fully forthcoming with his people. That realization takes time, over the course of both *Colors of Sacrifice* and *Vermilion Falling*.

To reach his epiphany, Vermilion must decide that the war with humans either already is, or should become, blue war. The more humans emphasize their willingness to *discuss* matters rather than *dictate* them, the more cooperative the Chromatic hero becomes. This may sometimes make sense to the characters and sometimes not.

For example, if a character simply says, "Tell us what we want to know!" she'll be met with silence, or insults at best. If she says, "Tell us what we want to know, and we'll move you to better quarters," she'll find Vermilion more inclined to cooperate. Oddly, however, if a character says, "Answer our questions or we'll cut off your leg!" Vermilion will respond (in all seriousness) with, "We negotiate now. Not cut off leg; hit me with hammer now; we hit human prisoners with hammer in future; information given now-and-future. Acceptable?" (As a result of similar statements, the current interrogators have incorrectly come to believe that Vermilion has an odd sense of humor.)

You should have Vermilion pass through the following stages over the course of this episode on his way to greater understanding:

1. Hostile, violent. Thinks humans are nothing more than beasts.

2. Hostile, but curious. Only violent under extreme provocation. Confused as to whether humans are aware of the blue-war/black-war distinction. Has decided humans are rational in their way, but are still beasts.

3. Mostly curious, but wary. Only violent if actually attacked. Believes humans don't know about blue war/black war, but thinks humans practice something like blue war by default. Wondering if they're not beasts.

4. Has figured out that the characters won't physically harm him. Wondering if Chromatics should be waging blue war with humanity. Definitely still regards humans as the enemy, but no longer as beasts.

5. Admires the characters as warriors, believes the conflict should be blue war, but still thinks the war itself is justified. Confused as to why the gods stated humans were animals.

By the time the Norça-sponsored kidnapping occurs (see page 39), Vermilion should be in either stage 3 or 4. The character's actions during the kidnapping should advance him one stage further. At the end of *Colors of Sacrifice*, after the ambush on Chrome-Prime, he should be in one of the last two stages. Thereafter, the events of *Vermilion Falling* should carry him the rest of the way to understanding.

Arrival at Haoa Flint Station

As noted in the briefing on page 2, the characters are to gather in the morning at bay R-106 in Yutu Yinchon Spaceport, the main traffic hub in Luna's Olympus colony. This may well be the first time the characters meet if they aren't already a team. Use whatever means you feel necessary to have them there — commercial flights from Earth or simply public LAMP tubes for characters already in the area.

The R spur is reserved for diplomatic traffic, so the characters must first run a security gauntlet. Any weapons they carry will be detected, but the characters have already been authorized, so security simply catalogs what each person carries and waves them all through. After any necessary introductions among the characters, they board *Selenaut*, an old but well-maintained Bakuhatsu GPT-02 "Deuce" (the precursor to the popular Trey) with UN markings. Aside from the characters, the only other people on the craft are two UN security personnel (one male, one female) and the pilot (also UN), Harve Dansel.

Captain Dansel explains that the trip to Haoa Flint will be relatively short, but cautions against attempting any transmissions during the flight. The site is a secure facility and all approaches and departures are strictly regulated. Unauthorized communications are not allowed. He points out that *Selenaut* has sophisticated sensors and comm-blocks that quickly detect and interrupt transmissions anyway. Dansel is simply informing the characters so that he and the security are saved the hassle of taking disciplinary action. With a smile that leaves the characters wondering if the pilot is actually joking, Dansel tells the team to strap in. He gets to the cockpit himself, and announces their departure to the tower.

Dansel and the UN security serve no other purpose than to establish that the characters are, indeed, part of a serious mission, and he's a way for them to get to Haoa Flint station. They know nothing about the characters' objectives, nor do they want to know.

You may develop this scene as much as you like, or simply fast-forward to the arrival.

The trip itself takes about two hours; the Deuce flies in a parabolic arc above the Lunar surface, then dives back down. Characters familiar with the Moon's geography may note that *Selenaut* heads for a point near Mare Ingenii. There's standard chatter from the cockpit as Dansel communicates with Haoa Flint on the approach, and the transport soon approaches a two-step structure built into the Lunar rock. The top layer bristles with communications gear and a selection of weapons placements; the lower layer is a fairly typical docking facility. The Deuce enters Haoa Flint without incident, and the characters soon find themselves entering what will be their home for the next fortnight.

As the team steps off *Selenaut* into the station, their first impression is of gloomy, cramped spaces and frenetic activity. Workers hurry to the transport to unload supplies, and there are also a fair number of onlookers who showed up to divert themselves from the monotony of life on Haoa Flint.

Emily Gaboriau steps forward to thank Dansel (who greets her back and then strolls off, motioning for the security detail to assist in supervising the off-loading) and welcome the characters. Gaboriau appears harried but generally pleased to see them. She immediately escorts them through the docking facilities to the stairs leading down to the main level (located underground), then to central security office.

As they walk, Gaboriau briefs the characters on the tight schedule they're all facing, but doesn't broach the topic of the actual mission as yet. Instead, she discusses Haoa Flint's general purpose and layout, and the protocols involved in interaction among the different projects going on. She cautions the characters against testing the station security, hinting in much the same manner as Dansel did at dire consequences if they try. Gaboriau's manner is professional, even friendly, throughout, but the characters definitely sense her weariness.

Haoa Station Security

The central security office is one man (Luis Ulloa) in a small room with a big computer. Ulloa has the computer take holostills of all the characters, then issues them temporary security cards and meal schedules. The whole process takes only take a few minutes, and Ulloa chatters amiably through the whole thing (about sports, current events, an old flatvid he saw recently — it appears he spends a lot of time cooped up in this room with little opportunity to talk). The security cards are just a formality, identification in case the computer system should fail for some reason.

The characters are likely chomping at the bit to find out details of their mission by now. Gaboriau is reluctant to discuss the subject until they get into the Operation Safeguard section, and will say as much if a character brings it up. After a few more meters of corridor and some security doors, Gaboriau responds freely. She relays that the first session with Vermilion is scheduled for the afternoon, so the characters have a few hours to settle in, eat lunch and get up to speed as necessary.

Gaboriau repeatedly advises the characters to be careful around Vermilion. She is obviously coolly hostile toward the alien, referring to him repeatedly as "the vermin" or "Verm." She also makes it clear that time is precious. The fleet is expected to leave in a week and a half, and she's not convinced that it's enough time to extract the needed information from the stubborn alien. (In actuality, the fleet will be delayed a few days, but no one knows this as yet.)

Quarters

The characters are bunked two to a room in the B Ring. Their schedules have them all down for lunch at 11:30 AM, but there's some flexibility in the time. Allow them to unpack (the characters' gear was off-loaded and sent to their quarters while they received their security IDs) and poke around the Safeguard section before mealtime.

At this point, Gaboriau must meet with Safeguard's biotech specialist, Sunil Payaparaji. William Pluteney, her second, may join characters headed for the cafeteria, though. He walks with a distinct limp, but it doesn't seem to bother him. Pluteney is also pleased to see the characters and chats with them in whichever language is most common to them all.

The cafeteria is very institutional, but the food is good for Lunar station fare. Pluteney is completely unwilling to discuss Vermilion while they're in the central core, and is visibly agitated if anyone brings it up. He's willing to discuss his injuries, but only in general terms. He uses circumlocutions like "our friend" to refer to Vermilion and "pleasant chat" for "interrogation." Irony is clear in his voice, but it should also be obvious he doesn't hold a grudge against Vermilion.

Unless the characters have questions about the station, Pluteney or Gaboriau's backgrounds or other non-work topics, you may move quickly through lunch.

Meeting Vermilion

After lunch, the characters return to the Safeguard section. They may watch (from a safe distance) as Vermilion is escorted from his cell in D Ring to an interrogation room in C Ring. He is treated as a threat at all times. A 1.5 meter pole is latched onto the restraining harness he wears (see "Technology," page 116) even before Vermilion is let out of his cell. One "handler" holds the pole while another keeps a stunner trained on him. The pole is longer than the station corridors are wide, and thus, would be a severe hindrance to Vermilion's mobility if he wrenched it out of the guard's hands. The pole does have a hinge in the middle for necessary maneuvering, but it is normally locked in the straight position, and Vermilion can't reach the joint.

The handlers have the trip from cell to room down to a science, and they only unlock the pole after they're all inside the interrogation room. During the actual interview, Vermilion is attached to his chair, which, like all the furniture in the room, is bolted to the floor. The bolts were recently upgraded from steel to olaminium-laced titanium to prevent Vermilion from breaking them again. The floor around Vermilion as well as the table are painted with red lines indicating the alien's maximum reach. These lines are conservatively and correctly drawn. On the table, beyond the red line, is the most recent version of Orgotek's translation device.

Gaboriau, Pluteney, and two or three of the characters are present for the first interview. The other characters (those not as well suited to interrogations) may watch from the observation and recording room and communicate suggestions via small headsets. Pluteney also offers sunglasses to the interrogators; Vermilion speaks partially in the ultraviolet, and the sunglasses prevent eyestrain.

If the characters were involved in **Ascent into Light**'s climax, you may decide that they've met Vermilion before! Since a number of Chromatics were captured during that invasion, the characters may have seen them being moved from one holding facility to another during the trip back to Luna or while they were at the Mare Ingenii base. If so, it's relatively difficult for the characters to realize it (especially after 10 months), but Vermilion has little trouble recognizing them. Chromat-

ics are much better at distinguishing between humans than vice versa.

This familiarity may breed contempt but not outright hostility — unlike Vermilion's reaction to total strangers. He knows that the current Safeguard team won't confront him physically, but he expects violence from unknown humans. If one of the characters comes within reach, Vermilion struggles to attack her as best as he's able.

Characters strong in Cryokinesis, Pyrokinesis or Photokinesis Modes also stand out to Vermilion. He can easily perceive the difference in their body temperatures and auras. Similarly, radical biokinetic changes or simple illness can change body temperature. Vermilion regards these differences as significant, and addresses those with higher temperatures and/or more complex psionic aura patterns as if they were higher in rank.

The Interrogation

Interrogating Vermilion is the focus of this episode. It's meant to give the players an opportunity to roleplay their own extended first contact with an alien. Additionally, it's vital to **Invasion** that a relationship form between the characters and Vermilion. The interrogations build upon this foundation, providing numerous roleplaying opportunities in the process. Explore this only as much as you feel that it is entertaining for all the participants. Don't simply relay everything that Vermilion knows, either. Try to create scenes where the players feel encouraged to communicate with this hostile alien and learn what makes him tick.

This communication need not be related only to finding out about Chrome-Prime and the Upeo infirmary, either. The interaction as the characters learn how to deal with Vermilion in his harness (the handlers are glad to pass this thankless job off on them) can be just as important as simply asking questions.

Characters interrogating Vermilion meet several obstacles, including dealing with an alien mindset, a light-based form of communication, a hostile subject, an unknown language and a translation device that is very much a prototype. Scale the difficulties in both roleplaying and dice rolling to match what your players find enjoyable. The exploration of a new form of thought can be just as exciting as scouting an alien world, but it is not to all tastes. The level of detail presented here may be very intriguing to some, but overwhelming to others. Don't hew exclusively to this information if you find it's boring the players.

Also, bear in mind that this is simply the first of many days spent interrogating Vermilion, with the final goal of getting enough information to successfully rescue the Upeo at the medical site. The characters shouldn't expect to get everything in one session that they need from their prisoner. The episode is geared so that the interview process requires roughly one week; you may adjust this to best suit your series. Feel free to weave intrigue in relating to the various teams in the station, or bring in subplots from previous stories. Don't let things drag out too long, however. The focus should remain as much as possible on Vermilion and the impending invasion.

Vocabulary

This information gets somewhat technical in spots, but you can use it to wow those who aren't scientifically minded or as an added bonus to those who get into scientific detail.

The first two aspects of the Chromatic language that the scientists of Operation Bridgework cracked were color and number. Chromatics refer to a color by "saying" that color. If it's outside their speech-range, they add a multiplier prefix. So, when shown the color red (4.5×10^{14} Hz), a Chromatic says the equivalent of, "That's half of 9×1014."

The aliens' numbering system appears to originally have been binary (base 2), and organized around the idea of doubling and halving frequencies of light. This seems to have evolved into base 6, as they frequently organize objects in groups of three or six. There are also hints of the original base 2 (or, perhaps, even base 8) numbering scheme for certain technical purposes, usually involving frequencies of light. This is similar to the way humans use base 10 for almost all purposes except low-level computer science, where base 2 is more practical. In Chromatic society, base 6 is apparently the most widely used by far.

The Bridgework team also observed Chromatics indicating numbers using their three-digit hands and feet. Curling up the thumb and index finger, but leaving the last finger extended, for example, indicates "110." These hand gestures are part of a small sign language vocabulary the aliens apparently use when stealth is required. Most of the gestures revolve around tactical maneuvers ("stop," "forward," "attack.")

Chromatics are also capable of a small range of audible sounds, but they are only used rarely. The sounds serve to punctuate Chromatic "light speech" in basic ways — for things like anger, lust, hunger and danger.

Though sophisticated in the discussion of light, the Chromatic light-based language is primitive in most other regards. Verbs are not conjugated, and complexities like person and tense are indicated by adding modifiers. ("I fight now." "He/she fight in past." "They fight in future."). There are relatively few nouns, and the words for any complex concept are compound. "Starship" is "high-raft," or sometimes "quick-high-far raft," "Building" is "above-cave." "Humans" are "high-far-beasts." The shortest Chromatic words are those dealing with home, family, hunting, conflict, and light, while the most complex are those for technology.

Armed with these details, you should be able to provide entertaining and convincing alien speech patterns for the players to enjoy.

The Translator

Operation Safeguard has the latest version of an Orgotek translation device, including several backups should one get broken. The device (developed by Orgotek in conjunction with the Ministry) is now in limited-scale production through a contract with the United Nations. It is designed to

Wavelengths

Chromatics can innately perceive a much larger range of light frequencies than humans can — from 10^{13} Hz to 10^{16} Hz. The numbers aside, this means the aliens can see through the same frequencies humans can (4.3×10^{14} to 7.5×10^{14}), and also a long way into both the infrared and the ultraviolet spectrums. Chromatics can emit light in a somewhat narrower spectrum, most of the infrared range, through visible light and into near-ultraviolet (that covers 10^{14} to 10^{15} if you're curious). Finally, the aliens speak in a narrower range — from visible light through to the colors indigo and violet and the near-ultraviolet (which encompasses 7×10^{14} to 10^{15}).

However, the *effective* degree to which a Chromatic can perceive and emit light frequencies depends on the individual alien's level of psionic ability. Unlike humans, all Chromatics are naturally attuned to subquantum energy. In the bulk of their population, this amounts to roughly one dot in Photokinesis, allowing for illumination control immediately around the individual — enough to shape light for speech. As noted in his template (see page 53), the hero Vermilion has the equivalent of five dots in Photokinesis, but he's only able to generate enough light for communication thanks to the dampening harness.

translate Chromatic-to-human languages (English, by default), and works much better than the various software and even telepathic solutions previously attempted. The details of its inner workings are not available to the characters, but it has both photokinetic and telepathic components.

The translator functions well enough to permit simple conversation. The transcript in the Setting section (page 15) was done using software, and is rife with errors. The Orgotek translator is overall superior to the "Chromie 3.0" software; the "Q & A" list below is intended to give you a good sense of how the new bioapp "speaks." As a given topic is explored, the device moves away from the clumsy compound nouns that Chromatic speech is full of, and toward a less immediately literal translation. This can be relayed precisely as accurate as you desire. Subjects that should be left vague are mentioned in the Q & A section; try to steer conversation away from direct answers on these topics.

Orgotek and the Ministry are quite interested in "field testing" the Chromatic translator they've created. As a result, you can add even more dynamics to these events by having characters from these orders pestered by officials curious about the bioapp's performance. No matter what the conversation is about, they invariably steer it back to the device with questions like "So how's the translator working?" and "Can you send us complete dumps of your interviews?"

Using Telepathy on Vermilion

Characters may wonder why Vermilion isn't simply being interrogated by a high-powered telepath. Chromatics have little or no apparent telepathic ability, so theory says this shouldn't be too difficult.

Unfortunately, theory is wrong. Telepathy has been used extensively on Chromatics, but has not proven 100% useful or accurate. Perhaps due to a radically different (and, arguably, more primitive) social structure, Chromatic thought and emotion are linked quite tightly. A telepath searching for information on subjects of importance (humans, their homeworld, the Bodiless Ones) triggers immense emotional responses (hatred, love, awe) within the alien mind that are both actively dangerous in their intensity and an impediment to further questioning. A Chromatic who has been "touched off" in this way tends to fixate on the topic until she has had a chance to calm down and gather her thoughts. This may take hours; Chromatics are passionate and direct beings. Between

the wear and tear on the psion and the necessary "cooling down" periods, it was found to be more efficient to simply talk to the aliens.

Vermilion, in particular, is extremely strong-willed. Feel free to apply at least +2 difficulty to **Mindshare** rolls against him. When such attempts are successful, be ambiguous. Emphasize the alien aspects of his thought processes. Slam home the emotional storms that ensue. Also, remember that Vermilion is skilled at believing what is most convenient, not from hypocrisy, but from a belief in speaking truth when reality is subjective.

Despite all this, Telepathy is not entirely useless. It can be quite helpful at double-checking responses Vermilion gives during more traditional communication. Doing so provides an additional die to rolls relating to the team's questioning, as the telepath can help clarify ambiguities and suggest more worthwhile lines of inquiry.

Characters who participated in **Darkness Revealed: Ascent into Light** may point out that the holographic re-creation device used in that adventure seemed to be pretty effective. True enough, but it was used to uncover information that the Chromatic subject was quite willing to divulge. Even then, the experience was challenging for the telepath to direct and was skewed strongly to the alien's opinions. Operation Safeguard gave up on that device early on, since it often gave as much fantasy and misleading data as it did accurate information.

A telepath isn't necessary for this story except to get the all-important psi coordinates from Vermilion (see "Departure," page 46). If the characters don't have a telepath on their team, use William Pluteney. His template is on page 56.

Q & A

The following is a list of questions the characters may ask Vermilion. (If the players aren't sure where to start, you may offer some of these as suggestions.) The answers provided assume Vermilion is in stage 3, psychology-wise (see page 30). If he's in an earlier stage, he'll be less forthcoming and more insulting. If he's in a later stage, he'll provide extra information. Note at each psychological stage what Vermilion is most curious about, as he'll try to direct conversation in those directions.

This list uses the compound-nouns representation of Chromatic light speech, with what the translator thinks is the most appropriate simpler word in brackets. The Orgotek device automatically substitutes the simpler word after the second or third time it's spoken.

General Questions

What is your name?

Leader Stonehand Sightblinder. (The device is "aware" that the interrogation team already calls him "Vermilion", and may incorporate that as well or simply use that instead.)

What do you do?/What is your position in your community?

I am a leader and a warrior.

Where did you get your psi powers?

My lights, which you have taken away? I have always had them.

Your gods didn't bring them to you?

Those-who-see [the Witnesses] speak to the gods. I do not speak for them.

Did the Witnesses bring you your powers?

No. People [Chromatics] have always had our light.

All Chromatics have psi powers?

All people glow.

About the War

Talk here will be relatively straightforward until things drift into the realm of "blue war/black war." That discussion gets somewhat vague at that point, due to fundamentally different Chromatic ideologies about which the Safeguard team isn't aware. The characters should not be completely clear on the blue-war/black-war concept until Vermilion Falling, when they have opportunity to see the distinction first-hand.

What was your mission in human space?

To kill. To gather spoor [strategic & tactical information] on high-far-beasts [humans].

Why do you wish to kill us?

You are the deceivers/corrupters.

What do we corrupt?

All in present, in future. [All that is or will be; the universe.]

Why do you believe this?

I have seen your corruption. I have been told of other instances.

Is this a holy war for you?

Black war.

So a war against evil?

A black war!

What do you mean, "black war?"

War with beasts. War to the end. War with you.

Are there other kinds of war?

There is war that is not with beasts. Blue war.

What is "blue war?"

It is war with Chromatics; war with people.

Humans are not people?

No! We are Chromatics, you are high-far-beasts [humans].

Are we not thinking beings?

All beings think. Stupid.

But are we not higher forms, like yourselves?

You are not like us!

Are we not different from animals?

No, beasts. You are much like the animals on our world.

How so?

You kill, you betray, you corrupt.

How do we corrupt?

By existing. By not being like us. By betrayal.

About Aberrants

The characters should have a good idea that Chromatics encountered Aberrants in the past, and that this is a significant reason for the current conflict. Characters may also figure that the aliens consider Aberrants and humans to be the same. Vermilion certainly reinforces this notion if asked, but is unable to provide much in the way of clarification as to why he thinks this.

This subject is easily prone to misinformation and confusion on Vermilion's part. The Chromatics see no real difference between Aberrants and other humans — from what Vermilion has come to suspect, Aberrants are the warriors, and humans are similar (though certainly not equal) to Chromatic priests.

When have we betrayed you?

Those-who-came-in-past spoke of trust, then turned on us.

Who came before?

Humans, like yourselves.

The Upeo?

Some were far-movers. Some were not.

Who were they?

More beasts.

Yes, but how were they different?

Not different; more beasts, corrupters.

Do you know what an "Aberrant" is?

You say in the past, still means nothing. All are beasts.

So you do know.

You words are not-bright [don't make sense].

Aberrants are not like humans.

No response.

Why don't you say anything?

Your words are not-bright [don't make sense].

About the Upeo

Why did you capture the teleporters?

They are corrupters, as are all high-far-beasts [humans]. They are useful.

How did you capture the teleporters?

We stopped them from far-moving [teleporting].

How?

With tools, built from wisdom carried to us by the Witnesses.

How do you control the teleporters, and make them do what you wish?

With more tools. With violence, and the threat of violence.

About Religion

Be vague on this topic. Chromatic religion is as complex as their talk about light. (Indeed, Project Safeguard has noted that a number of terms seem to be interchangeable between the two.) Although some players may already gather that some Doyen are posing as the Chromatics' gods, don't provide confirmation of this at this point. The full truth of this will come out in *Vermilion Falling*.

You can remain sketchy on this even if a character continues pressing the issue. After all, Vermilion has never seen one of the Bodiless Ones. He's simply relaying what his priests have told him.

Why did you start the war?/Who says humans are corrupters?

Those-who-see [the Witnesses] tell us the word of those-with-no-form [Bodiless Ones, gods of light].

Who are the Witnesses?

The ones who bring us the words of the Bodiless Ones.

Who are the Bodiless Ones?

Those who told us where to find your far-movers [teleporters]. We follow their orders.

Why?

They are bright [pure]; we are less so [flawed].

How did the Bodiless Ones know where the Upeo were?

They are pure; they know many things.

Why did they tell you where to find them?

You are the corrupters. You need to be destroyed.

Have you ever seen a Bodiless One?

No.

About Technology

Where do you get your ships?

Those-who-see [the Witnesses] give us the knowledge.

Where do they get it from?

They are the Witnesses.

Why does your technology look like ours?

You deceive! It is the other way.

So you're saying our technology looks like yours? Are you saying we stole from you?

You deceive. It is your way.

Couldn't your Witnesses have taken the knowledge from us?

People do not take from beasts. You take from people!

What else have the Witnesses brought to you?

Wisdom. New ways. New weapons. Goals. Missions. Knowledge.

The Next Step

Once the characters have established a rapport of sorts with Vermilion, it's time for them to learn what they can to help them in their mission. Clarence Greaves (the Upeo rescued in the end of **Ascent into Light**) knew of the place he was held, but it was determined to be too heavily guarded for an initial strike. He'd heard of others including an infirmary, but had never been to them. Æon proposed that they see if they could find reliable data on less securely held sites, rescue teleporters there, then use their knowledge and skills to get the others.

The medical site was determined the most promising. Vermilion stated in a previous interrogation that as many as half the remaining Upeo may be there. Safeguard got the impression that security is relatively light there because the teleporters are in poor physical condition and are deemed very low threats by the aliens. The char-

acters have to find out all that they can about the location, and what kind of activity they can expect from Chromatics in the area. If it looks like the characters are straying too far from the plot, and you'd like to steer them back on course, have Gaboriau or Pluteney make helpful reminders.

Vermilion answers these questions reluctantly, even though he suspects that the site was designed for an ambush. Vermilion doesn't understand why a disused warehouse was made into a medical facility unless it was meant to be a decoy — that's what he'd do, anyway. But he's far from certain of this and is not inclined to tell his captors anything simply on general principle.

Normal and telepathic techniques won't pick up anything untoward regarding the information Vermilion reveals, since he never actually lies. He does omit certain details and suspicions of his own with a degree of skill that professional con artists would envy, though. This twisted but firm desire to maintain truthfulness is a key component of Chromatic culture, as becomes more clear by the end of **Invasion**. A telepath might register danger, some fear and that Vermilion may not be telling them everything — none of which is surprising. After all, the characters are trying to find out about a sensitive installation from a captive who's facing bizarre alien tormentors.

Over time, Vermilion spells out the medical complex's precise location, the nature of its security, and dictates a rough sketch of the facility. This should take days to drag out of him, and be interspersed with wild tangents and circular arguments. Vermilion is a Chromatic hero even if he is a thrall, and he won't give up easily.

The alien claims that the internal security consists of 12 permanent guards and a patrol of six guards passing under the site roughly every two hours. Another 60 guards patrol the exterior, but Safeguard knows that those can be easily circumvented by having Clarence Greaves teleport inside the site. Vermilion further says that there should also be about a dozen non-combatant Chromatics at the site, mostly "doctors."

All of this information is very important, but the characters don't have the most important element — usable psionic coordinates, a sensory impression of the site with which Greaves can teleport. To add to the frustration, Vermilion is kidnapped before the characters can get this key data.

The Kidnapping

Luis Ulloa, the Norça on Haoa Flint Station, is assigned to spy on the groups there. This is not as treacherous as it sounds. Ulloa frequently runs these internal operations to test what is seen as shoddy security in the other orders (including getting Norça agents hired in from the beginning, as Ulloa was into Æon). The data gathered is usually kept for future reference. Sometimes, Proxy del Fuego cheerfully presents the evidence of their findings that indicate the holes throughout the other orders' security.

Unfortunately, Ulloa is a fanatic who's exceeded the bounds of this mandate. As part of his sometimes-misguided efforts to further his interpretation of the Norça's goals, Ulloa had already tried to sabotage projects at Haoa Flint that he saw as counter to the Norça's interests. The station's unique, segregated environment hampered his efforts, preventing anything more than minor complications to date. Thanks to his post, though, Ulloa has managed to almost completely subvert the station's computer security. This proves most helpful to Ulloa's kidnapping efforts.

Ulloa hired a group of freelance psion mercenaries led by one Joan Milovanovic. Oscar Riddle is her second-in-command; Vashti Matts, Shams ud-din Mohammed Hafiz and a man known only as Etacar round out the team. (See "Dramatis Personae," page 53, for a full description.)

This group has no particular connection with the Norça, having been hired by various orders and agencies in the past. They were smuggled to Haoa Flint one week ago in crates marked as office furniture, and have been hiding in the empty section since. (Refer to "Haoa Flint Station," page 19, for more details on the station's layout.) Ulloa wiped the records of the furniture shipment, and is preventing the security systems from registering the mercenaries' presence.

Detecting the Norça tampering requires the character to first have access to the complex's security (a tremendous challenge even for a ranking Æon member, requiring at least Status [Æon] 3 and a successful **Bureaucracy** or **Command** roll at +1 difficulty). Once in the system, the character is at +3 difficulty on **Intrusion** to detect any tampering; even so, determining who caused it requires a separate roll at +4 difficulty. (Ulloa is very good.) **Interface** may also be used at one lower difficulty on both rolls.

The Plan in Motion

The actual kidnapping occurs about one week after the characters arrive on the station, at around two in the morning. The mercs break through a security door connecting the empty section to Project Safeguard, then access Vermilion's cell (both actions are accomplished by Ulloa subverting the security codes on the doors). Once in the cell, the kidnappers give the alien a dose of RATRI (see "Technology," page 116). Vermilion resists the drug's effects violently, and succeeds in breaking three of Etacar's ribs before finally going down. This complicates things slightly for the squad, as they must now not only carry Vermilion, but help Etacar as well.

They slip back out, Matts carrying Vermilion. Hafiz is helping Etacar along, and Milovanovic and Riddle are providing cover to the front and rear. An already dicey situation goes flat-out wrong for the mercenaries as they try to leave Operation Safeguard. You may have one of the characters notice them as she battles insomnia; Vermilion could make his distinctive warning croak, waking someone; a hapless technician could run afoul of the mercs and get off a shout before being struck down.

The specifics are up to you, but make sure that the characters don't quite have a chance to stop the mercenaries in the station itself. They'll get to enjoy the unique environment of the Pit before they catch up to the kidnappers.

Once the alarm is raised, the merc team kicks into high gear and the rest of the station isn't far behind. The kidnappers have the edge, though. They've rigged a shaped charge on a section of the ceiling that lies under the docking area. Once the jig is up, Milovanovic detonates it remotely, opening a hole directly to the docks from the empty section. Ulloa had encoded a special subroutine in the computer system for exactly this circumstance. The explosion would normally trigger safety alarms; instead, the tremor trips the subroutine that scrambles the entire system. All computer-controlled security systems (including communications and weapons) go off-line for the remainder of this scene.

The mercs hustle through the empty section, climb through the gap and "commandeer" the Banji Raven 11 transport sitting in the bay. In actuality, the ship was arranged by Ulloa, the pilot pretending to be forced into service. The Raven then has a clean getaway. The scrambled computer prevents any cries for help, the station's defensive weaponry are similarly off-line, and no other crafts are ready to pursue (or are as fast as the getaway ship).

To whet the players' appetites, have a brief fight between the characters and the mercs. The most likely location is the hole from the main level to the docking level — the characters scrambling to catch up from below with the kidnappers fleeing up and out. Make this fight as even as possible. The characters should only have minimal armaments thanks to having been alerted from a sound sleep with no idea of what's happening. And while the mercenaries are quite well armed and armored, their only concern is getting out with their captive.

The mercenaries should escape with Vermilion, but have one of the team captured in the process — Etacar makes the most sense, as his injuries slowed him enough to be caught. If the characters consider using area-effect attacks, Pluteney pops his head out of a side corridor and shouts them down. Vermilion is right in the midst of the mercs and is far too valuable to be killed. This could be just the distraction the kidnappers need to slam shut the transport's door and trigger the bay's hatch. Once the departure sequence begins, alarms blare and warning lights flash. The characters have no choice but to flee back into the Safeguard section and get behind the emergency pressure door.

Particularly aggressive characters may want to try getting through the hole into the bay and boarding another ship before the area depressurizes. The hole is in the center of the bay, though, and as they might all recall from their arrival, only one ship is allowed in the bay at a time. There's simply nowhere to run inside the bay before decompression gets the best of the character. There is an L-B NEL (see *Trinity*, page 285) at one of the exterior docks, but with the computer off-line it takes 10 minutes to manually open the numerous hatches to it. By then, the kidnappers are long gone.

In short, the characters allow the mercenaries to get away. That doesn't mean they're not without recourse, however.

Afterward

The Æon personnel running Haoa Flint (four security guards, two comm operators, three security-office personnel — including Ulloa — two medics, three maintenance workers, four cooks/housekeeping staffers — all neutrals) spring into action after the kidnapping. All go to their posts to make sure everything's in order, except the security guards; two take Etacar to the infirmary, the other two split off with the maintenance crew to sweep the entire station. Maintaining Flint's in-

tegrity is their top priority, but allow the characters to help. Those with appropriate talents and who aren't deemed security risks (Status [Æon] 3 or being vouched for by Gaboriau and Pluteney) may help get the computer system back on-line, find out what Etacar and his crew were up to, or help sweep the facility.

Etacar was taken to the station's core infirmary where his wounds (and those of anyone else who suffered injury in the recent combat) are tended by the medics. Again, characters with appropriate training are welcome to lend a hand. Etacar doesn't say a thing during treatment or when the guards make some effort to question him. Security is obviously not trained in interrogation, so the characters can easily step forward and take control. The medics won't allow them to harm Etacar physically, but otherwise the characters have free reign. Verbal interrogation gets nowhere very quickly. Despite threats and mind-games, Etacar proves completely unwilling to talk. He doesn't appear angry or fearful, merely a bit nervous.

During this initial period, be sure to address what's going on in the security office. The system operators have no idea what happened to the computer. (Ulloa planned the swipe for a time when he wasn't on night shift; computer records show him entering his room hours before the event.) Ulloa, the other two computer techs and any characters with relevant skills work to bring the systems back on-line. Even if characters aren't there, Ulloa follows his co-workers' lead in the repairs, acting just as puzzled as they.

The Norça spy is unconcerned until he learns that one of the mercenaries was captured alive (either from a character helping with the computer or when one of the Proteus guards stops by on a sweep). Ulloa only dealt with Milovanovic, after all, and only identified himself as "Senõr Misterio." He then realizes that it could be a huge problem if Milovanovic herself was captured.

Flustered (noticeable with a standard **Rapport** roll), Ulloa tries to leave the security office at earliest opportunity. If a character's there and confronts him, Ulloa claims he's not feeling well. The Norça agent is very smooth when he wants to be, even when panicked. Short of **Telepathy**, it's difficult to tell (**Subterfuge** at +3 difficulty) that Ulloa's pale skin and sheen of sweat is anything other than a touch of flu.

Luis Ulloa makes a tactical error here. Instead of jumping in the NEL docked outside the station and getting the hell out, he's confident that he can get through any potential confrontations with his guile and wits. He's a Norça, after all. He heads for the infirmary, to bolster Milovanovic's confidence (if it's her) or to just be a fly on the wall (if one of the other mercs was captured).

Ulloa enters the infirmary just as the characters find they're getting absolutely nowhere with Etacar, or when they decide to use **Telepathy** (whichever comes first). If one of the characters has **Telepathy** and you have a fair idea that she'll use it instead of bothering with conventional questioning, leave Etacar in a haze of pain for a while as his injuries are tended. Once enough time passes that Ulloa could've learned of the capture and come to the sickbay, indicate that Etacar seems lucid enough that **Telepathy** shouldn't be hindered by the prisoner's pain.

Ulloa and Etacar are each relieved when they see one another — the former because the prisoner isn't Milovanovic, the latter because he recognizes Ulloa. Unknown to the Norça, the mercenary leader ignored the command to keep Ulloa's identity secret. Milovanovic relayed Ulloa's description so that any of the mercs could impress the Norça spy into service if things went awry, using him as a "hostage."

Etacar has no intention of deliberately betraying his employer, but he is both surprised and relieved when Ulloa arrives. Thanks to the pain relievers coursing through his system, it's impossible for Etacar to hide his expression entirely (characters note it on standard **Rapport** and **Subterfuge** rolls). Ulloa is much more smooth, but Etacar's look is damning enough.

If the characters don't have **Pilfer** or prefer to confront Ulloa directly, he simply denies everything (regardless of evidence). He excels at circular logic and debating, throwing doubt on any claims the characters make. ("Why did the prisoner look relieved to see you?" "Perhaps I look like someone he knows"; "Why does his mind show that you hired him?" "Who's to say that an unscrupulous psion didn't implant that thought in him in the first place?") Even so, it all begins to sound rather flimsy — especially since it's obvious that the kidnapping had to be an inside job.

At this point, Ulloa admits to everything. He explains that he was heading up a plan to benefit the glorious Norça Order, that capturing the dread

Chromatic would have gone a long way to furthering the Norça's cause. Ulloa is clear to take all the blame for himself and even confirms the rendezvous point; Vermilion is too important a resource to lose even if the alien does go back into Æon's hands. Ulloa is confident that his order will see the wisdom of his plan and initiate a new one of their own to rescue him and Vermilion. As characters who've dealt with the Norça in the past suspect, Ulloa may well be visited once word gets back to Proxy del Fuego, but it won't be a pleasant encounter. *Pai de Norça* doesn't like his children acting up like this.

Regular interrogation may not be necessary, though. Neither Etacar nor Ulloa has heightened resistance to psi (though the drugs make Etacar even more pliable). Effects like **Sense Emotion**, **Mindspeak**, **Pilfer** and **Mind's Eye** easily pick up on their states of mind, but **Pilfer** reveals exactly who hired the team and where they were headed. Conventional questioning is possible, but takes much longer — an extended **Interrogation** roll garnering six successes reveals the plan.

However the characters go about it, they eventually learn that the mercenaries were to take Vermilion directly from Luna to Colombia. Ulloa would send an encrypted laser transmission to his fellow Norça (something he'd been doing regularly since he'd first come on the job here, wiping the record of it each time). A representative would be on hand at the coordinates the mercenaries were given. They'd exchange Vermilion for a staggering amount of money and vanish for a time, while the alien would disappear into the Norça complex.

Once this is divulged, Etacar starts to chuckle. He's feeling no pain from the drugs, and in his current euphoric state of mind has to laugh at the fact that although this is the official plan, it's not what really happened!

The Real Kidnapping Plan

In truth, Etacar's leader, Joan Milovanovic, had a contingency plan in case one of her people didn't make it out. Instead of Colombia, the mercs would head for the Pit. From there she'd send an anonymous transmission to Ulloa's minicomp urging him to check certain LunaNet boards. (These coded messages on LunaNet had been how they'd handled previous communications.) Etacar recalls that Milovanovic would want an update and determine how best to spring their comrade.

Since Milovanovic couldn't be sure that Ulloa would be willing to help free a mercenary, she'd keep Vermilion secured in an undisclosed place until arrangements were made. Checking Ulloa's minicomp, the characters find no message and can't be sure when Milovanovic might send it.

It'd be cut-and-dried if Etacar knew where the mercs went to ground, but he doesn't. Milovanovic made a point to not be predictable, so she and her team could be anywhere in Yeltsingrad. Pluteney observes that someone must've noticed the Raven II dock somewhere, and it couldn't be that easy to keep a trussed-up Chromatic a secret for long in such a place.

Time is of the essence, Gaboriau urges. They'll keep tabs on the minicomp in case anything comes in, but she encourages the characters to head for Yeltsingrad to try tracking down the mercenaries and recover Vermilion. No one else in the station is as suited to the mission, and further support won't arrive for nearly a full day. (Both the UN and Æon are stretched very thin at the moment.) Further, Vermilion will at least *recognize* the characters, which is only true of about a dozen other humans in the entire Solar System.

Chain Hotel

The mercenaries have been in the Pit — in Chain Hotel, in fact — for two hours by the time the characters arrive in Yeltsingrad. Vermilion is sedated and restrained, but the mercs have a limited supply of RATR1 and no way to get more. Keeping Vermilion restrained once the drugs run out presents a problem. Fortunately, the Pit has many solutions for that kind of dilemma — although how drugs designed for human physiology might affect an alien is anyone's guess.

Chain Hotel is located roughly between the second and third ring outside the Floor. It's close enough to be fairly clean and well run, yet far enough to lack any real charm or flair. It caters, quite explicitly, to the extreme bondage crowd. The decor runs to black and red pseudo-leather, vinyl, fake human skin, chains, ropes, tentacles and assorted mechanical restraining devices. The lobby has an iron maiden on display, as well as what appears to be a harness for a Chromatic. (The latter was created by the decorator on a whim, working from pictures of Chromatics, and is far too weak to actually be functional.)

The mercenaries chose this hotel not because of the decor, however, but because every room comes with more-than-adequate equipment to keep someone chained up indefinitely. They get a two-room suite and lock Vermilion to the wall in one while they occupy the other. Milovanovic sends the prompt (from a public terminal) to Ulloa's minicomp shortly before the characters reach the Pit, then she heads back to the room, posts the first code message and waits.

An Angry Alien

Vermilion is in a state of confusion and fury difficult to describe by this point. He's been repeatedly drugged and manhandled, and now appears to have been captured by a *new* group of humans. He doesn't understand the differences in motivations between humans, having been taught to expect that they all act with unified intent.

He's not sure where he is now, but Vermilion knows that it's not up to the security of his previous cell. The chains holding him are strong, but careful testing reveals that he could break them with a determined effort. The alien is eager to kill the mercenaries, but they're armed and formidable and he's still drugged. Vermilion waits to regain his faculties more fully, and to learn what he can before breaking loose into an inexplicable environment full of enemies.

Finding the Mercs

Once the characters reach the Pit, they have a lot of options available. Thanks to Etacar and Ulloa, they should know the makeup of the mercenary team, but they don't know the full details of the backup plan (only Milovanovic does) or where the team may have holed up.

The following scenario is not the only option available to the characters or to you. You can devote as much time to this part of the episode as you like. There's a wealth of source material on the Pit starting on page 21. You could run a drawn-out game of cat-and-mouse with the characters and the mercs trading intrigues on the LunaNet board, with tense meetings and pursuits through the morass of decadence that is the Pit. You could focus on a more straightforward but still suspenseful investigation, where the characters track down the mercs from clues they find along the circuitous route from the abandoned Raven II, through danger and depravity, and so to the Chain Hotel. Gear things to best suit the characters and what you think the players will most enjoy.

Asking Around

So long as the characters don't represent themselves as "the law," almost everyone in the Pit can be bribed to talk (and are otherwise silent or send the characters into a hold-up if they look like easy marks). Cost and trustworthiness vary widely, but spending anything less than ¥50 for each piece of information is tantamount to insult and usually puts the characters on a wild-goose chase. The few who can't be bribed are either honest (rare) or too paranoid to talk to anyone (not uncommon).

There is a maintenance worker at the docking port where the Raven II was left (an alcoholic who maintains the seals in exchange for food and drabs of cash from the locals). The scruffy, Asian woman virtually ignores any questions (and any threats of violence) until offered ¥100. At that point she delivers a detailed description of the mercs, the big box they had with them and what direction they left in. She didn't hear their conversation. After delivering this information, she slips away to have a little party with her infusion of cash.

Asking "Where could I keep someone locked up?" results in varied answers. There isn't a single establishment in the Pit that doesn't have at least one room with a suitable space for keeping troublemakers. Most responses are variants on "I've got a room you could use. Cost ya ¥100 a night." More useful answers include various storage lockers around the outer rings, the Secs lockup in the Floor, hotels and a few of the kinkier brothels (including the Chain Hotel). Specifically asking, "Where could I keep an alien locked up?" gets mostly strange looks and hurried exits (and maybe even a report to the Secs). Even so, with luck, someone will mention the fake Chromatic harness at the Chain Hotel.

Going to the Top

The characters may ask the local authority (the President's people) for help. This isn't necessarily a bad course of action, although the Secs and various underlings on the Floor are hostile toward representatives of "law and order" (which is what they assume the characters are even if they don't say it). Still, the characters will get passed slowly up the chain of command if they manage to convince any of the security, pit bosses, dealers or other members of the President's staff that they have a legitimate problem (**Command**, **Etiquette** or **Subterfuge** rolls are most appropriate here). "Legitimate problems" include "dangerous alien in the Pit," "threat to humanity," and any other threat to the President's life or livelihood.

This process finally ends with the Secretary, the President's major-domo. He's adopted the President's air of secrecy, wearing a blank white mask with a single red stripe across the forehead, gloves

Using Psi

• Clairsentience can be used to track down the mercs, though it can take some time. **Envision** with an extra success used at the abandoned craft discloses what the mercs discussed and where they went afterward. Details are sketchy, but the psion learns that the team planned to check into a hotel "where the demon lizard won't bother us." **Dowsing** can lead the characters directly to Vermilion; he's the only perceptible alien in the Pit.

• Yeltsingrad no longer has a unified computer network, so Electrokinesis is of little help. Checking the LunaNet board with **Interface** may bear more fruit once Milovanovic posts the first coded message. With three successful rolls at +1 difficulty once in the system, the character can track the post's origin to the Chain Hotel.

• The Biokinesis talent **Transformation** could be used to disguise the character as Etacar or Ulloa to get close to the mercenaries. This would most likely involve setting up a meeting through the LunaNet board, or approaching the mercs' room in Chain Hotel once the characters have narrowed down the location.

• Using Telepathy on random Pit-dwellers is safe if the subject remains unaware. It's unlikely that the characters will meet another psion (at least one not employed by the President), and it's not easy for neutrals to notice telepathic intrusion if they're not tipped to it. Random scanning is bound to look suspicious sooner or later, though. At that point, the individual likely gets violent and/or calls for Secs, adding a level of complication the characters can little afford right now.

Remember that any psi use is detected on the Floor (see "The Floor," page 25).

and a white Nordamerican-style suit of conservative cut. He meets the characters in a suite overlooking the casino. The office is done in *faux* wood paneling with dark blue with red accents. The Secretary is very quiet and very menacing, but if the characters are honest, he agrees to "make some calls." The characters are firmly escorted down to the casino to wait, and even given a few betting chips (¥20 each).

After a few hours (just long enough for the characters to start getting nervous) security gives a folded Zip-Strip to the team leader (see "Technology," page 116). The slip says simply:

"Chain Hotel.

Don't come back.

—The President"

If the characters are less than polite and honest at any point in this, they're removed from the Floor with whatever degree of force is necessary. If a physical altercation ensues, ending in death, the killer faces a quick trial probably leading to execution (see page 108 of **Luna Rising** for details on the President's "justice" system).

At the Chain Hotel

The Chromatic harness in the Chain Hotel's lobby is immediately obvious. Even a cursory inspection by anyone familiar with Vermilion reveals it wouldn't hold him for a second. It's made for decoration.

The clerk at the desk is apparently female, and dressed from top to toes in shiny green tightness. Any questions about the mercs is met with, "Our clients don't pay us to talk. A suite here goes for ¥300 a night, and our reputation for silence is worth at least twice that." This is a thinly veiled request for a bribe — a room and another ¥600 for information. If the characters pony up, the clerk says "Room 304" and hands them a code key — for Room 303 (where the mercs are staying). She then informs the characters that physical stuff is okay, but she'll call the Secs if she hears any loud noises.

If the characters try to bull their way through, planning to get the mercs on their own, the clerk calls the Secs immediately. Four well-armed thugs appear (use the Police template in **Trinity**, page 304) as the characters are engaged with the mercs, and don't really care what's going on until everyone is subdued.

Confronting the Mercs

The mercenaries have planted bugs (see **Trinity**, page 274) in the single elevator and on the landing to the back stairs, so it's tough to sneak up on them (**Awareness** at +4 difficulty to see the bug, **Stealth** at +3 difficulty to sneak). The hallway is an L-shape, running 10 meters from the elevator, turning left for another four meters to the stairs. The rooms have no back doors and the walls are reinforced and sound-proofed. At any given moment, one mercenary stands watch over Vermilion in the rear room closer to the stairs. The remaining three are in the front room; one is asleep and the other two sit generally facing the monitor receiving the bugs' transmissions. Those awake are combat-ready in one turn. The sleeping one can be jostled awake and is ready to go in three turns.

If the characters simply run in and break down the door, the fight starts immediately. Otherwise, if the mercs think they have time, they'll try to gather up Vermilion and head for the back stairs (or the elevator, if that looks like a better shot). The mercenaries only use guns if they are fired upon; they know about the President's Secs, too.

If Vermilion hears a fight start, he waits for the guard to be distracted then breaks free and attacks. With the damper harness on, Vermilion can only use his strong rear legs to attack (kicking and clawing). This fight is about even; Vermilion is

tougher, but the merc has a knife and body armor. When and if Vermilion sees the characters, he is reluctant to kill them and instead tries to escape.

Instead of simply breaking down the door, the characters may call the mercs. Joan Milovanovic is very disappointed that they've been found, but she's a reasonable woman. If she is convinced that Ulloa has given up on them and that the characters will treat her people fairly, she surrenders. Milovanovic has no desire to have her team killed in a stupid fight in a bondage hotel.

Otherwise, the situation may devolve into a standoff — but the Secs show up after a while if neither side budges. This could turn into a three-way fight, but the mercenaries are unlikely to battle two enemy forces and will again surrender. Unless the characters try to take on the Secs (a suicidal notion since the President has a lot more Secs than the characters have teammates), the latter force a peaceful resolution. The Secs, under the President's orders, give Vermilion to the characters (noting that the characters should remember this favor) and escort both parties out of the Pit by two different routes.

Departure

By the time the characters recover Vermilion, the invasion fleet is fast approaching zero hour. Only 23 hours remain before the characters must ship out, and they still haven't gotten a clear sense-impression of the Chromatic medical site. They must return to Haoa Flint post haste. There's no time for personal issues — such as vendettas against the mercenaries. (If the mercs surrendered, the characters should turn them over to Æon security when they return to Haoa Flint, to join Etacar and the self-martyred Ulloa.)

Gaboriau and Pluteney are concerned about the mission if they don't get the information they need from Vermilion in time. They direct the characters to initiate further interrogations after the Chromatic's physical status is determined to be stable — which, aside from a few scrapes and cuts, it is.

The characters get only a few hours of sleep, and return to the interrogation chamber. It's difficult to tell, but it seems that Vermilion has undergone a subtle change (having progressed another stage in his opinion of the characters and of humans, thanks to his recent rescue). He's disposed to learning more about humanity (through the characters), but he is still far from trusting them outright. This extends to telepathic probes.

Teleporting requires a telepathic sensory impression. This is tricky to get (see "Using Telepathy on Vermilion," page 35), as it requires reading Vermilion's mind and he's not into that sort of thing. He hates being telepathized and he isn't simply going to give up his recollections of the medical site no matter how puzzled and intrigued by humanity he's become.

This requires using **Pilfer** at +2 difficulty (Vermilion is resisting), and takes three successes beyond the those needed to overcome the difficulty. If the character is having trouble getting these many successes, have Pluteney suggest that he try distracting Vermilion with his own Pilfer attempt on some other topic while the character "slips in through the back door" — effectively negating the difficulty for the moment. If this is all being handled by Pluteney, make a few roles, play out a description of how challenging it is, and then allow the attempt to succeed.

When the characters finally get the sense-impression, play up a sense of victory, as if the characters have achieved a truly significant goal in the episode. It should make all the trouble they've gone through seem worthwhile.

When it's time to go, an E-19 drop ship arrives at Haoa Flint to take the team and Vermilion to *Chicago*, one of the invasion fleet Leviathans. The rest of the fleet is already heading off the plane of the ecliptic by the time the characters leave Luna. It takes a few hours to meet up and dock, and the jump ships continue their outward course through the next scene.

The Invasion Plan

Once they arrive on *Chicago*, Vermilion is taken directly to one of the drop ships, *Red Hornet*, while the characters are escorted to a cramped briefing room. If they have never been on a bioship before, emphasize the quasi-organic twists and folds of the interior. At the briefing, they get a very complete rundown of the invasion (even though most of the details are irrelevant to them). The lecture, intended as a final recap before departure (it covers the high points, as all those present should already be familiar with their respective duties), is delivered by Admiral Wallace Mkumba in a coded broadcast from the flagship *Europa*.

The fleet consists of five Leviathans, named *Chicago*, *Europa*, *Himalaya*, *Bolivar*, and *Aegypt*. *Bolivar* and *Aegypt* are not fully equipped, having no Tessers. Instead, they're being jumped by two Upeo who've returned recently to Earth — one is Susan N'gamba, former mayor of Karroo; the other is anyone who you might think would make for an interesting plot thread in the future.

The Leviathans will jump in extremely close to Chrome-Prime; only a few hundred kilometers above the surface. This is a deliberate strategic move. The "dirty" subquantum wave produced by the jump ship's translation from subquantum to normal space should leave the entire psionically sensitive Chromatic population off-balance (see **Trinity**, page 192, regarding backlash).

Each Leviathan carries 12 fighters (mixing Bakuhatsu E-15s and Orgotek Locusts) in its internal bays. Its external docking clamps have four Nova Starcraft A-5L Phoenix frigates, two Orgotek Seahawk bombers, four L-B Military Equipment Lifters and two Bakuhatsu E-19 Stealth drop ships. Its exterior capital-ship docks hold two L-B Novastorm 1AC frigates (holding a mix of eight fighters), one L-B Aerie 1FC frigate (with a mix of 24 fighters) and one Orgotek Scarab frigate (with a pair of Locusts).

All of these vehicles are listed in **Trinity**, the **Trinity Technology Manual**, or in the "Technology" section of this book. They relate only peripherally to the characters, though, so don't be concerned if you lack specific statistics on, say, the L-B Novastorm.

The drop ships each have specialized missions, including the rescue mission. The L-B MELs (car-rying reinforced infantry platoons) are assigned to the pinpoint insertion of demolition teams to destroy hardened, valuable ground targets. The bombers will hit "softer" ground targets. The bulk of the battle will be conducted by the frigates and their fighter squadrons, destroying any and all military targets on the ground or in orbit. The frigates will operate in pairs, each defended by one third of their fighter force. The Leviathans will stand off once they've dropped their flock and prepare to receive damaged craft. The remaining fighters are assigned to defend the Leviathans.

Once orbital space is secured, the fleet is to reform and begin detailed scans of the surface. This intelligence-gathering is intended to determine what non-military targets require attention, and of what sort. In all cases, the mission is to eliminate the Chromatic threat. While the UN does not intend to engage in xenocide, it is prepared to use nuclear weapons on even civilian sites that are determined to be threats, but that can't be eliminated in any other way.

The characters will miss virtually the entirety of this conflict. Clarence Greaves (who doesn't help with the inter-system jump since he'll need his

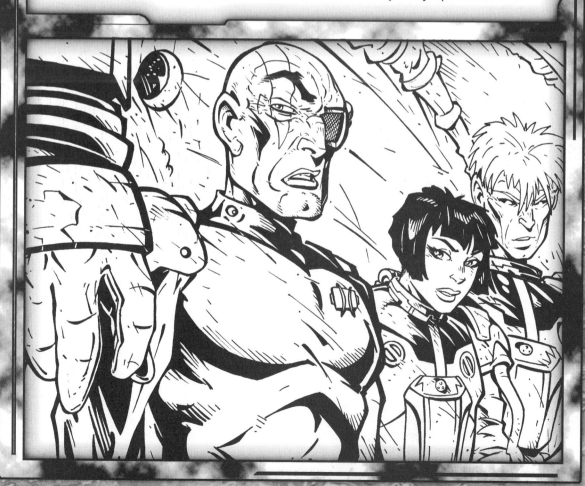

energy on Chrome-Prime) will teleport them and Vermilion (as an on-site guide and possible insurance in case of trouble) directly to the medical facility. Once on the ground, the characters are in charge of their own timetable. They're strongly encouraged to recover as many Upeo as possible from the site and then teleport out without dawdling. Marsden believes the fleet should be able to take and hold orbital space, but it's not a given.

Once back on board the Leviathan, the rescued Upeo will return to Earth with the first load of injuries and casualties (although the Tessers require some time to power up, N'gamba, Greaves and the third Upeo should have enough energy to jump within a day or so). The characters are to interview the teleporters during this time and use the information gained to return for further rescue attempts on Chrome-Prime.

The Jump

After the briefing concludes, the team meets Clarence Greaves as it heads for *Red Hornet*. He's a skeletally thin, dour Englishman who provides enough gloom and doom for everyone to enjoy. There's time for little more than first impressions and small talk before Mkumba transmits a broad-band announcement that the jump ships have finally reached safe departure range. Everyone buckles in, and the ships plunge into subquantum space.

For any characters who haven't journeyed through "sub-space" before, this is a moment of dread and expectation. As the energies gather, the drop ship vibrates like a leaf. The radical alterations in the noetic field can be clearly felt by all psions, even through the Leviathan's shielding aura. There is a single bright flash (more in the mind than in reality), and the trip begins. There's no clear sense of how long the translation from Earth to Chrome-Prime takes, but clocks measure it as only a few hours. The characters are almost entirely disconnected from complex thought during this time. After remanifestation, recovery takes only a few minutes, though. Even for those characters who traveled via long-distance teleportation before, this is a dramatic experience.

Welcome to Chrome-Prime

Aegypt has already arrived and is deploying by the time *Chicago* and *Bolivar* appear, each within a few seconds of one another. *Europa* comes through about a minute later and *Himalaya* slams into being a full five minutes after that.

The jump ships' shielding protects the humans from the worst of the subquantum flux their arrivals create — including those that come in late — but it's still rather disorienting (characters are effectively Dazed for a couple of minutes). While the characters and their pilot are recovering, the drop ship detaches automatically from *Chicago* and starts a rapid, evasive dive toward Chrome-Prime. This is less to shorten the distance (for the most part, distance doesn't matter to a teleporter) than it is to get clear of the scrambled noetic field around *Chicago*. *Himalaya*'s tardy arrival complicates things somewhat as the characters must make **Attunement** rolls in reaction to the backlash it sets off.

The pilot, intentionally a neutral just in case the Leviathans arrived in stagger formation, is little affected by the psionic fluctuations. He takes the controls and brings *Red Hornet* in hard and fast, avoiding the sporadic anti-aircraft fire that starts up. Once the characters are all recovered and ready to go, Greaves jumps them and Vermilion. As the team teleports out, the drop ship lurches from a direct hit. The characters won't know the extent of the damage; allow them to suspect the worst. In truth, *Red Hornet* limps back to *Chicago*, but is out of service for the rest of the invasion.

The Medical Site

The materialization is rough. Greaves blames this on the inherent difficulty of a combat jump — but, unbeknownst to them at the moment, the teleportation damping field that the Chromatics set up over the planet's surface is the primary cause. The team appears on the second level of the site. They have a clear view of several rooms on the second level and a partial view through the collapsed floor and light shafts to the ground level. It is just prior to local dawn, and the sunlight is very red. There are no Chromatics in the immediate vicinity (aside from Vermilion).

Overall Design

The building has four levels, not counting the tunnels beneath. About 25 meters square at the base, it's shaped like a stepped pyramid. The ceilings are low, just under two meters. Each floor has a square opening in the center that serves as a light shaft. If this building were in regular use, Chromatics would look into the light shaft to talk to each other from floor to floor. Neither these holes, nor the outside balconies, have railings. Chromatics are excellent climbers and guard rails would never occur to them. The building also doesn't have stairs. To get from floor to floor, Chromatics exit the doors on each level and climb or jump up to the next balcony. If they're feeling energetic, they leap across the light shaft to the floor they want. There are a few spindly ladders lying about on each floor to accommodate the Upeo who were treated here. They collapse if subjected to any rough treatment, though.

The overall style is simple and chunky. Construction is of red and yellow stone blocks reinforced with visible iron girders. Interior walls are of smaller stone bricks. The iron is beginning to rust, but only slightly; Chrome-Prime's surface is dry. The bricks are mortared, but the large blocks aren't, and what mortar is visible is crumbling. There are several narrow windows on each level. Looking out, the team sees a dry, rocky landscape, with other stepped pyramids scattered across it. Some show signs of activity, but most look abandoned. The orbital battle is just visible in the sky as flashing lights and bomb blasts can be heard in the near distance.

Equipment, all biotech, is placed haphazardly about the three lower floors. It all appears primitive in design, roughly equal in sophistication to human equipment from the late-19th and early 20th century. There's no sign of electronics more advanced than a vacuum-tube and transistor stage. There are simpler hardtech tools, but those look even more alien than the bioapps do.

An **Engineering** roll is required to get a general idea what function a device serves. Some is abandoned medical equipment, but the newer-looking devices are security systems (primitive motion and vibration sensors) with wires leading off in all directions. Unless the team is extremely careful and paranoid, the devices are tripped shortly after they teleport in. This isn't obvious unless one of the characters gets two or more successes on an **Engineering** roll. ("Hey, the pool of mercury in this gadget just tipped over.")

Three simple traps are set on the first level, consisting of chemical land mines hidden under rubble and are triggered if someone steps on one. Treat them as fragmentation grenades that do only five dice of Lethal damage. The only other innate dangers come from the building's lack of structural integrity. Any kinetic weapon with base damage of six dice or more that misses its target causes part of the building to fall inward. Collapsing rubble does three dice (or more, depending on how large you decide the collapse is) of Bashing damage. Clever characters may use this to their benefit.

This building was abandoned as a warehouse when several of the floors fell in, and the rubble was only partially cleared away during the brief period that it was a hospital. In particular, a distinct "ramp" of rubble exists going down from the northeast corner of the second level, through the first level and to the tunnels. Characters can travel down this slope at normal running speed with two successes on an **Athletics** roll. One success permits walking speed, and a failed roll means the character must move at two meters per turn. Storytellers are encouraged to be creative with a botch.

The third level was storage and remains the most cluttered. If the team has time to search they can find some extremely primitive medical supplies for humans here. Most have gone bad and you should reward experimentation with nausea at a minimum.

The fourth and uppermost level, as in most Chromatic aboveground structures, was used as a guard post and for sending and receiving long-range messages.

It's obvious to everyone after initial searching that there are no prisoners here. The sensors and mines lend the idea that this is likely an ambush (a clairsentient with Danger Sense can pretty much guar-antee that idea). At that point, Greaves tries to teleport the team out. The damping field responds immediately, clamping down on him like an angry alligator, inducing a massive migraine, spotty vision, and (if you want to truly complicate matters) unconsciousness.

This does not look good. If you decide that Greaves is still conscious, he explains for the slow-witted that he's being blocked from leaving. It might just be the building, but whatever the case it's a bad idea to stay there. The characters have to get out. The only problem is getting past the enemy.

Chromatic Forces

With the teleport dampers operative, the aliens assumed it was impossible to teleport into the building. There are a significant number of Chromatics on the site, but they're scattered and their attention is to the exterior (until the characters give away their presence inside). There are twice as many Chromatics in the guard as the team's number. When the security devices are tripped or if a Chromatic senses the characters' arrival (standard **Attunement** roll), all but two of the guards proceed downward to attack the team. This pair starts signaling out the windows for assistance, but other Chromatic forces fail to notice their message for several minutes due to the planet-wide chaos the invasion is causing.

There are another six Chromatics in the basement tunnels, one leader and five warriors. They don't notice anything until the shooting starts, or if the team stumbles across them. Outside, there are up to 60 more Chromatics in groups of three, spaced under cover in an outer and inner ring around the building to guard approaches.

As the fight begins, the Chromatics hesitate momentarily at the sight of Vermilion. They assume he is a thrall, though, and shoot at him if the opportunity arises. Vermilion is perfectly capable of talking to them during the battle, but what he says depends strongly on his current attitude towards humans as well as what he's decided about his own status. At worst, he says nothing. At best, he tries to stop the battle; he may be convinced by this point that the war is a gross error. This isn't entirely successful, as the guards cannot be convinced in the middle of hostilities that they aren't fighting a black war.

The characters must fight their way out, but such a battle doesn't go well. Every time a Chromatic falls, another two appear from tunnels or from outside. They are fierce and strange warriors, fighting for the safety of their race. Play up the sense of having disturbed a wasp's nest.

This could get exceedingly grim for the characters very quickly. If you like, have some of what Vermilion says strike a nerve in the Chromatics. They retreat slightly, going on the defensive to assess the situation and get orders. This also gives the characters time to escape from the building.

There are several exits — on the surface and beneath. Of the five tunnels under the site, one is completely filled with rubble. A second leads steeply downward and a third has sounds of Chromatic activity. The tunnels to the north and east are relatively clear and safe. After several hundred meters each comes out under a building of similar construction to the medical site, although each is empty and unguarded. The characters can exit to the surface here.

If the characters decide to stay and fight, more Chromatic grunts, in groups of six, arrive on the scene from the third tunnel mentioned above. These new groups don't have effective leadership or discipline, and you should play them as confused and hesitant (perhaps knock a die or two off their Physical Ability rolls). The idea is to convince the characters that it's time to run, not to kill them.

Once the characters are on the surface, Greaves still finds it impossible to teleport away. The characters must retreat across the surface. Luckily, they can evade the surviving Chromatics fairly easily. The aliens were ordered to ambush anyone appearing at the medical site, and they aren't going to pursue unnecessarily (especially if Vermilion gave them something to think about). Instead, the Chromatics continue to try to report the situation to their superiors, but communication is confused right now.

The team finds that the surface appears largely undeveloped. There are scattered buildings, either small and blocky or larger and pyramidal, and the occasional beaten-dirt or gravel road. All the buildings appear to be storage or industrial and are mostly abandoned. This area was passed by in the rapid Chromatic technological advancement. There are no residences, and nothing resembling "office space." It's a desolate world, teeming with hostile aliens, and the characters are stranded in the middle of it.

Conclusions

This is the end of *Colors of Sacrifice*. It's intended as a cliffhanger, leaving the players concerned over their characters' fate for the moment. This fate is settled in the next episode, *Vermilion Falling*. Although this episode leads specifically into the next one, there are other options you may choose if you don't want the characters immediately stranded on the planet's surface.

Other Endings

• **The Characters are Rescued:** The characters are thoroughly berated for not accomplishing anything, and then assigned to other parts of the invasion effort. Possible subplots that can occur on board the Leviathan include ferreting out a Doyen plant attempting sabotage, or recapturing Vermilion if he should break loose.

• **The Characters Return:** Once the team has been bandaged up and re-equipped, it can be sent back down to a different possible Upeo site. This will probably turn out no better than the last attempt, and can lead back into *Vermilion Falling*.

If you decide not to run the second adventure, the events of that episode, including the startling revelations about the Chromatics' motives, will still occur. However, instead of the characters, another surface assault team will take on the central role in these dramatic events.

Dramatis Personae

The following are profiles and statistics for key individuals involved in the events of *Colors of Sacrifice*.

Luis Ulloa, Norça Spy

A charismatic, handsome Brazilian man in his mid-50s, Ulloa sees himself as a master manipulator. He stays very much behind-the-scenes, trying to finesse events without getting caught. In his role as computer security for Haoa Flint, Ulloa has met everyone at the station. They all know he's from South America, but that doesn't automatically mean he's Norça. (It's a big continent.) The Norça made sure Ulloa's background was impeccable when he joined the Æon Trinity, and he's been the perfect mole for many years. Unfortunately, Ulloa's charm has been overwhelmed by his fanaticism. His efforts to become Proxy del Fuego's prodigal son prove disastrous during the course of this episode.

Robert Linsey Marsden, CinC of Ground Forces, Operation Caravel

Marsden is a career officer, and played a pivotal role in the recent Karroo expedition (seen in **Darkness Revealed: Ascent into Light**). Due to his brilliant work against the Chromatics there, he is now commander-in-chief of the ground forces for Operation Caravel, and thus, the character's direct superior during the invasion.

He's not the brightest light on the block, intellectually, but Marsden has an excellent grasp of strategy and tactics, and his fellow troops respect his abilities. In the field, Marsden doesn't put much effort into idle chit-chat or boasting — he's more concerned with addressing the problem at hand.

Clarence Greaves, Designated Teleporter

Clarence Greaves is one of very few teleporters currently available to humanity, having been rescued during the Chromatic attack on Earth in the previous year. He is an argumentative man of English descent with a biting command of invective. Although committed to the mission, Greaves is definitely nervous about it. If questioned about why the teleporters went into hiding, he claims ignorance. He and his fellow Upeo captured on Chrome-Prime left Earth before any of that occurred.

Greaves is weak in combat skills; the Neptune Division template (**Trinity**, page 304) fits him reasonably well. As for his teleporting ability, handle it by *fiat*. It works when it needs to, within the general limits described in the course of the adventure.

Stellar Frontier contains specific Teleportation powers for those Storytellers interested in exploring the Aptitude in greater detail.

Stonehand Sightblinder (a.k.a. "Vermilion")

This Chromatic hero was hatched during the darkest period of the Howler War. Many of the hatchlings born in that time were not expected to survive, going into battle as untrained yearlings. Stonehand earned his first deed-name at the age of 14 months, slaying a marauding howler single-handedly before it could reach the dynasty's hatching ground.

A natural warrior, Stonehand also proved to be a natural leader and quickly attracted loyal followers who lent the young Chromatic considerable status and prestige. By age seven he was a high-ranking warrior in the Longstrider dynasty; he took the role of chieftain a short time later when their leader fell in an ambush at Singing Falls. Stonehand's cunning and resourcefulness helped turn war against the howlers and made his people prosperous once again.

Not long after the howlers were driven off, the Aberrants appeared. The beings' treachery soon manifested, and they attacked the Chromatics without provocation. Stonehand saw many of his children slain and his entire dynasty decimated in a single night of treachery. He was among the first of the chieftains to call for black war against the corrupters. The ferocity of his photokinetic assaults against the Aberrants earned him his second name, Sightblinder.

When the Witnesses began the work of the Bodiless Ones, Stonehand devoted himself completely to their cause. His status helped persuade many hidebound chieftains to follow his example. Stonehand was well known as a leader but not as a politician — and the Witnesses knew that such unwillingness to compromise could be problematic for them. So they made sure Stonehand remained in the field instead of allowing him access to the inner circle.

The Chromatic hero fought valiantly during the initial Crab Nebula forays, and was one of the first warriors chosen to lead the invasion of Earth. Stonehand's mother ship was wrecked during the battle and the hero taken prisoner. His attempts at suicide failed; Stonehand found himself in thrall to his hated foes, a fate worse than death.

Image: Stonehand is of impressive size for a Chromatic, standing just under two meters in height, with rich reddish-brown skin. While there is little of his physical appearance that is inherently distinctive to humans, his movements are fluid and powerful, and he holds himself with a poise and assurance that suggests intelligence and authority.

Roleplaying Hints: You are a living legend, a hero. You are proud of your achievements, and carry yourself with a dignity and self-confidence born from years of experience. You lead by example, and nothing is more important than the safety and prosperity of your race. This does not mean you are hotheaded or impetuous; you are intelligent and insightful, but once you have determined a course of action you act decisively. In fact, your time in captivity allowed you to observe numerous humans, and their behavior has surprised you. They don't act in the way you have come to expect from beasts, and you don't know what that means. But since there are no others of your people to help you puzzle it out, you will have to find the answers for yourself.

Nature: Leader
Allegiance: Chromatics

Physical Attributes	Abilities
Strength (Powerful) 5	Might 5
Dexterity (Lithe) 5	Athletics 4, Firearms 2, Martial Arts 5, Melee 4, Stealth 3
Stamina (Hardy) 4	Endurance 3, Resistance 4
Mental Attributes	**Abilities**
Perception (Alert) 4	Awareness 4
Intelligence 2	Bureaucracy 2, Engineering 1, Medicine 1, Survival 3
Wits (Cunning) 4	Meditation 2, Rapport 2
Social Attributes	**Abilities**
Appearance 3	Intimidation 4
Manipulation (Authoritative) 4	Command 5, Subterfuge 4
Charisma (Confident) 4	Etiquette 3

Aptitude: [Electrokinesis] Electromanipulation 3, Photokinesis 5; [additional Mode] Pyrokinesis 3 (for more on Chromatic powers, see page 111)
Backgrounds: Influence 5, Status (Longstrider) 5
Willpower: 10
Psi: 8
Gear: None

The Mercs

Three years ago, Joan Milovanovic left the Second Legion to form an independent mercenary group. The team of disaffected psions does not have a special name; it calls itself simply "Milovanovic's Mercenaries." Her team has had modest success working for various governments, corporations and psi orders (infiltration, wetwork, kidnapping). They'd never worked with Ulloa before; he got Milovanovic's name from intra-order gossip as a reliable merc who kept her mouth shut.

The merc team is small but adequate. One set of stats is provided; the only notable differences between the mercs are their Aptitudes. The team includes:

• **Joan Milovanovic:** Milovanovic is a tough, competent, professional mercenary. Her team is not the best set of guns-for-hire, but they are fiercely loyal to each other and to their employer of the moment. As mercs go, she and her team are ethical, moral, and trustworthy. She runs the team firmly but fairly, and gives everyone input into planning and choice of jobs.

Aptitude: [Psychokinesis] Pyrokinesis 2, Telekinesis 4

• **Oscar Riddle:** Riddle is second-in-command. He freely admits that his last name is not the one he was born with, but refuses to explain it. "My name is Riddle, and my name is a riddle," is his only comment. His origins are unclear, but he is apparently of European origin, probably Germanic. He was triggered by Orgotek but transferred to the Legions, where he served with Milovanovic in the Second. He stuck with Milovanovic when she left, and is the heart of her team. They are not romantically involved; indeed, he seems interested mainly in military maneuvers.

Aptitude: [Electrokinesis] Electromanipulation 2, Technokinesis 2

• **Vashti Matts:** Despite her Asian appearance, Matts is a third-generation native of Argentina. Her family lived barely above poverty, and she worked from a young age to keep them from slipping further. At 18, Matts had a chance to make substantially more as part of one of Argentina's many mercenary groups. Seven years ago, while her team was under contract with the Norça, a shifter sensed Matts' latency and brought her to Proxy del Fuego's attention. The proxy considered her suitable and asked her to join. She leapt at the chance, but over time found the intense focus and often rigid family structure of the order stifling. She finally fled the order, adopted a new name and identity, and ended up with Milovanovic's team.

Aptitude: [Biokinesis] Adaptation 2, Psychomorphing 1, Transmogrify 3

- **Etacar:** Etacar was raised virtually in the shadow of the Jomo Kenyatta Spaceport. His family was in the import-export business, and he lived in luxury all his life. In 2110 he decided to see something of the universe, and wandered across Africa as a tourist. In Cairo he met Shams ud-din Mohammed Hafiz (below), and they became a couple. Hafiz was already a psion in the Æsculapian training program. Etacar was tested and registered strong psychokinetic potential. This led to a rift in their relationship. Etacar dropped his first name and joined the Legions, where he encountered Milovanovic and Riddle. When he heard from Hafiz years later that the doc had joined Milovanovic's Mercenaries, Etacar left the Legions to fight beside his soulmate. Etacar recently converted to Islam.

Aptitude: [Psychokinesis] Cryokinesis 2, Pyrokinesis 2, Telekinesis 1

- **Shams ud-din Mohammed Hafiz:** Hafiz was raised in Cairo, middle son of a large liberal Muslim family. He let his parents guide him to a career in medicine though he felt it stifled his passionate nature. Discovered to be latent, Hafiz took it as a sign from Allah and agreed to be triggered. During a break from Æsculapian training, he met Etacar and they quickly fell in love. Hafiz's training didn't allow him to spend time with Etacar, and the Legions were forceful in recruiting Etacar once they were told of his potential versatility. This caused a rift, and Hafiz returned to school bitter. After his internship ended, Hafiz wandered North Africa treating those he encountered. There he met Milovanovic, who recruited him as her combat medic. All of Hafiz's combat training has come from her.

Aptitude: [Vitakinesis] Iatrosis 3, Algesis 2

MERCS TEMPLATE

Physical Attributes	Abilities
Strength 3	Brawl 3, Might 1
Dexterity 3	Firearms 4, Martial Arts 2, Melee 2, Stealth 2
	one of: Athletics 1, Drive 1, Pilot 1
Stamina (Hardy) 4	Endurance 2, Resistance 2
Mental Abilities	**Abilities**
Perception 3	Awareness 2
Intelligence 2	Intrusion 2, Medicine 1, Survival 2,
Wits 3	
Social Abilities	
Appearance 2	Intimidation 2
Manipulation 2	Command 1, Interrogation 1, Subterfuge 1
Charisma 2	Savvy 2

Aptitude: Varies
Willpower: 5
Psi: 5
Backgrounds: Allies 2, Contacts 2, Resources 2
Gear: Fighting knife, Banji Cyclone, L-K MAC-803, armor vest, RATR1 doses, miscellaneous first aid and commgear.

Investigator Emily Gaboriau

Emily Gaboriau is a typical Lunar citizen, born in Sokotown to a family noted for its mixed-cuisine restaurant. She was a bright but unremarkable student until she took an anthropology course in her second year at Oxford Luna. She became fascinated by humanity's cultural diversity, and pursued a career in biology and anthropology. Gaboriau spent decades immersed in a variety of societies, and her formidable training attracted the attention of the Æon Trinity. Triton Division finally approached her to join. She's spent the past decade as a skilled researcher and field investigator for Æon.

Image: Emily Gaboriau is a Caucasian woman in her early 50s. She is 154 cm tall, of medium build, with white-streaked black hair and stern blue eyes. Of late (around the time she first started investigating Chromatic culture) she has adopted a determined, forbidding air. In less tense situations, or in the rare moments when she relaxes, she can seem quite personable, and even has a mischievous sense of humor. When Vermilion is present or even being discussed she cools noticeably. She dresses in simple, dark-colored suits, frequently with a white lab coat.

Roleplaying Hints: You are a professional doing an important job. You find that you're offended by the Chromatics on a visceral level. This troubles you somewhat, since you've always prided yourself on your objectivity. However, you just can't get past this disgust. You consider Vermilion to be a savage, but you try to keep your mind open to other viewpoints. The characters are colleagues, but don't have the background in interrogation you do, so you'll try to keep them from making mistakes.

Nature: Analyst
Allegiance: Triton Division

Physical Attributes	Abilities
Strength 2	
Dexterity 2	Athletics 1, Drive 1, Firearms 1, Legerdemain 1
Stamina 2	Resistance 2
Mental Attributes	**Abilities**
Perception 3	Awareness 4, Investigation 5
Intelligence (Insightful) 4	Academics (anthropology) 4, Bureaucracy 2, Intrusion 1, Linguistics 2, Medicine 1, Science (biology) 3
Wits 3	Meditation 1, Rapport 2
Social Attributes	**Abilities**
Appearance 2	Intimidation 1
Manipulation 3	Command 2, Interrogation 4, Subterfuge 3
Charisma 3	Etiquette 2

Willpower: 7
Psi: 1
Backgrounds: Contacts 2, Followers 1, Mentor 2, Resources 2, Status (Æon) 3
Gear: Wazukana DX70 personal computer with Hera agent

Assistant Investigator

William Pluteney

Born in western China, Pluteney has the blood of the ancient Tibetan nomads in his veins. Starting in his early teens he wandered China, learning a dozen dialects and several languages before his 20th birthday. He was recruited by the Ministry more for his language skills than for his relatively minor latency. Joining the Ministry gave Pluteney the opportunity to explore the greater universe, and over time he was directed to some joint Ministry-Æon assignments. After a few years of bureaucratic wrangling, Pluteney finally left the Ministry and joined Æon's Triton Division full-time. The Trinity's broader focus on research appealed to him, and he hoped to someday pursue alien linguistics. With Pluteney's assignment to Operation Safeguard, this has been made reality.

Image: William Pluteney is a Chinese man in his late 30s. He is just under two meters tall, of thin build, with black hair and brown eyes. He seems optimistic but guarded, and has a quiet sense of humor. He is fluent in many languages and speaks with a lilting accent in all of them. He tends to dress colorfully, favoring purple shirts. He is cautious around Vermilion, but does not seem to hold a grudge toward the recent injuries the alien inflicted (During *Colors of Sacrifice*, Pluteney walks slowly and carries himself cautiously.)

Roleplaying Hints: You enjoy language for its own sake, and are delighted to have the opportunity to interact with an alien. You don't understand why Vermilion tried to kill you, but you want to learn. You suspect he's a lot more complex than Gaboriau thinks. The characters are fellow explorers, and you like to share speculation with them.

Nature: Explorer
Allegiance: Triton Division

Physical Attributes	Abilities
Strength 1	
Dexterity 2	Athletics 1, Drive 1
Stamina 2	Resistance 2

Mental Attributes	Abilities
Perception (Astute) 4	Awareness 3, Investigation 2
Intelligence 3	Academics 4, Linguistics (English, French, German, Portuguese, Swahili) 5, Medicine 1, Science 4
Wits 3	Rapport 3

Social Attributes	Abilities
Appearance 2	Intimidation 1
Manipulation 3	Interrogation 4, Subterfuge 2
Charisma 3	Etiquette 4

Aptitude: [Telepathy] Empathy 1, Mindshare 3
Willpower: 6
Psi: 4
Backgrounds: Contacts 2, Mentor 2, Resources 2, Status (Æon) 1
Gear: Wazukana DX70 personal computer with Churchill agent
Note: Due to his injuries, Pluteney is at the "Injured" Health Level.

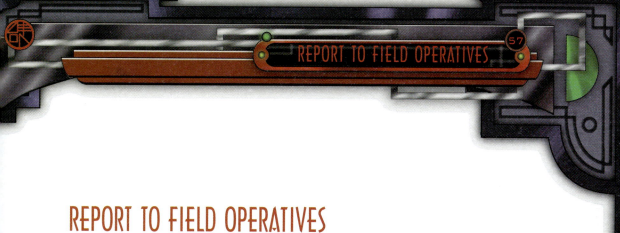

REPORT TO FIELD OPERATIVES

PROTEUS DIVISION MESSAGE ARCHIVE, FILE GROUP 98-5054

Message Source: *Chicago*, Chromatic Home System, 09:05:31 5.9.2121

>>> MESSAGE BEGINS <<<

— I say again, this is Commander Marsden, transmitting from jump ship *Chicago*. I don't know if you are receiving this; we're getting a lot of local interference on planetary transmissions. We will continue transmitting this message until the fleet passes out of range.

All ground assault and rescue teams are being withdrawn from the surface of Chrome-Prime by orders of Admiral Mkumba. Our attacks on Chromatic industrial sites in orbit and on the planetary surface caused significant damage to the aliens' war effort, but we have not recovered any Upeo prisoners. None of the installations designated to hold human prisoners appeared to have contained humans in quite some time.

Unfortunately, we do not have the resources to make a full-scale search. Even now, Chromatic forces are recovering from the subquantum backlash of our jump and are organizing resistance efforts.

Rescue and recovery efforts are further hampered by the appearance of Aberrants. Several assault teams have been ambushed, and casualties have been heavy. It is unclear whether they are working in concert with Chromatic forces, but their mere presence has convinced Mission Command that we must regroup and review our battle plan before continuing.

As of 0930 LST the fleet will complete recovery of all drop ships and retire to the designated fall-back position in the Chromatic system. There will be no further support flights after that point. All forces left on Chrome-Prime are ordered to go to ground and avoid contact with the enemy until such time as a recovery effort can be mounted.

Do not lose heart. Once Admiral Mkumba and his staff have had time to review the attack and the intelligence gathered by the strike teams, we will know better how to proceed. We will be back; I promise you that. Not one single human will be left behind on that Godforsaken rock if I have to take down a drop ship myself.

In the meantime, all I can say is keep the faith. We're not giving up on you, so don't give up on us. We will get you out of there — just find somewhere to hole up and avoid enemy patrols. I wish I could say that we'll be back soon. The truth is, I just don't know.

This is Robert Linsey Marsden, Ground Forces Commander, out.

>>> MESSAGE ENDS : ENCRYPT SEQ AO132 : MESSAGE REPEATS <<<

The Eve of Invasion

Biocam File Transcript: MKUMBA.bpg (2.25GB Compressed)
Created: 5.7.2121
Last Modified: 5.8.2121

Blake: Good evening, ladies and gentlemen. This is Marty Blake, coming to you from the eye of the storm beyond Luna — the flagship *Europa*, the Leviathan leading the first human invasion into Chromatic space. In the corridors and compartments of this tremendous jump ship, hundreds of determined men and women are readying themselves for their greatest battle.

Over the last eight months, the United Nations has stood together in deed as well as in name, assembling a fleet of soldiers and ships from every major power in settled space. The men and women I have encountered in the last few weeks seem little older than teens, but their fresh faces are hardened with determination. They know there is a real chance that none might ever return home, but many volunteered even before their militaries issued the assignments. They have joined up to fight, to put their lives on the line for a loved one, for the home they hold dear, for everyday joes on the street they have never met.

Now this great fleet rests on the brink. Soon the great Tesser engines will flare, and then there can be no turning back. Here with me tonight is the man who will lead these troops past the point of no return. Thank you for taking the time to talk with us, Admiral Mkumba.

Mkumba: It is a pleasure, Marty. Anything to escape another four hours of logistical briefings. [laughs]

Blake: Admiral, you are a highly experienced officer. You graduated with top honors from the academy at Cape Town and earned your nation's highest honor for the defense of Libouye Hospital during the Aberrant attack on Luna in 2104. They say you faced down an Aberrant single-handedly.

Mkumba: [smiles] Well, if you do not count the platoon of tanks I commanded.

Blake: But when the creature approached the hospital, you went out to meet it alone.

Mkumba: [nods] That is true. It wanted the hospital and the doctors — I still do not know why. I told it that it could not have them, and that I would fight it if I had to. The Aberrant — it called itself Dezago — laughed, pointing out that my forces could not hope to stop it. I agreed, but the hospital would be wrecked in the battle, and it still would not have what it came for. Dezago asked if I was willing to die, to which I said "yes." We stared at one another for a little while, and finally it left. That was the longest five minutes of my life.

Blake: And the whole time you were talking, you didn't even have anyone in those tanks. Your soldiers were in the hospital evacuating the doctors through maintenance tunnels. You were out there facing down a monster, trying to buy time with your life.

Mkumba: That is what soldiers do, Mr. Blake.

Blake: But the point is, you place a very high value on the lives of the people under your command. In just a few hours, you'll be leading the single largest military expedition since the Aberrant War on a mission that might well decide the course of the entire Chromatic conflict. That must be a heavy burden to bear, Admiral.

Mkumba: I have a job to do, Marty. Earth depends on us to rescue the captured Upeo and send a message to the Chromatics that humanity will not sit idle and wait for their next invasion.

Blake: What is your plan when you reach the system?

Mkumba: [smiles, shakes his head] You know I cannot go into that, Marty.

Blake: Oh, come now, Admiral. We're all humans here. Can you speak in general terms, then? What are your intentions?

Mkumba: I can do that much. We will use mechanical and psionic means to identify and perform surgical strikes on military bases and industries vital to the war effort. Some of the assaults on Chrome-Prime will be carried out by ground forces who will destroy key structures. But for the most part, the attacks will be carried out by frigate and fighter-bomber strikes.

Blake: Why send troops down to the surface, Admiral? They're certain to be outnumbered and outgunned, and on the enemy's home turf to boot. The fleet has missiles that can hit buildings from hundreds of kilometers away without putting anyone's life at risk.

Mkumba: Even smart missiles are only accurate up to a point. An E-15 can put a missile through a bio-factory's front door, but will that guarantee it will hit the computer systems that generate the growth matrices? If I put a man on the ground, he can find the most valuable components in the installation, the ones that will be the hardest to replace, and blow them to pieces. I cannot settle for *probably* destroying some of these targets. I must be certain. We only have a limited window of opportunity, and we are going to make sure that the enemy is out of the war business for a long time.

Blake: I understand that Susan N'gamba, a fellow countryman and recently revealed Upeo psion, is helping teleport your forces to Chrome-Prime. I've also heard that you have as many as six other Upeo who've revealed

their existence to help in the war effort. What roles will they assume in this conflict?

Mkumba: There are teleporters who have come forth to aid us, yes. They are too valuable to reveal their identities or their involvement at this time.

Blake: After discovering that captured Upeo were forced to teleport Chromatic forces to our system last year, most people assumed that the Chromatics had captured all the teleporters. Where did these other Upeo come from?

Mkumba: I cannot say.

Blake: Cannot or will not? All right, how about this, then: I've heard from certain sources that casualties among the ground forces are expected to be heavy — as much as 70%.

Mkumba: I... cannot comment on that. Where did you get all this information?

Blake: For a man with such widely documented concern for his troops, that's a steep price to pay to blow up some buildings.

Mkumba: Mr. Blake, do not take offense, but you are

not a military man. It is difficult, but sometimes an officer has no better alternative but to place his soldiers in danger, knowing some might die in order to achieve a necessary goal—

Blake: So you are saying that you haven't got a choice. That losing 70% of your ground troops, or more, is better than some other alternatives before you?

Mkumba: What is it that you mean—

Blake: According to my sources, Admiral, if enemy resistance is too great — and, especially, if you cannot rescue the still-captured Upeo — you've been ordered to use nuclear weapons on the Chromatics. The death toll could well be in the hundreds of millions—

Mkumba: This interview is at an end.

Blake: Would you actually resort to using nukes, Admiral? What if there were still UN forces on the ground at the time—

Mkumba: I said that is enough! [exits]

>>> FILE ENDS <<<

CHROMATIC STAR SYSTEM

ADMIRAL'S LOG, 5.9.2121

— **Wallace Mkumba, Admiral Commanding, UN 5th Fleet, Flagship *Europa***

There is not much time to write. As we had hoped, the psionic backlash of our arrival knocked the enemy off-guard. Our frigates and fighters are deployed and missions are now underway to strike at Chromatic shipyards in their asteroid ring. We were surprised to find almost no active patrols around the homeworld, or even an early warning sensor array. It is as if they never considered the possibility of an attack on their planet.

We can detect no modern cities, advanced transportation systems or supplementary industry. I do not know what to make of these people, and frankly, I do not care. If this raid will put an end to the war I will do whatever it takes to make it possible.

The mission must succeed. My intelligence officer reports that even with surprise on our side, casualties among the ground forces will be heavy — projections are currently at 80%. It is too high a price to pay for failure. We are fighting on their home ground, and while our enemies are poor fighter pilots, with solid earth under their feet they fight like nothing I have ever seen before. If the fleet suffers significant losses, especially among the space forces, I do not know when we will have the material and political means to mount such an attack again.

The key to turning the tide is the Upeo. You cannot have an interstellar war without the ability to attack enemy territory. We have a few assisting with the mission — N'gamba, Greaves, others — but they are not enough. In rescuing the teleporters on Chrome-Prime, we leave the Chromatics stranded on their world — and in the Crab Nebula — with no means by which to strike back.

Initial reports indicate that every site predicted to have Upeo prisoners is empty. Our clairsentients are scanning as best they are able, but they have not found them yet. The telepaths assure me that there is no way our Chromatic prisoners could have willingly deceived us. It may be that the enemy believed that captured troops would break eventually, and moved their captives elsewhere. The Chromatics continue to be a mix of contradictions and revelations.

My orders are clear. The Chromatics must be deprived of their interstellar capability. If I cannot rescue the Upeo, I will have no choice but to employ nuclear weapons, striking likely targets where they are being held — including population centers. Intel assures me that the Chromatics planned the same thing for Earth when they invaded last June. Their fighters carried primitive nuclear missiles that could have turned Pretoria into a plain of radioactive glass. I pray to God it will not come to that, but I shall do my duty, no matter the cost.

I will be damned if history records me as the man who lost the Chromatic War.

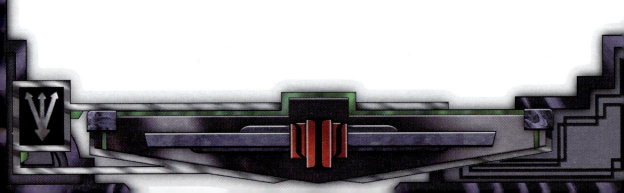

Chrome-Prime

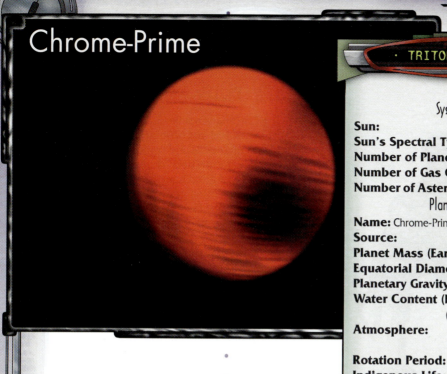

System Data

Sun:	CSGC 4:5112:35:21-G
Sun's Spectral Type:	G0
Number of Planets in System:	5
Number of Gas Giants:	0
Number of Asteroid Belts:	1 (5AU from sun)

Planetary Data

Name:	Chrome-Prime (no known native referent)
Source:	psionic survey
Planet Mass (Earth = 1):	1.1
Equatorial Diameter:	11,300
Planetary Gravity (Earth = 1):	0.84
Water Content (Earth = 0.75):	0.45 (subsurface) 0.002 (surface)
Atmosphere:	nitrogen, oxygen, some sulfites
Rotation Period:	26 hours
Indigenous Life:	Chromatics, various flora and fauna
Population:	1 billion (approx.)
Closest Distance to Earth:	8,600 light years
Primary Satellites:	none

Stellar System Profile
Chromatic Home System

Notes: Primary population concentrations are sub-surface, localized along the shores of large, equatorial seas. Surface structures are almost entirely industrial or military in nature, cited with respect to utility (near available resources) and population density. Industrial sites show a surprising range of technological development, from metal foundries similar to 18th-century European structures to advanced biotech fabrication plants. The remnants of a moon, likely shattered in an astronomic event millennia ago, created scores of asteroidal bodies that still orbit the planet. The natives have hollowed out many of these asteroids for mining and ship-building purposes.

Initial mineralogical and geological surveys indicate the presence of large amounts of industrial-grade ores (lead, copper, iron, titanium) and crystal formations highly conducive to hardtech industry, as well as large amounts of precious metal deposits (silver, gold, platinum). The planetary surface remains in a moderately high state of geological transition, with a large number of active volcanoes planet-wide and signs of large-scale earthquakes in the recent past.

Flora and fauna on the surface are sparse, consisting of primarily insect and reptilian life forms and a narrow range of plant life hardy enough to survive the extreme temperature range. The profusion of tunnels and caverns beneath the surface appear to be capable of holding heat and gases sufficient to stimulate a much broader assortment of life, but more in-depth surveys are required to confirm this.

Long-range scans have not located any extraterrestrial outposts, with the exception of the aforementioned orbital installations.

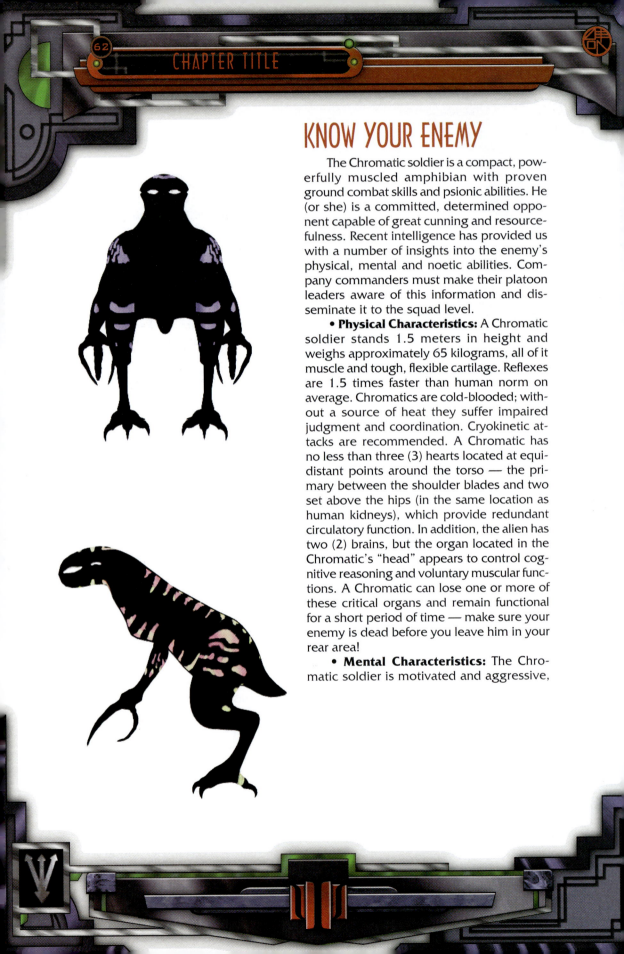

KNOW YOUR ENEMY

The Chromatic soldier is a compact, powerfully muscled amphibian with proven ground combat skills and psionic abilities. He (or she) is a committed, determined opponent capable of great cunning and resourcefulness. Recent intelligence has provided us with a number of insights into the enemy's physical, mental and noetic abilities. Company commanders must make their platoon leaders aware of this information and disseminate it to the squad level.

• **Physical Characteristics:** A Chromatic soldier stands 1.5 meters in height and weighs approximately 65 kilograms, all of it muscle and tough, flexible cartilage. Reflexes are 1.5 times faster than human norm on average. Chromatics are cold-blooded; without a source of heat they suffer impaired judgment and coordination. Cryokinetic attacks are recommended. A Chromatic has no less than three (3) hearts located at equidistant points around the torso — the primary between the shoulder blades and two set above the hips (in the same location as human kidneys), which provide redundant circulatory function. In addition, the alien has two (2) brains, but the organ located in the Chromatic's "head" appears to control cognitive reasoning and voluntary muscular functions. A Chromatic can lose one or more of these critical organs and remain functional for a short period of time — make sure your enemy is dead before you leave him in your rear area!

• **Mental Characteristics:** The Chromatic soldier is motivated and aggressive, willing to attack forces much larger and better-equipped than his own. Chromatics operate in tactical units similar to a squad formation — five to nine troops, led by an officer of indeterminate rank. Six soldiers per squad seems to be the Chromatics' preferred formation. One soldier supplies photokinetic illusions and blending for the squad, while the others protect that soldier and engage the enemy. Targeting this individual first is a top priority — but do not assume that it is the only one of them capable of generating illusions.

Officers have effective leadership ability, but lack technical proficiency. Chromatics as a whole use relatively little technology — some laser weapons and portable equipment, but virtually no support vehicles or artillery. Chromatics favor swift, hit-and-run raids and ambushes, which are especially effective when combined with their ability to psionically conceal themselves. Do not pursue a retreating Chromatic force unless specifically instructed to do so by higher command, and never take any enemy camp at face value.

• **Noetic Characteristics:** The Chromatic soldier possesses high natural talent and proficiency in photokinesis and, to a lesser degree, pyrokinesis. Despite information being disseminated by civilian sources, psionic strength is as individually varied in the Chromatic race as it is in human psions, but their soldiers appear to be selected for their noetic strength as much as for their physical abilities. Assume every enemy encountered is a photokinetic of exceptional ability, and act accordingly.

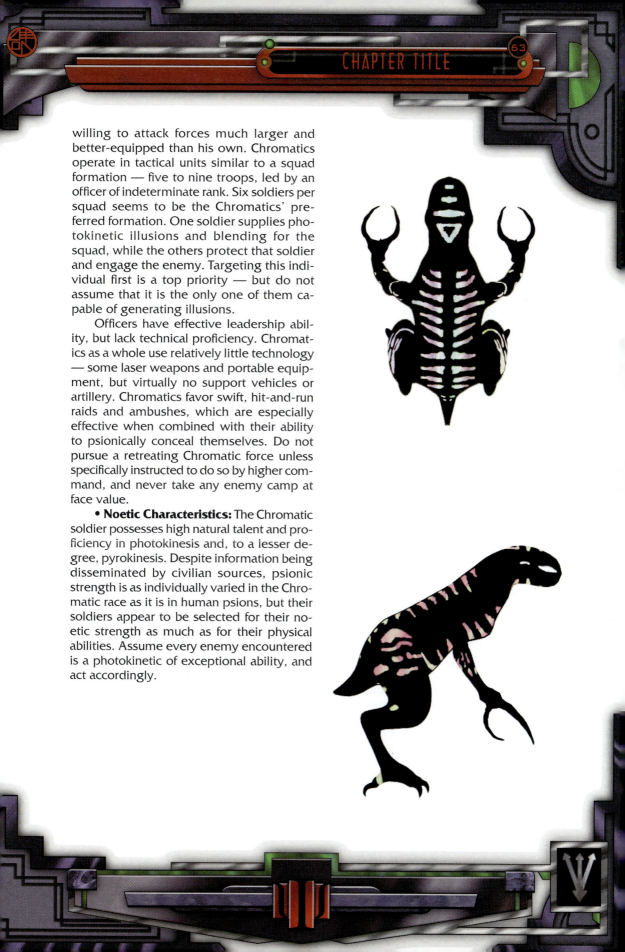

>>> CLASSIFIED MATERIAL — EYES ONLY <<<
>>> NOT FOR DISSEMINATION <<<

TRINITY FIELD REPORT: CHROMATIC TECHNOLOGICAL EVALUATION

— Dr. Sunil Payaparaji, Operation Safeguard, Triton Division, 3.5.2121

Ongoing research into the Chromatic's technological capabilities was greatly enhanced by captured equipment and wreckage recovered in the Sol System after the aliens' unsuccessful invasion on 6.29.2120. Prior investigations were hampered by a lack of available evidence on which to build a comprehensive picture of current Chromatic technology.

Observations of the Chromatics' day-to-day life, and viewing that they lack any personal technological devices (aside from weaponry or mission-specific tools) presented what we believed were huge gaps in our knowledge of their technological base. Having the hull of a largely intact mother ship enabled our researchers to examine the Chromatics' scientific advancements from a cultural context. Our studies were illuminating, more because of what we did *not* find than what we *did*.

The Chromatic mother ships are of biotech construction, larger even than our Leviathans. When I refer to biotech, I mean *everything* — internal systems, sensors, engines, weaponry. Even our bio-ships still use hardtech propulsion and weapons since they're still superior to current biotech development. The Chromatic counterparts show that they suffer a similar limitation in biotechnology. The engines are, overall, much larger for their output than human hardtech engines are, and function differently than Qin bio-engines do. In fact, I believe it's safe to assume, based on this and other corresponding data, that the Qin and Chromatics have had no contact prior to their meeting humanity.

· CONFIDENTIAL ·

Subject: Re: Target Tasking Profile
From: Giselle Rigny, Director, Clairsentient Reconnaissance Department
To: Major Xi Xemin, Staff Intelligence Officer
Encryption: DSE
Transmission type: textfile
Date: 5.1.2121

Major—

I recognize your concerns regarding information revealing the source of Chromatic technological development. I am no expert, but I concur with the anthropologists that there is no way that race could have gone from knives to starships in two decades without help. At the moment, none of my people have had any indications of third parties present on Chrome-Prime, but the search is ongoing. Rest assured that we'll scan every microbe upon arrival in the Chromatic system. Still, we don't know if we're looking for another alien influence or a set of computer databases. Whatever you may think about how we operate, this kind of job is like trying to find a lost button in a videodrome parking lot. The minute we know something, so will you.

bon chance,
Giselle

CHROMATIC MOTHER SHIP INTERIOR > > > ÆON ARCHIVE

The mother ship can carry many fighter craft internally, but there are no external docking points as we have with our craft. These vessels are also clearly designed to carry large numbers of Chromatics for extended periods of time, yet the on-board facilities provided for the crew are exceedingly minimal. Staterooms were nothing more than large, oval chambers set with numerous niches and cabinets that contained handcrafted jars and bowls of herbs, plant dyes and fragments of what appears to be eggshell. There were no zero-g hammocks or other facilities for sleeping, nor were there storage areas for personal effects, nor did the rooms have computer access terminals or entertainment systems.

The only technological items present in these rooms were a zero-g lavatory and a biotech bubble three meters across. This device could be entered and pressure-sealed from within, at which point the bubble filled with water to a pressure approximating that of Earth at sea level. Whether this was some form of hygienic device or an emergency life-support system is unknown.

The walls of each chamber were decorated with pictures not unlike the cave drawings of primitive humans, depicting hunting scenes and battles with large, anthropomorphic monsters. The pictures were made from a paste combining natural dyes and a phosphorescent, alkaloid substance that gave off a faint glow. One room we studied had a

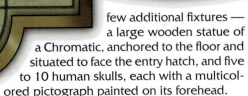

TRINITY FIELD REPORT

few additional fixtures — a large wooden statue of a Chromatic, anchored to the floor and situated to face the entry hatch, and five to 10 human skulls, each with a multicolored pictograph painted on its forehead.

Examining the ship's duty stations and engineering spaces revealed a high degree of automation, with control consoles set up to handle basic, menu-driven functions. Dr. Madeleine Russell, an astronautics expert formerly of Orgotek and now with L-B, was especially fascinated by the staggering amount of redundancy in the ship systems. According to Dr. Russell, if a component was damaged, it wasn't repaired — function was simply shunted to a backup system, without impairing system performance. The backup systems added bulk to the designs, but reduced the required amount of technicians necessary for each trip. Similarly, the ship's medical facilities were rudimentary at best, with two dozen more of the "water bulbs" in each chamber and cabinets containing a wide assortment of organic medicines.

Oddly, most interesting of all was the ship's stores. The mother ship had larders the size of a hangar bay, containing carefully preserved but freshly killed meat and seafood in prodigious quantities. There were absolutely no indications of ration bars, processed meal packs, or other advanced food storage techniques. The amount of wasted space and energy was mind-boggling in terms of starship design. One member of the project team suggested that the Chromatics did not simply prefer fresh meat, but required it, because their digestive systems were not conditioned to handle processed foods. After consideration, I am inclined to agree.

· CONFIDENTIAL ·

Subject: Sunil Payaparaji
From: Katsuhiro Ueshima, Field Research Office, Mare Ingenii Base
To: Alice DeValere, Triton Division Field Office, Olympus Colony, Luna
Encryption: DSE
Transmission type: textfile
Date: 3.7.2121

Alice—

Don't let him sweep this under the rug. I know you respect Sunil's abilities, but he's wrong on this one. Someone *from Earth* is giving the Chromatics their technology. You should have seen the staterooms on that ship! The Chromatics are a primitive people — culturally, they look like pre-agriculture hunters. That big wooden statue was a charm against evil spirits. I'm the anthropologist here, for Buddha's sake, but he wouldn't put any of my observations in the report!

I know you're going to start telling me I'm on my "Orgotek Conspiracy" thread again, but think about this for a minute. Everyone, from Legionnaires to Karrooans, have been describing the toadie bioguns as "cheap Orgotek knock-offs" and their ships as "early Orgotek designs." Well, we recovered quite a few of them up here, and guess what? They *are* Orgotek knock-offs! No serial numbers or anything like that, but the designs match some of the Big O's initial prototypes.

So you tell me which one of us is crazy.

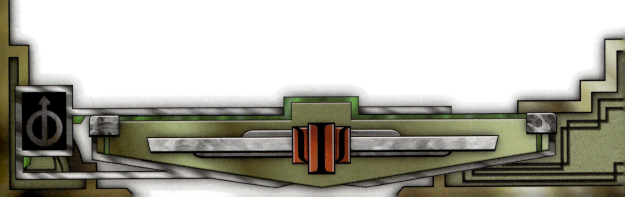

u8509437893129

6u9284373

CHROMATIC MOTHER SHIP INTERIOR>>>ÆON ARCHIVE

My conclusion, in light of this new evidence, is that the Chromatics as a race are not technologically refined, as we would view a modern society. The only possible explanations are that their culture actively avoids the use and understanding of technology except where absolutely necessary. Alternatively, the Chromatics are, in fact, a primitive people with technology thrust upon them. That having been said, I am intensely opposed to any suggestion that this race has been supplied their technology by persons or organizations from Earth, despite such speculation on the part of my staff. Such allegations are specious in the extreme, and could only serve to inflame the conspiracy-minded within the public and armed services.

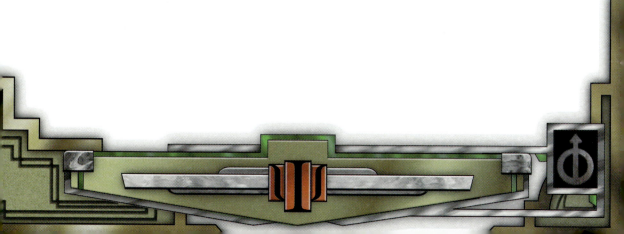

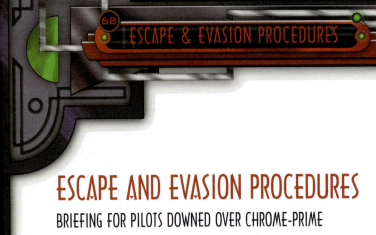

ESCAPE AND EVASION PROCEDURES
BRIEFING FOR PILOTS DOWNED OVER CHROME-PRIME

— Major Edwin Langstrom, 33rd Military Transport Squadron

This squadron will shortly conduct assault team insertion and recovery at the ground installations that Major Walters just covered. Our clairsentient reconnaissance teams have located surprisingly few enemy anti-aircraft weapons covering these sites, for which I am certain you are grateful. Still, the fact of the matter is that we are dealing with an enemy that can fire a laser from its fingertips and we have located at least three enemy fighter squadrons based in our area of operations. We must prepare ourselves for the possibility that some of you might get shot down. I'm here to brief you on survival procedures should you find yourself on the surface.

Chrome-Prime has a thin atmosphere and almost negligible ozone, so it has temperature variations similar to Earth deserts. At night the temperature quickly drops below freezing. You might think your first concern here is the Chromies, but since they're cold-blooded they won't be running around at night much. No, your worries are hypothermia and hypoxia. You're going to get cold and feel like you can't get enough air. Conserve your energy and control your breathing. Keep your vac suit in good condition; it'll insulate you from the cold and protect you from UV radiation. Move in short, fast dashes away from your craft and breathe off your suit air while running or if you start to feel lightheaded.

It's a totally different story when daylight hits. Temperatures get extremely hot, and unlike the nighttime, the toadies thrive here. UV poisoning is a serious risk, so keep your eyes shielded at all times and, once again, rely on your vac suit to mitigate your UV exposure. If at all possible, move into a rocky area likely to have caves or overhangs, so that you can get out of direct sunlight and conserve moisture. Once again, keep your movements to a minimum if at all possible.

Your survival packs should contain enough rations for a couple of days. If for any reason you should run low, your overriding concern is water. The surface of Chrome-Prime has just enough moisture per square kilometer to fill my coffee cup here. The only water sources are underground, and those areas have been identified as being Chromatic population centers. The good news at least is that if you can get to the water, you can drink it without too much risk. Be certain to use your purifier pills to kill any native bacteria, though.

Initial scans show that there is considerable flora present in the tunnels beneath the surface, but at this time we do not know if any are edible. Autopsies of enemy bodies show no plant matter in their stomachs — the docs say this is because the Chromies are carnivores, preferring numerous varieties of fish. I can tell you that the seafood is edible, though catching it will likely prove problematic. My advice: If you must eat something, sample the local plant life. Getting sick isn't nearly as dangerous as getting caught by a pack of toadies.

That's about it, people. I wish I had more to offer, but we're in uncharted waters here. Good luck out there, and Godspeed.

Terrible Swift Sword

Aberrant cult believes themselves to be Angels of God

— Howard Rosemont, senior editor, *Dark Times Journal*, June 5, 2049

The man who once called himself Jason O'Hare prefers to address his followers by torchlight, the flickering reddish glow giving the upturned faces an unsettling, crimson cast.

"Put your faith in the Lord, brothers and sisters," says the man who now calls himself the angel Uriel. "In this dark age when nations tremble and the Earth is torn asunder, where can humanity place its strength? In steel? In stone? In the strength of weapons of war? No, my brothers. The path to heaven is the way of righteousness, of faith in the wisdom of the Lord. Through the word of Jesus Christ we may find a faith everlasting that will raise us up from the shadows that bind us. For the time is coming soon when God's anger will pour down upon the Earth, drowning the wicked in lakes of fire. God's will is clear, my brothers and sisters. You may choose to worship — or feel his terrible swift sword."

Uriel speaks with utter conviction born of the belief that he is God's agent of worship — and punishing sword combined.

"We are all children of God," Uriel tells me at a recent evangelical meeting in Provo. "But for some of us, the Lord sees fit to give us a special calling, a responsibility that transcends that of most mortals. That is why He sent angels to Earth to mate with humans, to produce a mingling of mortal and holy blood that gives his servants the power to fulfill their special duties."

Such is the reasoning of the cult that calls itself the Seraphim, after the highest rank of angels said to serve God in heaven. Uriel and his followers hold themselves to a strict moral and religious code that keeps their bodies pure and receptive to God's commands. Uriel requires that his people be open to instruction from the Lord "every moment of every day." Since their formation in September of 2047, only Uriel has received visions which he's used to send the Seraphim on "crusades" across the United States. Many times these crusades are little more than traveling tent revivals, preaching to the faithful and occasionally recruiting human followers. But sometimes, the mission is one of punishment and destruction.

Uriel is still passionate about the Seraphim's attack on Aspen in 2048. "A den of iniquity," he says in an ominous voice. "A modern-day Sodom where the rich indulged in sins of the flesh and practiced blasphemy." Eight thousand people, rich and not-so-rich, died in the explosions and avalanches brought on by Uriel's righteous anger, leaving a permanent scar on the Rocky Mountain range. When curious (and bold) attendants at the Seraphim's tent-meetings confront Uriel with the cult's infamous act, he makes no attempt to deny it. "They were sinners," he replies simply, and launches into another sermon on faith.

Whatever the case, the man who calls himself an angel says that the Seraphim will continue to travel and render God's judgment for as long as the Almighty wishes it. "Whenever and wherever he wills it," Uriel says.

Coming soon to a city near you.

GROUND ASSAULT

PROTEUS DIVISION MESSAGE ARCHIVE, FILE GROUP 98-1010

Message source: data feed broadcast to ground forces, UN assault group Delta Five, Chromatic Home System, 07:30:45 5.9.2121

Delta Five: *Chicago*, this is Delta Five on secure laser with situation report.

Chicago: Roger, Delta Five. What is your condition?

Delta Five: Target area secured and explosives set. The little glowing bastards never knew what hit them. They were still recovering from the jump backlash when we hit the ground. None of my people got so much as a scratch. We had some time to check the area out while Lawson set the charges, and we found some stuff that the intel boys are going to want to see.

Chicago: What have you got, Delta Five?

Delta Five: A lot of industrial equipment, all biotech. Heavy fabrication matrices, equipment haulers and so forth. The control panels are nothing like ours, but the basic layout is the same as what we've got on Earth, down to the locations of the exit indicators. We're getting as much video of this as we can before we're picked up. Damnedest thing I've ever seen.

Chicago: Are you saying they are Earth designs, Delta Five?

Delta Five: I don't know, you tell me — Douglan, get over here! Get the camera on that cargo hauler. No, the big yellow one, shit-for-brains! *Chicago*, are you seeing this?

Chicago: We see it, Delta.

Delta Five: You remember those old Orgotek commercials, way back when they first got started? This thing looks an awful lot like one of those prototypes they showed off back then. Same basic design, but don't ask me how the toadies got hold of it. That kind of work's above my pay grade. But I thought you might want to pass the info on to the powers that be. Delta Five is awaiting pickup.

Chicago: Roger that, Delta Five. Ah… good work. Pickup is on the way.

Delta Five: Roger, *Chicago*. Tell the flyboys we aren't ready to head back to the barn yet. This was too easy. If this is the best the Chromatics can do, you just keep supplying us with ammo and we'll end this war by lunchtime!

>>> communication ends <<<

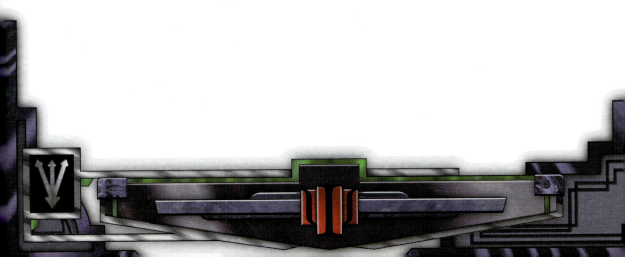

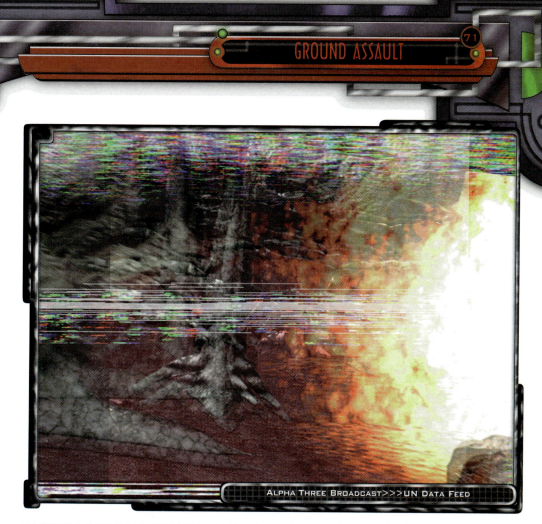

ALPHA THREE BROADCAST>>>UN DATA FEED

PROTEUS DIVISION MESSAGE ARCHIVE, FILE GROUP 98-1015

Message source: data feed broadcast to ground forces, UN assault group Alpha Three, Chromatic Home System, 07:30:45 5.9.2121

Alpha Three: *Europa*, this is Alpha Three. My perimeter is secure and I need immediate pickup. We've got casualties.

Europa: Roger that, Alpha Three. Pickup is on the way. What is your situation?

Alpha Three: Four dead and two wounded. Fucking demon lizards came out of nowhere. There's holes all over the installation, and they must've come up from underground somewhere, 'cause—

Europa: Alpha Three, I did not read that last. Say again.

Alpha Three: We've got movement in the hills to the south. About 500 meters.

Can't make anything out yet. When is that drop ship getting here? There's only four of us, and we're getting low on ammo — [sound of explosion] Oh my God!

Europa: Alpha Three, what's happening? Alpha Three, come in—

Alpha Three: [sound of small arms fire, screaming]

Europa: Alpha Three, come in! We have help on the way. What is your situation—

Alpha Three: Aberrants! Oh my God! Get away from me — get away — somebody help me— [unidentifiable sound]

Europa: Alpha Three, come in! Alpha Three! Did you say you were under attack by Aberrants? Please respond!

>>> communication terminated <<<

The Front Line

Biocam File Transcript: MARTYCAM.bpg (1.75GB Compressed)
Created: 5.9.2121
Last Modified: 5.9.2121

Blake: This is Marty Blake reporting from — *whoa!* — a jumpseat in the troop compartment of a drop ship over the Chromatic's own home-world! The UN offensive is less than six hours old, and outside the viewport here I can see plumes of smoke and fire rising into the sky from numerous successful human attacks.

The initial strike, coordinated by Admiral Wallace Mkumba, has thrown the enemy into complete panic, though there are indications that the primary objective of this daring and costly raid might not have been entirely successful. With me here is United Nations medic Else Boehm, a crew member on the drop ship whose responsibility is to tend to injured soldiers. Else, what can you tell us about this mission we are on?"

Boehm: This is a recovery mission. We are going to pick up one of the rescue teams and return to the fleet, as you well know—

Blake: Dr. Boehm, the people back home want to hear about the war in your words, not mine. Which rescue mission was this team performing?

Boehm: I believe they were attempting to free trapped human teleporters from a prison facility. We'll be there in just a few minutes.

Blake: But the team wasn't successful? They didn't report that they had recovered any prisoners.

Boehm: No, I don't believe so. You were the one listening to the radio; you tell me.

Blake: Didn't the rescue team have a teleporter of their own, allowing them to simply jump back to the fleet? Why do they need a pickup?

Boehm: Either the teleporter is dead, or there is something keeping the teleporter from using his abilities. Is common sense a requirement for being a reporter?

Blake: Ladies and gentlemen, as you can see, we're about to participate in a daring rescue to recover a trapped band of daring commandos who gave their all in an attempt to rescue fellow humans suffering under the yoke of Chromatic tyranny. No doubt they are injured, some perhaps dead. This drop ship with its heroic crew is their only way of getting home. Else, is there anything I can do to help?

Boehm: You can climb into this locker here and stay the hell out of my way.

Blake: Ha! You've got to admire the wit of people like Else Boehm, who have to laugh to keep from crying in the pressure cooker of war. Wait — the drop ship appears to be slowing, and its nose is pulling up. We are about to land at the pickup point. I'm just grateful you, the viewing audience, don't have to be here in harm's way like Else and me. I can't describe what I'm feeling — a mixture of terror and anger, really. I find that I'm not afraid. There is danger, certainly, but more important is our sacred task — to bring our fellow soldiers home. What the— What was that? Why are we pulling up? Are we shooting at something?

Boehm: We're being shot *at*!

Blake: We've got to get out of here! Nobody said anything about getting shot at!

Boehm: What about bringing our fellow soldiers home?

Blake: Screw them! Tell the pilot to get us out of here! I'm a reporter, not a grunt! He isn't supposed to take me into real combat!

Boehm: *We're hit—*

Blake: My God; it *can't* be! Aber—

>>> FILE ENDS <<<

This is the second episode in **Invasion**, the first book in the two-part **Alien Encounter** series. The preceding color pages should be shared with the players as you, the Storyteller, see fit.

Vermilion Falling places the characters in the midst of confusion and catastrophe. Even so, it presents them with the chance to wrest victory from certain defeat if they are willing to place the good of their fellow humans above their own — the essence of what being a hero is all about.

The following information is for Storyteller eyes only. If you're a player, stop reading now!

Overview

Vermilion Falling begins with the characters' headlong flight (along with the teleporter Greaves and the alien Vermilion) into the hostile landscape of Chrome-Prime. This follows the ambush at the medical facility as described at the conclusion of *Colors of Sacrifice*. With Chromatic hunting parties nipping at their heels, the characters must battle the elements and the aliens, evade capture and try to get a transmission through to the fleet for pickup.

The assault on Chrome-Prime as a whole achieves mixed success. Bombing missions and commando attacks against military and industrial targets go very well, causing a great deal of damage, but teams searching for evidence of Upeo hostages come up empty. When reports of the Chromatics having a teleportation damper come in — as discovered by teleporter characters and/or Clarence Greaves in the previous episode — doubt spreads among the UN commanders. What if the Chromatics anticipated the human assault? Were humanity's successes really nothing more than bait to draw the fleet further into a trap?

Aberrants throw things even further into disarray — ground troops are under attack from the creatures! The UN commanders knew that the Chromatics had encountered the Aberrants at some point, but the presence of the beings on Chrome-Prime comes as a shock. Many senior officers fear that the Aberrants have allied with the Chromatics. This isn't actually the case, but amid the con-

fusion of the assault there is no way the humans can know for sure.

Worse, Chromatic forces recover from the initial shock of the attack and offer steadily increasing resistance to humanity. What begins as a series of swift, surgical strikes soon threatens to bog down into a war of attrition, something the Earth fleet does not have the resources to win.

The characters are little aware of this — and may not care, since they're running from hostile aliens at the moment. The characters, blocked from teleporting out thanks to a planetwide dampener array, find time in their hasty retreat to get a message through to orbit. The characters manage to set up a rendezvous with a drop ship, though the pickup point is several kilometers from their current position. The team must make a dangerous cross-country run through enemy-infested terrain to get to the LZ in time.

What they don't know is that the Aberrants on Chrome-Prime — the group known in previous generations as the Seraphim — listen in on the transmission, and also make their way to the rendezvous. Having been on Chrome-Prime for several years, these Aberrants lived in hiding after the Chromatics defeated their attempted invasion. Now, with human ships in orbit, the Aberrants are taking advantage of the confusion to strike at isolated groups of humans and Chromatics alike.

The characters reach the pickup point with scant minutes to spare, scrambling to the top of the broad, flat plateau as the roar of the approaching drop ship rumbles down out of the sky. The team's ticket home comes in from the east, descending slowly — then moments before landing it suddenly pulls up, firing a pair of smart missiles toward the characters! The craft saw the hidden Aberrants and attacked. Explosions and bolts of plasma fill the air as the Aberrants respond in kind. The drop ship is shot down, limping out of sight and crashing a couple of kilometers away.

The characters escape from the ambush, but before they can call for more help, a grim-voiced Marsden sends an emotional message to all human forces still operating on Chrome-Prime — the report at the very beginning of this episode (see page 57). All surviving ships are being recalled and teams still on Chrome-Prime are ordered to go to ground and hold out as best they can until the fleet returns.

Impassioned speeches and well-wishes mean little to the characters right now, who are under fire from Aberrants and hunted by vengeful Chromatics. Vermilion proves to be most helpful at this point. He has seen enough of the characters' actions of late to doubt that they're the same corrupters as the Aberrants. Although the Chromatic isn't on the humans' side, he understands that retreat is the best option at the moment. He helps lead characters to a ruined Chromatic city-fort where they can hide and tend their wounds.

As if the recent trials weren't enough, though, upon reaching the ruined city the characters run afoul of a pack of howlers — savage, Neanderthal-esque creatures related to Chromatics. Once the howlers are dispatched, the characters *finally* have a chance to rest. During this time, they can explore the abandoned galleries and story-gardens and confront Vermilion about their recent failed mission. Surprisingly, the Chromatic hero has some questions of his own.

Vermilion watched the characters save his life first from rogue psions (in *Colors of Sacrifice*) and recently from Aberrants, the same creatures who attacked his world years ago. The Bodiless Ones, the spirit guides who came to save the Chromatics from the corrupters, claim that humans and Aberrants are two faces of the same evil. Now Vermilion is not so certain. He questions the characters carefully about why they protected him against their fellow corrupters when they fled from the Aberrants who attacked the drop ship. This is the first real open dialogue the characters have with Vermilion, and it presents an opportunity for the characters to convince the alien that humans are not the same as the Aberrants who tried to conquer his people.

While Vermilion and the characters broach this topic, the ruined fort fills with Chromatics — outcasts, not pursuers, stripped of their rank and status by the Witnesses, the spiritual leaders who speak for the Bodiless Ones. The outcasts are led by a Chromatic hero named Fireclaw, a chieftain like Vermilion who questioned the absolute authority that her people gave to the Witnesses.

Fireclaw believes the Witnesses became more concerned with their own personal power than with the good of the people, and fears that their holy war against the corrupters achieved little except the

deaths of many thousands of Chromatics. Fireclaw intends to break the Witnesses' hold over the people by taking away the Chromatics' ability to travel between stars — by getting rid of the captured Upeo. Since Fireclaw doesn't know where the humans are being kept, she has decided instead to enable the captives to escape. Her band will attack and destroy one of the teleportation dampers, setting off a chain reaction that will shut down the entire damper network. This is a suicide mission, but Fireclaw believes that the current war is a travesty, and this act is necessary for the survival of her race.

Fireclaw's plan could allow the characters to salvage their rescue mission — if they can find a way to work with the Chromatic outlaws. The key is Vermilion. After some intense dialogue with the characters, the Chromatic hero now believes that the Witnesses might have been wrong in their zealous pursuit of the holy war. He is willing to speak to the outcast chieftain on the characters' behalf, but there's a problem. As the characters' prisoner, Vermilion is regarded by his people as a thrall, an individual of no status or identity in Chromatic society. The characters must make a leap of faith by setting free their former enemy, thereby returning Vermilion's identity and influence.

After tense introductions, with Vermilion acting as mediator, the characters and Fireclaw's band agree to join forces. It is a marriage of convenience only — neither side should be under the illusion that they are friends now. After some more rest, the characters and Fireclaw's band penetrate the tower, but quickly find themselves surrounded by Chromatic forces. A desperate battle begins, with the outcasts giving their lives to buy time for the characters to locate and disable the dampening field. With the field generator destroyed, the planetary dampening network overloads and collapses, although it takes some time for the subquantum interference to subside enough to allow teleportation. Meanwhile, a small army of Chromatics gathers outside the tower. The stage is set for a defiant last stand.

At that point, the Aberrants attack. The remaining Seraphim consider the collection of Chromatics, seemingly pitted against one another, too good a target to pass up. Bolts of plasma rain down on the Chromatic forces (and on the characters) from 50 of the malformed creatures. The Chromatics fight back valiantly, but so many are killed in the Aberrants' first volley that the outcome of the battle seems certain.

Just as all appears lost, the characters hear Marsden's voice over the radio. The fleet is under attack by Chromatic ships, but has fought its way back into orbit. A drop ship is *en route* with a fighter escort to pull out the team and take them home.

Once again, the characters must make a fateful decision. They can likely escape in the confusion, letting the Chromatics get wiped out by the Aberrants — or they can use the incoming fighters to turn the tide of the battle. If the characters chose wisely, the fighters scatter the Aberrants with a few well-aimed strafing runs. The drop ship descends nearby, ready to evacuate the characters. Emerging from the tower with Vermilion, the characters see Chromatics in stunned, shellshocked silence. They're reeling both from the battle and from the confusion. The Chromatics don't know what to make of the fact that the corrupters — in ships much like the Chromatics' own — drove off the other, malformed corrupters. The universe no longer makes sense.

This is an opportunity for the characters to make their case to the Chromatics — that *humans* aren't the real enemy, the *Aberrants* are. Vermilion and the survivors of Fireclaw's band aid in this, echoing the characters' assertions. Before the Chromatics on the field can truly process what they're being told, an entity appears above them in a blaze of light.

The Chromatics know it as one of the Bodiless Ones — though characters who took part in **Ascent into Light** recognize it as one of the Doyen! The Doyen's telepathic voice thunders in the minds of humans and Chromatics alike, claiming that the characters are lying, trying to earn the aliens' trust the same way that the Aberrants did when they invaded many years ago. But Vermilion has seen enough in recent months to no longer accept the word of a god without question. He stands up to the fearsome being, confronting the Doyen with hard questions. Vermilion doesn't doubt that it is a being of great wisdom and power, but the Chromatic hero wants to understand why a spirit meant to guide his people would lead them into pointless slaughter. The Doyen, fearing that it is losing control of the situation, strikes down what it thinks is the lone dissenting voice. It blasts Vermilion with a massive cryokinetic strike.

The Chromatics react to this with horror. The Bodiless Ones are supposed to be gentle advisors, not dictatorial monsters, and Vermilion is well known as a staunch hero of the people. Many of the aliens

throw down their bioweapons, rejecting the Bodiless Ones' gifts. The Chromatics gather around their fallen hero as the Doyen thunders and threatens, but its failure is obvious. With no other recourse, the Doyen vanishes. The characters are allowed to leave, while the surviving Chromatics take their fallen hero. Chromatic society is soon in a new kind of struggle, as dynastic chieftains challenge the Witnesses' power and others side with the spiritual leaders. The black war with humanity is questioned, and humanity itself has a chance to lend its voice to proving that they are not the Chromatics' enemy.

Thanks to the characters' valiant efforts, a dialogue — perhaps even peace — is possible with the strange aliens known as Chromatics.

Theme

Hope, sacrifice and unity — the fundamental themes of the Æon Trinity — are especially important in *Vermilion Falling*. Ambushed and isolated on a hostile alien world, the characters must hold together until help arrives, relying upon one another to survive. They must hope that Vermilion, Fireclaw's band and the rest of the Chromatics, are willing to see another truth than the one presented by the Bodiless Ones. The course of the Chromatic War and the fate of the imprisoned teleporters lie in the characters' hands — if they are willing to potentially sacrifice their lives in a desperate raid to disable the aliens' teleportation damper.

Mood

The mood of *Vermilion Falling* is the quintessential chaos of war — a potent mix of confusion, anger, defiance and despair. Before the raid, the characters are members of a powerful UN invasion force, supported by numerous spacecraft, soldiers and fellow psions. Soon their plans are in ruins, their mission ostensibly a failure, and they are only a handful of humans on a world with billions of implacable enemies. Events are moving very rapidly, with no time to pause and think. The characters must swallow the bitter taste of defeat and keep fighting, doing the best they can for one another while trying to complete their mission, no matter the cost.

Setting

Vermilion Falling is set on the surface and subsurface of the Chromatic homeworld, referred to as Chrome-Prime by human forces. The main focus is on the region surrounding the Chromatics' *de facto* capitol city, White Rocks Holding.

White Rocks

D

Hot Sands

□ = 200 Meters
D: Dampener
P: Pickup Point
T: Transmission Point
U: Upeo Medical Building

N

T

P

Map 1: Area Map, Chrome-Prime

Chrome-Prime

Chrome-Prime is a young world geologically, roughly the size of Earth, but with extremely little surface water. At some point in the planet's history, its single moon was destroyed, leaving behind a ring of asteroidal bodies in low orbit and robbing the planet of the tidal forces necessary to draw water to the world's surface. As a result, Chrome-Prime's water table remains fairly deep underground, warmed by geothermal activity to form large subterranean seas. These were the source for much of the life on the planet. Tectonic activity over many millennia caused some seas to alternately swell and shrink, eroding caves and passages where the water found soft or porous rock. These chambers now trap heat and gases to produce a greenhouse effect conducive to plant and animal life.

The surface of the planet is radically different, giving no hint of the vibrant, primordial life below. With what little atmospheric gases and moisture available being provided by volcanic activity, Chrome-Prime's landscape can best be described as hellish. The air is thin and sulfurous and ambient temperatures are similar to those found on Mars. A few very hardy species of plant and animal life have evolved amid the rust-colored peaks and gullies of the planet's surface, as resilient and diverse as any found amid the deserts of Earth.

From orbit, Chrome-Prime provides clues that it is home to a space-faring race, but the hints are more tantalizing for what they *don't* reveal. While eight of the planet's trapped asteroids have been hollowed out and turned into orbiting shipyards, no city lights gleam from the red-ochre surface below. New biotech fabrication plants nestle close by squat, stone ziggurats that appear little more than a few decades old. Large-capacity roadways connect the industrial sites with raw material refineries and a half-dozen launch facilities, but for every active manufacturing site there are 10 more, each progressively less sophisticated, that simply lie abandoned. The one thing they all have in common is a focus on a single, specialized industry: arming for interstellar war.

Chromatic History: An Overview

Early in Chromatic cultural development, competition for resources and breeding ground was fierce, shaping them into a fierce race of hunters and warriors. They organized into large tribes that controlled specific breeding areas and passed ownership to their children in a dynastic fashion. Even within these dynasties there was not enough room in the hatching grounds for everyone to breed, leading to a system of social rank that established an individual's worthiness to breed. Many of the lowest-status Chromatics were driven off dynasty lands, becoming exiles until they had demonstrated sufficient prowess to receive higher rank.

Individual social status is driven by the species' instinct to survive, granting rank and breeding rights based on individual ability and reputation. Strength, speed and stamina are valued, as are sharp wits and noetic prowess. Leadership skills and the ability to communicate effectively are also held in high esteem, and can frequently offset a Chromatic's physical shortcomings.

An individual's raw talents, however, are not as important as how well he or she puts those talents to use. Young Chromatics are not given names, but instead must perform some exploit that demonstrates their prowess and proves that they deserve recognition. It is very rare, but not unheard of, for a Chromatic to gain more than one deed-name over the course of her life — the mark of a truly great warrior.

The Howler War

The Chromatics had evolved into near-surface dwellers, while a parallel species' evolution stagnated far below even the underground seas. Just under the planet's crust, Chromatic society grew to the point where overpopulation and finite resources triggered cycles of territorial wars. (The concept of thralls, as described on page 29, developed during this time.) That and ever-expanding searches for resources brought the Chromatics into contact with their distant relatives. The creatures' vocabulary of guttural cries (an outgrowth of their echolocation sensory ability) earned them the label "howlers."

The primitive howlers attacked in frenzied swarms, overrunning entire dynasties. The Chromatics, mired in dozens of internal disputes, could not resist the invaders. Facing extinction, the Chromatics were forced to negotiate with one another, and develop rules of warfare that evolved into the concepts of blue war and black war.

The need for collaborative efforts and improved defenses during the Howler War allowed for numerous technological and social innovations. Communal defensive sites, called "holdings," were centered generally around a cavern or adjoining series of caves in an area conveniently accessible to neighboring dynasties. Once the Howler War ended, the holdings' roles gradually expanded, effectively becoming Chromatic cities. Chromatics met in the holdings as a sort of neutral ground to trade, share news or take shelter during long journeys.

The process of expansion also led the Chromatics to discover the surface of their world. The fiery glow of the sun attracted many holy seekers, but the lethal conditions for the cold-blooded species brought on at nightfall hindered settlements on the surface.

The Corrupters

After a time, Chromatics exploring the surface further encountered a group of Aberrants — the Seraphim, recently expelled from Earth. As these new beings bore no resemblance to the Chromatics' mortal enemy, the howlers, the Aberrants were not automatically considered a threat. The Chromatics were cautious at first , but Gabriel, a member of the Seraphim with a telepathic gift, enabled the two races to converse. Eventually, the Chromatics accepted the Aberrants' friendly overtures and welcomed them into their subterranean world. The goodwill was not to last, however. Once the Aberrants judged the Chromatics to be primitive and easy to conquer they showed their true faces, killing thousands in what the Chromatics named the "Night of Lies."

The scope of the deceit overwhelmed the Chromatics, but as the killing continued, their shock turned into righteous rage. They faced an enemy more evil and dangerous than any howler, and the Chromatics declared black war against the onslaught of the corrupters. The unity and single-minded fury of the Chromatics took the overconfident Aberrants by surprise. They slew several in a series of bloody battles. Again, the Chromatics suffered terrible losses, but their all-out effort drove the Aberrant clan into hiding in the high mountains of Chrome-Prime, ending the war in a stalemate.

The Bodiless Ones

The aftermath of the black war against the Aberrants was a period of despair and desperation, as the Chromatics faced dire threats both from above and below. Bodiless spirits of light appeared to a select group of Chromatic holy seekers — individual Chromatics who left their dynasties in search of greater spiritual truths. These "spirits" offered the power to destroy the corrupters. In truth, they were members of a race called the Doyen — who believed that Aberrants would inevitably corrupt the entire universe unless they were destroyed. The "spirits" were part of a splinter group that considered all of humanity

corrupt and believed it must be wiped out to prevent more Aberrants from arising. Despite their convictions, the Doyen were not fighters (indeed, they are often quite cowardly and panic easily when combat occurs). Instead, the beings sought to enlist the Chromatics to fight for them.

The Doyen chose Chromatics of exceptional intelligence and imagination to renew the black war — not just against the corrupters in the hills, but against the ultimate domain of the corrupters and its wardens — Earth and humanity. Until Earth was destroyed, the Doyen said, the corrupters would keep coming until the Chromatics were no more. These chosen Chromatics became known as the Witnesses, and their Doyen mentors gave them secrets that would carry their war to the stars — technological information taken from humanity itself.

There were only 30 Witnesses, each of whom was specialized in an area of technology and industry, making use of human-refined biotech designs imparted telepathically by the Doyen. The vast and unique knowledge given to these individuals granted them higher status than the greatest chieftain. That, coupled with the Witnesses' origins as self-exiled pilgrims, set them outside the bounds of "proper" Chromatic society. This enabled them to gather multitudes of willing followers not only from powerful chieftains, but also from the ranks of outcasts.

The Witnesses drove their followers ruthlessly, setting into motion an industrial revolution that catapulted the Chromatics to the stars in less than 20 years. The first weapons produced were turned against the howlers, resulting in victories that further cemented the Witnesses' influence and their status above the chieftains. The Witnesses told their people that the corrupters made their lairs on distant places, a long journey through a cold sea of darkness. The thought of such a trip terrified any sane Chromatic, but black war demanded every ounce of their bravery and determination. Thousands might be lost, but for Chromatics to survive, the corrupters must be destroyed. Nothing else mattered. Given the Chromatics' brutal history (and Doyen propaganda) it is easy to understand their implacable hatred of humanity.

White Rocks Holding

Situated near the shore of a vast subterranean sea, this Chromatic city-fort was built during the howler swarms and was the first location visited by the Witnesses with their message from the Bodiless Ones. Since then, the city became the holy ones' seat of power. Built by seven of the most powerful existing dynasties, White Rocks Holding can house up to 5000 Chromatics in times of enemy attack.

The site has living spaces, hatcheries, warehouses and assembly areas surrounded by three concentric mud walls in a huge, high-ceilinged cavern 115 meters beneath the surface. Numerous passages in the cavern's walls wind their way up through the flanks of the mountain above and lead to the living areas of the Witnesses themselves (who prefer to remain near the surface as much as possible in case the Bodiless Ones should return). The tunnels around the holding bustle with activity at all hours. Shifts of workers move back and forth between industrial sites on the surface and representatives from distant dynasties arrive to receive new instructions regarding their role in the war effort. At the time of humanity's raid, the Upeo wa Macho prisoners are being kept secretly in a number of warehouses near the innermost ring of the fort.

Industrial Sites

Seen from orbit, the slopes of the mountain above White Rocks Holding is crowded with a jumble of industrial structures — many now abandoned, having outlived their usefulness in the Chromatics' headlong technological advancement. The configuration of the more advanced facilities closely resembles their counterparts on Earth; however, all are primarily biotech in construction. Any hardtech buildings are made in more traditional Chromatic style, using stone, iron and broad ziggurat shapes.

There are four large biotech fabrication plants on White Rocks Mountain, their matrices operating around the clock, and several dozen raw material refineries supplying organic material for the plants. Warehouses near the plants receive a constant flow of weapons and miscellaneous equipment to eventually supply the next assault on Earth. In the initial stages of the assault, all four fabrication plants are attacked by human strike teams and wrecked beyond repair.

The Starport

A wide crushed gravel road extends from one of the fabrication plants to a nearby orbital launch facility, which operates 12 laser launch systems to boost work crews and starship modules up to the assembly yards in the asteroid ring. Again, much of the base layout and design of the laser launch units are reminiscent to systems in operation on Luna and Mars from the past two decades. The starport also houses a squadron of fighters for local defense and a garrison of troops. During the attack, this site is subjected to bombing runs that destroy all but a few dozen fighters and most of the laser systems. The fighters and laser systems that remain operational serve to harry incoming Earth craft once the Chromatics recover from the first attack.

The Teleportation Dampener Network

A tall square tower situated by itself some eight kilometers from the holding's other surface structures, the damper is one of a network of field projectors around the planet. These towers relay specially calibrated noetic waves, creating a net that disrupts attempts to form teleportation conduits. This keeps the captured Upeo from escaping their holding areas, and strands any free teleporters on the planetary surface.

Hot Sands Holding

This was the original city-fort constructed by the seven dynasties generations ago. It is situated near a series of geothermal vents that keep the holding comfortable, and which once provided stable temperatures for hatching eggs. Unfortunately, Hot Sands was also situated near a major fault line, and suffered recurring damage from Chrome-Prime's frequent earthquakes. The holding was hit by a pow-

The Guiding Light

Chromatics are a curious and perceptive people, and have developed numerous myths that attempt to answer the universal questions of existence. Most of these religious beliefs center on a number of common themes: Light in all its forms is a pure and life-giving force. (This no doubt touches on race memories of using photokinetic powers to survive in the seas' dark depths.) Darkness is associated with coldness and hunger, and is personified as evil. There is no worse fate for a Chromatic than freezing to death, surrounded by blackness. Since light is the source of life, mythical spirits are described as luminous beings.

The "gods of light" in Chromatic myth are not seen as all-powerful, judgmental beings, but as helpful advisors, giving wisdom and aid to protect the people from darkness. As far as most Chromatics are concerned, the gods help those who help themselves.

erful quake over two decades previously that decimated the place. Rather than rebuild, the Chromatics moved four kilometers west, and built White Rocks Holding to take Hot Sands' place.

Since the earthquake, the ruins of Hot Sands sit deserted, home to outcasts and exiles willing to risk the cavern's instability to have some temporary refuge. When the characters become trapped on Chrome-Prime, Vermilion leads them to Hot Sands to rest and tend their wounds (see "The Ruined Keep," page 91, for details).

Running
Vermilion Falling

Vermilion Falling is a direct continuation to the story begun in Episode One, _Colors of Sacrifice_. This episode can be run as a stand-alone adventure, however, with some modifications.

Bypassing _Colors of Sacrifice_

If the characters didn't interrogate Vermilion and later jump with him to the suspected Chromatic medical site, there are a number of different ways to involve them. Some of the more plausible origins are listed below.

Whatever the specifics, the characters prove to be the only ones close enough to help one of the beleaguered rescue teams. The characters arrive in time to help the last surviving human, Clarence Greaves, and his prisoner, a Chromatic referred to as "Vermilion." While the characters flee, Greaves relates to the characters the events of _Colors of Sacrifice_, including Vermilion's role.

The characters might initially find the alien to be a liability but Greaves insists that it's vital they keep the Chromie. The characters have the daunting task of winning the alien's respect and trust while trying to stay alive in enemy territory. Assume that Vermilion has come to trust Greaves as he would have the characters through _Colors of Sacrifice_; this can be used to help the characters in any tight spots. At this point, you can start the characters in the first part of "Miles to go Before I Sleep."

• **UN military personnel.** The UN raid represents the largest multinational military offensive undertaken since the Aberrant War. Numerous active-duty and even reserve soldiers from all over the world are chosen for their expertise in orbital and ground combat to join the assault force. This provides an excellent opportunity to bring together characters from diverse backgrounds and allegiances.

• **Æon Trinity operatives.** Æon's influence with the UN allows it to dispatch teams of special operatives along with the fleet to provide "support activities" — everything from logistical planning to elite commando teams. The characters might comprise just such a team, assembled and supervised by the fleet's ground forces commander, Æon operative Robert Marsden.

• **Scientists and scholars.** Though unquestionably a military operation, the mission to Chrome-Prime, nevertheless, represents the first expedition to an alien homeworld since the Chinese traveled to Qinshui. A select group of xenobiologists, anthropologists and first-contact specialists have received permission to accompany the fleet and gather as much information as possible on humanity's implacable enemy.

• **War correspondents.** It is a sad fact that there are more reporters and columnists traveling with the fleet than scientists. The UN and Æon are both eager to present an image of world governments and psions united in the cause of protecting humanity and rescuing the trapped teleporters, and members of the news services are actively courted by high-ranking members of the multinational force. Reporters also have broad access to the regular troops in the fleet, and some enterprising hype-types have bribed drop ship crews to tag along on missions over Chrome-Prime.

Behind the Scenes

Alien forces take center stage at this point, as each pursues agendas that will affect events surrounding the characters:

The Chromatics

Humans have the impression that the Chromatic race is a unified entity, monolithic and fanatical in its pursuit of holy war. This is not entirely the case — Chromatic society is by nature intensely dynamic, as individuals compete constantly for rank and status within dynasties. The Witnesses, with their uniquely powerful position as servants of the Bodiless Ones, instantly supplanted the highest chieftains and imposed their will on the race as a whole. Suddenly, the path to high rank lay in mastering the knowledge that the Witnesses taught, and in building the tools and weapons for war. The word of the Witnesses was law, utter and absolute, and the Chromatics were united in a single purpose. This idea ran counter to the Chromatics' concept of society, but the threat of the corrupters was enough to override individual ambition.

The Witnesses' iron grip began slipping, however. After the capture of the Upeo and early successes against the Karroo Mining Colony, the fortunes of war appeared to turn against the Chromatics. Rather than overrunning the colony, the resourceful Karrooan scientists and miners fought back, turning the tide to a stalemate. The Witnesses appealed to the Bodiless Ones for guidance, but no help was forthcoming. Not knowing what else to do, the Witnesses continued with arming the vast invasion fleet and waiting for word to carry the battle to the corrupter's home ground.

Finally, the Bodiless Ones returned. They seemed uninterested in the failures in the Crab Nebula, dismissing the campaign as a "field test." The real objective was Earth, and the Chromatics were commanded to assemble an elite force of their finest warriors for a raid to obtain vital information about the corrupters, which would ensure the invasion's success. For all the Chromatics' valor, the raid was a failure, forcing the Chromatics to prepare for the invasion of Earth, without the vital data promised by the Doyen.

The great mother ships gathered shortly after, and hundreds of the finest warriors set out amid great ceremony. In a fierce battle in human space, most of these warriors met their deaths at the hands of more skilled human pilots. Only two of the nine mother ships returned to Chrome-Prime with just a portion of the elite force. What was a bitter victory for Earth was a terrible disaster for the Chromatics.

Setback after setback caused the peoples' faith in the Witnesses to seriously waver. Many spoke softly that war ought to be the province of chieftains, not holy seekers. Now the corrupters have come again to Chrome-Prime, filling the sky with their ships and raining death onto the surface of the world. Many sites on the surface are destroyed. All doubts about the Witnesses' capabilities are momentarily put aside to drive off the invaders, but the right set of circumstances could cause the Chromatics' doubt to blossom into full-blown revolt.

Howlers

The howlers are a species that branched off from Chromatic evolution millennia ago. These beings were cut off from the underground seas by a series of geologic upheavals and forced to evolve as land-dwelling predators in the deep darkness below the planet's surface. Different evolutionary pressures caused the howlers to develop echolocation abilities as well as greater strength and endurance than ordinary Chromatics possess, at the cost of photokinetic ability and intelligence. (The howler template on page 112 has details.) A howler's metabolism forces it to hunt for food nearly every waking moment — the beings even feed upon one another when their hunger becomes too powerful to endure.

When the howlers encountered the Chromatics, they saw their cousins as a source of easy and plentiful prey, attacking dynasty lands in great swarms, or sometimes using their powerful limbs to tunnel into hatching grounds. Individually more powerful than ordinary Chromatics, it took the fanatical efforts of black war to drive the howlers back into the lower tunnels. Encounters with the howlers are currently rare, but with so much effort now focused on the black war against humanity, packs of howlers occasionally stalk the fringes of populated areas hoping to catch lone travelers or isolated work parties.

The Seraphim

The Aberrants who call themselves "the Seraphim" have been lurking on Chrome-Prime for years, stranded by the death of Uriel, the only member of their clan who could warp. Their attempt to find a "new Canaan" failed, as did their efforts to subjugate the Chromatics — including being unable to steal one of the Chromatic mother ships to continue their pilgrimmage. Similarly, the Aberrants are too few to take on the entire human invasion fleet.

The Aberrants' pent-up fury at being stranded and defied by lower life forms finally boils over. The Seraphim venture out in groups during the UN invasion to attack isolated Chromatic and human stragglers. The initial ambushes are very successful, and bloodlust makes the Seraphim increasingly bolder. By the time of the attack on the teleportation damper (covered in The Tower Raid), the thrill of violence exceeds the Aberrants' cunning. A large force of degenerate Seraphim stages a major attack against the Chromatic war band that the characters themselves face.

The Doyen

The Doyen are mysterious, bodiless entities possessing tremendous psi abilities. Tuned far more closely to the universe's subquantum resonance than humans are, the Doyen sensed the growing Aberrant threat from light-years away. As they neared Earth, the Doyen sensed the human proxies' burgeoning noetic talents, leading to a surreptitious first contact. The proxies agreed to keep the Doyens' existence secret since the aliens appeared benevolent — and the proxies themselves were a clandestine group.

The Doyen seldom made contact after that first time, and the proxies were soon involved in matters closer to home. Only recently have the proxies learned that there are Doyen who have taken malevolent interest in humanity. All Doyen vehemently oppose the Aberrants, seeing them as a danger to all sentient life, but a faction has decided that humanity itself will eventually succumb to the taint. The race doesn't favor direct action, though, preferring to manipulate others to achieve its goals. This faction searched for a race to act as its exterminators — and found the Chromatics.

Cursory telepathic probes revealed that the Chromatics held extensive myths about "light spirits" — conveniently, a not-dissimilar description for the Doyen themselves. They took on the role of the Bodiless Ones to recruit the Witnesses. Armed with schematics swiped from humanity itself, the Witnesses were charged with developing the war effort. Once the Chromatics were far enough along,

Some of the Doyen possessed Upeo teleporters (in much the same way as Robert Wei was possessed in **Ascent into Light**) — tricking "fellow" teleporters to jump to Chrome-Prime where Chromatics waited with special psi-dampers.

Then, providing guidance when necessary, the Doyen sect unleashed the Chromatics against Karroo to test of the warriors' abilities and to give them some experience with their new weapons. After that came a full invasion of Earth.

The Doyen are a careful, methodical race, with vastly different perceptions of life and the universe than what humans have. The beings prefer to think through their plans in meticulous detail, taking into account every possible ramification. This makes them potent schemers, but leaves them unable to react quickly when unexpected events overtake them. The failure of the Chromatics' invasion of Earth, for example, caught the Doyen faction off-guard.

Despite these setbacks, the Doyen are unwilling to release their grip on the Chromatics. They have returned to Chrome-Prime to order the Witnesses to begin building a second invasion fleet, larger and better-equipped than the first. The

Doyen faction is perfectly willing to sacrifice all Chromatics if that is what it takes to destroy the tainted enemy. Ever the schemers (or cowards, depending on how one looks at it), the Doyen do not involve themselves directly in the conflict until it becomes apparent that they are losing their control over the Chromatics (as detailed in "The Bodiless One," page 105).

Miles to go Before I Sleep

Vermilion Falling begins immediately where *Colors of Sacrifice* left off. The human offensive is in full swing, striking industrial and military targets all across the planet. But the rescue attempt at the suspected Upeo medical facility has come up empty, luring the characters into an ambush.

The characters reach the surface, fleeing Chromatic pursuers, just minutes before dawn. The medical facility is situated in an abandoned industrial park, surrounded by empty, ruined stone structures (see map, page 76). The night sky is full of stars, and the planet's asteroid ring gleams overhead like a necklace of rubies. Without the reflected light off a moon overhead, the darkness on the ground is almost total. Off to the north and northwest, the characters see a dull orange glow on the horizon and hear the rumble of explosions. The characters' radios crackle with frenzied, overlapping messages between the other strike teams and the fleet. Anyone trying to listen carefully and make sense out of the jumble must make an **Awareness** roll (+1 difficulty). If successful, the characters figure out that other ground teams sent to specified targets also encountered ambushes, and even hear a terrified voice shout "Aberrants!" before being drowned out in a shriek of static. Any attempts by the characters to call the fleet at this point are lost amid all the other radio chatter.

The Chromatics are right on the characters' heels, emerging onto the surface moments later and firing a number of poorly aimed shots in the characters' direction. There are three times as many pursuers as there are characters, but there are no high-ranking leaders among the aliens and their orders were not to leave the medical facility. The Chromatics fire at the characters until they are out of sight amid the ruins, then most stop and wait for further instructions.

Only a small group of Chromatics, equal in number to the characters and unable to resist the thrill of the chase (and potential for glory), sets off in pursuit. Refer to the Chromatic character template in **Trinity** (page 306) for statistics.

Fire and Ice

The thin surface atmosphere of Chrome-Prime creates a harsh and potentially deadly environment for both humans and Chromatics. The oxygen content in the air is similar to that found at high elevations on Earth. Humans under strenuous exertion (running, climbing, fighting) can suffer Bashing damage — treat this as a Bashing attack with a Damage Rating of one die per cumulative turn of effort. Characters wearing life-support equipment such as vac suits or assault suits are unaffected.

Additionally, the planet's thin ozone layer and meager greenhouse effect pose hazards from extreme temperatures and UV radiation. At night, the surface temperature drops swiftly below zero, while during the day the noontime heat reaches in excess of 90° Celsius. Unprotected humans suffer one Lethal Health Level of damage every two hours they're exposed to the elements.

Chromatics on the surface at night suffer two Lethal Health Levels of damage for every 30 minutes of exposure. A Chromatic who has developed pyrokinetic skill can use **Temperature Control** to warm his immediate area, however, effectively allowing them to roam for a couple hours with little risk. The aliens' metabolic systems allow them to withstand daytime conditions without harm.

Keep the Chromatic pursuit through the first portion of the episode dynamic and intense, a confused chase through dark ruins punctuated by sudden bursts of weapons fire. Put pressure on the characters to keep moving. The aliens move much more easily in the dark than humans do despite the cold, nipping continually at the characters' heels, trying to gang up on stragglers and taking quick shots at any glimpse of their quarry. Try to keep them at a breakneck pace, unsure of the enemies' exact numbers and locations, distracted by panicked radio messages and the distant sound of explosions. The characters should feel as though they're only one step ahead of certain death.

Also, throughout the chase (and over the course of the entire episode, for that matter), you must spare Vermilion from sustaining fatal or incapacitating damage. He has to live long enough to defy the wishes of the Doyen in the episode's climactic finale — and *then* suffer a dramatic death.

Race Through the Ruins

The Chromatic pursuit pushes the characters toward the mesas to the east. Moving through the ruins is a difficult and even dangerous proposition in the darkness, though. The ground is sandy and uneven and broken pieces of stone litter the narrow alleys between buildings. Running requires a successful **Athletics** roll (+1 difficulty) each turn to avoid tripping on unseen debris. Characters with night-vision equipment, Sense Mastery or enhanced senses negate this +1 difficulty; using a flashlight also works, but gives away their location to the Chromatics. Characters who fall aren't injured unless they botch. (In which case, inflict Bashing damage equal to the 1s rolled.) Instead, they lose ground to the pursuers, or drop pieces of equipment — which may not be noticed considering the panic of the situation.

The characters consider their options while on the run. If they have a difficult time making decisions, you can have one or more characters try standard **Command** rolls and then lay out their options.

Choices are few: The characters could try to hole up in one of the ruined buildings and hope for rescue, but staying so close to the medical facility makes the chances of discovery very high. They can attempt to ambush and eliminate their pursuers, but enemy reinforcements could arrive at any moment and overwhelm them through sheer weight of numbers. Finally, they can hope to escape into the mesas and call for pickup at a more remote location.

Surprisingly, Vermilion enters the discussion — unless the characters turned it off, the translator device flickers softly, automatically translating their dialogue. If it is off, the alien barks harshly after a moment and begins speaking, demanding that they turn it on. He's a seasoned warrior, after all, and has a good idea that the characters are discussing retreat even if he can't understand what they're saying.

Vermilion strongly endorses moving into the mesas. He informs them that he is familiar with the terrain (his dynasty's holdings are not far away) and can guide them through the mesas to a likely pickup point. Perceptive or empathic characters — standard **Awareness** or **Rapport** rolls — might notice that, since arriving on planet, Vermilion has been agitated and skittish. Further, after the initial encounter in the medical site he actually tried to *avoid* catching the attention of fellow Chromatics.

The last thing Vermilion wants is to be recognized as a human prisoner, since in Chromatic culture it marks him as a thrall and bereft of status and identity, a fate worse than death for someone of his stature. Whatever his current feelings are about his captors, for the moment it's in his best interests to keep the characters out of Chromatic hands.

Lost in Translation

By the time of the events covered in *Vermilion Falling*, the Orgotek translation device has assembled enough of a "vocabulary" for the Chromatic visual language that simple conversations occur with a 67% degree of certainty. ("Vermilion, are you hungry?" "Yes, I am hungry.") Subtle concepts, particularly the Chromatics' "inflection" of unequivocal statements, do not translate as yet, still forcing the characters to puzzle out Vermilion's more complicated responses. ("Vermilion, is that tower the source of the dampening field?" "Above-cave holds high-far-steppers.") As a rule of thumb, if Vermilion is called upon to discuss or explain specific technological or social concepts to the characters, his "speech" reverts to strings of compound nouns and verbs that attempt to draw a picture of what the Chromatic is trying to describe.

Vermilion admits this grudgingly if pressed, though he assumes the characters are already familiar with the concept of thralls and are taunting him. Naturally, some characters might be wary of trusting the assistance of an enemy prisoner, fearing that Vermilion could lead the team into a new ambush. A successful **Subterfuge** roll (+2 difficulty) or the use of **Mind's Eye**, **Sense Emotion** or **Pilfer** confirms that Vermilion is not being duplicitous.

The Mesas

As the characters near the outskirts of the industrial area, dawn breaks over the horizon, filling the sky with harsh light (as thin as the atmosphere is, the sun is an orange flare in a searing orange-white sky). Within minutes, intense solar radiation interferes with the characters' radios, garbling messages with spikes of squealing static. The sunlight casts long, sharply etched shadows along the high mesas and the narrow gullies that run through them. For a moment the Chromatic pursuit abates, as the hunters pause to soak in life-sustaining warmth and to decide their next moves.

Vermilion describes a plateau 10 kilometers east by south (see map, page 76) that is big enough for a drop ship to land on. First, however, the characters must contact the fleet. Transmission from the base of the mesas isn't possible due to the surrounding rock and solar interference. A successful **Engineering** or **Science** roll allows the characters to conclude that their best bet for getting a signal through would be to transmit from a tall rock formation visible four kilometers to the east.

Meanwhile, a number of high-ranking Chromatics arrive via subterranean tunnels at the medical facility and take charge, organizing a thorough search of the buildings and eventually the mesas. Calling on additional reinforcements, the searching force numbers nearly 600 low-status Chromatics from local dynasties (including Vermilion's). These hunters organize into bands of five hunters led by a squad leader (described in "Dramatis Personae," page 112). The search party has a large amount of terrain to cover, so the characters will never encounter more than six to nine Chromatics at any given time, but as the aliens begin their search, the chorus of barks and grunts sounds like a small army of Chromies are on the characters' trail. Because each building must be searched before the aliens proceed to the mesas, the characters have some time to put distance between themselves and their pursuers, and should use it as wisely as possible.

The characters have two choices for navigating the mesas: work their way through the maze of narrow gullies, or try to climb the steep slopes and travel along the hills' flat tops. Climbing the hills requires a successful **Athletics** roll (+2 difficulty due to the steep incline and loose sand). Once on top, the characters can move quickly and navigate easily, but they are in full view to anyone atop the other hills. Moving through the twisting gullies has its own advantages, not the least of which is some amount of protection from direct sunlight (characters keeping to the shade of the gully walls can avoid the Lethal Health Levels incurred by heat and UV exposure), but the high walls make navigation very difficult. Clairsentient characters using **Farsensing** can aid in leading the team to the transmission point, and the use of **Danger Sense** can provide warning if the team is heading toward Chromatic hunting parties.

If the characters travel the gullies, Vermilion tries to take the lead, working from memory to choose the correct path. Again, successful **Subterfuge** rolls (+2 difficulty) or the use of appropriate psi techniques confirms that Vermilion is entirely truthful in wanting to aid the team.

The Chromatic search party takes half an hour to search the buildings along the eastern edge of the industrial area, then proceeds into the mesas. The aliens' strategy is to send a third of their force up onto the tops of the hills, while the rest split up and work their way quickly through the gullies, acting as "brush beaters." These hunters make considerable noise in an attempt to flush the characters out of cover. The Chromatics on the mesas, moving stealthily, watch the adjoining gullies for movement. If the characters are spotted, the Chromies coordinate the brush beaters' movements to try to surround their prey. This provides an opportunity for a tense "fox hunt" as the Chromatics stalk the humans through the mesas, though you must be careful to limit any encounters to small, intense exchanges between the characters and small hunting groups. The idea is to keep the characters under pressure and on the run, not to bog things down into a battle that the humans cannot win.

Transmission Point

The characters arrive at the transmission point exhausted and possibly on the verge of panic as the gullies behind them echo with the cries of pursuing aliens. Climbing the hill requires two **Ath-** letics rolls (+2 difficulty), and doing so brings the characters into view of the Chromatic hunters patrolling along the mesas. Characters with **Stealth** may conceal their movements, rolling at +1 difficulty. Otherwise, hunters along the mesas flash urgent messages to nearby brush beaters, and the Chromatics swiftly close on the rock formation.

Once at the top, the characters' radios must punch through the solar interference to get through to the ships in orbit. This is an extended action, requiring six successes for either **Engineering** or **Interface**. (The fleet is thousands of kilometers from the surface, too far for even the most powerful psion to use **Transmit**.) Fiddling with the transmission should take a couple of minutes at least — creating a tense situation as the Chromies draw ever closer — but the characters establish a weak contact with the jump ship *Chicago*. (Marsden's transmission on page 65 isn't broadcast until the end of "One Foot in the Trap," page 88.) The officer contacted sounds harried and somewhat confused. After considerable difficulty explaining the situation (go ahead and play the conversation to the hilt, complete with gaps in sentences and garbled words), the officer confirms the characters' location and designates a pickup point. An E-19 drop ship is on the way, ETA 20 minutes. Before signing off, the officer shares a chilling warning; Aberrants have been sighted on-planet, operating in large groups. Three strike teams have been attacked and casualties are heavy. She wishes the characters good luck.

The pickup point is six kilometers away. There is no time to lose.

So Close, So Far

Speed and stealth are now of paramount importance. The characters must reach the pickup point ahead of the drop ship (it isn't going to wait around in the middle of hostile territory), yet they cannot draw the Chromatics along with them or the ship will come under heavy fire as it tries to land. Moving along the tops of the mesas covers a lot of ground quickly, but makes the characters easy to track. Vermilion, clearly as interested in avoiding the pursuing Chromatics as the characters are, again offers to guide the characters through the gullies.

The group must move as quickly and as stealthily as possible to avoid pursuit. The Chromatic search party descends swiftly on the transmission point, but continues along to the east unless the characters leave a clear trail showing their change of direction. (A successful standard **Survival** can help disguise their tracks.)

The Black Tower

When the characters are on high ground, anyone scanning the surrounding terrain notices a tall, square tower by itself on an alkali plain 15 kilometers to the north (see map, page 76). A character covering that distance with Psi or the Sight can roll **Attunement**. If successful, the character senses a subquantum fluctuation that Greaves confirms is what's inhibiting him from teleporting. With one extra success on the roll, the character feels that the emanations seem to be "routed" through the tower. If the characters question Vermilion about it, he grudgingly admits that the tower "keeps the corrupters from far-stepping," but that is all he knows. If anyone suggests trying to sabotage the field, the Chromatic vehemently argues that even if there was enough time, the tower is close to a major holding and the area is very heavily guarded. The characters can try to inform the fleet about the tower, but the fleet is already in the process of regrouping. There aren't any resources available to mount an attack at the present time. The information will be noted for use in developing a secondary attack strategy, however.

Complications

There are still numerous possible dangers on the way to the pickup point, even if the characters elude the search parties. You may challenge the characters with some, none or all of the encounters listed below, at your discretion. For detailed information on the animals and plants, refer to "Dramatis Personae," page 109.

• **Chromatic fighters:** Three Chromatic fighter craft scream out of nowhere, passing low over the characters' position. The characters can't be sure what the crafts' intended target is or whether the pilots spotted them.

• **Magma vent:** Chrome-Prime has widespread volcanic activity. A vent opened nearby recently, spewing thick clouds of toxic ash and smoke that is deadly to breathe, and it fills several gullies with an impenetrable fog. These clouds can sweep into adjoining gullies with a change in wind direction, swiftly and silently engulfing the characters. Anyone breathing the sulfurous fumes suffers one Lethal Health Level damage per turn of exposure. Normal visibility within the ash clouds is nil.

• **Rock devils:** As the characters make their way through a depression, they stumble upon a pack of these monitor-like reptiles picking at scraps of flesh from a large skeletal carcass. The creatures prefer live prey and set upon the characters; when more than half of the rock devils are killed, the rest flee.

• **Sandeaters:** The characters find the gully ahead filled by a herd of enormous, ovoid creatures. The sandeaters are feeding when the characters find them, and the team must either run a gauntlet between the beasts or climb the gully walls and bypass them (without getting spat on in the process).

• **Diggerbees:** Characters encounter these rapacious insects when resting for a moment in the shade of a shallow cave or rock overhang, or they may swarm up from the desiccated carcass of an animal as a character passes by.

• **Tangleweed:** Characters who step into a hole or run a hand into a dark crevice might receive a rude surprise when the limb is swiftly enmeshed in a net of tangleweed tendrils, which draws tightly enough to cut off circulation.

• **Desert belladonna:** Many of the gully floors are dotted with dark green, cactus-like plants. An enterprising character may try to recover water from a plant, though Vermilion advises against it, fearing that it might be poisonous. Cutting open the plant reveals pale flesh that is indeed saturated with water. The plant's moisture tastes metallic and slightly bitter, but the water can be ingested by eating the plant's flesh, or by wringing the water out and drinking it. Characters who consume a cup or more suffer powerful hallucinations, paranoia and psychosis an hour after ingesting the water.

• **The "empty-heads":** The characters literally run headlong into a group of six unarmed Chromatics all prostrate on a flat stretch of ground under the full light of the sun. When they see the humans, the aliens stumble to their feet and dance in a jerky yet rhythmic fashion, flashing a range of soft colors. Some create holograms of bright, multicolored orbs gleaming through a dark void, while others offer the characters trinkets of bone, volcanic glass, or possibly even gemstones. These Chromatics are all quite mad, exiles who came to the surface in supplication to the Great Radiance above (the sun). They are harmless and treat the characters with some semblance of awe. Vermilion glows contemptuously at the holy seekers and sends them scampering away with a few threatening barks. Vermilion is dismissive if questioned about the odd aliens, referring to them as "empty-heads."

The characters reach the pickup point with only minutes to spare. As they begin their climb to the top they can hear the distant roar of the drop ship's engines to the east. The climb to the top of the plateau is an extended **Athletics** action requiring five successes within four turns (the point at which the drop ship reaches the plateau). Characters can grab their buddies and help pull them along, combining their Dice Pools but suffering +1 difficulty due to the awkwardness of such a climbing method.

If the Chromatic search parties fails to pick up the characters' trail at the transmission point, the sound of the descending E-19 brings them southeast at a ground-eating run, taking a direct route across the tops of the mesas. (If the characters fail to elude the hunters at the transmission point, you can slow down the pursuit by subjecting the aliens to one of the encounters listed in Complications.) When the characters finally struggle over the lip of the plateau and see a glint of light in the sky that is their ticket home, they should feel tremendous relief. They're virtually home-free!

Which is, of course, when all hell breaks loose.

One Foot in the Trap

The Seraphim, Aberrants stuck on Chrome-Prime, take advantage of the confusion raised by the UN attack. They listen in on human communications and ambush isolated strike teams and pickup efforts. (They are also attacking Chromatic holdings and surface sites, but reports of this haven't yet filtered back to the fleet.) A pack of Seraphim hears the characters' call for help and reaches the plateau first, laying a hastily organized ambush. (Use the Aberrant character template in **Trinity**, page 303, for statistics and abilities.) Characters may detect the Aberrants' presence through **Attunement** (since they appear as "holes" in the subquantum stratum). The roll is made at +3 difficulty unless a character states specifically that she's using it; the characters are more focused on the exertions of the race to the plateau and the hurried climb. If the ambushers realize that they have been discovered, they will immediately attack.

The Seraphim are split evenly between ranged attackers (using plasma and quanta-lasers) and physical attackers. The ranged attackers take up positions on one or more of the three mesas overlooking the pickup point, intending to catch the characters in a crossfire. The rest are concealed along a narrow ledge near the lip of the plateau's east face. Unfortunately for them, that's also the side from which the drop ship approaches, and its pilot sees the waiting Aberrants moments before landing.

The exact number and abilities of the Aberrants involved is at your discretion, depending largely on the condition of the characters by that point. The Aberrants serve the story only to force the characters into hiding with Vermilion and to meet Fireclaw — and to give the characters a much-needed victory. By the time the characters reach the pickup point and see their ticket home shot out of the sky, they'll need something on which to take out their frustrations! Don't obviously pull punches to let the characters win, but adjust the number of Aberrants so that the team has a very good chance of defeating them. If nothing else, you can have a large number initially, but the missiles fired from the E-19 grievously wound enough to shift the odds.

If the characters fail to detect the Aberrants, the first indication that something is wrong is when the drop ship's engines suddenly howl at full power and pitch the craft from a slow descent into a sudden climb away from the plateau. The drop ship launches both of its smart missiles; for a terrifying moment it appears as though they are shooting at the characters, but the weapons strike around the lip of the plateau's eastern end. The Aberrants on the nearby mesas strike at the same moment, firing laser and plasma bolts at the characters and the drop ship. As the characters either throw themselves to the rocky ground or return fire, the drop ship pulls into an almost vertical climb — until three plasma bolts stitch a ragged line along the ship's right side. One engine explodes and the drop ship pitches over, spiraling down 50 meters then limping off to the northeast. The E-19 leaves a trail of thick black smoke and loses altitude steadily as the pilot obviously struggles to regain control. It finally disappears out of sight a few kilometers away. Shortly thereafter, the characters hear an explosion and a ball of fire rises into the sky.

With the drop ship down, the remaining Aberrants turn their full attention to the characters. The group waiting at the lip of the plateau (if you decide there are any left) climbs up and attacks in close combat, complicating the aim of the other ambushers on the nearby mesas. (You could have stray shots strike Aberrants engaged in melee to even the odds if necessary.)

The one person most surprised by these events is Vermilion. From his perspective, a band of corrupters just shot down one of their own rescue ships! As confusing as the situation seems, when the Aberrants come over the plateau, the Chromatic hero attacks them without thinking —

these mutated creatures have been his foes for many years. Without access to his psionic aptitudes, however, Vermilion is at a severe disadvantage. The characters are obligated to defend him as well as themselves.

A character might be tempted to remove Vermilion's dampening harness to help fight off the Aberrants — certainly in the present situation the team needs all the help it can get. You needn't dissuade the character, but you should point out that once the Chromatic is out of the harness, he's not going to meekly put it back on again. Freeing him negates much of the control the characters have over their prisoner, who might just as easily turn against them once he has full command of his abilities. Then again, he's been increasingly helpful as the characters have fled Chromatic pursuit. At the very least, the character could take off the manacles covering Vermilion's hands so that he may use his foreclaws. Let the characters make their own decision, but don't allow much time for contemplation — after all, they're in the middle of a fight!

Just as the last Aberrant falls (or the remainder flee — they're vicious, but not suicidal), a high-powered radio signal crackles over the char-

acters' radios. The voice belongs to Robert Linsey Marsden, the commander of the UN ground forces. Marsden tries to sound positive and encouraging, but there is an unmistakable tension in his voice. The transmission on page 65 covers this transmission; read it aloud or allow the players to look it over. The gist of the message is that the fleet is pulling back into deep space to regroup, but will return as soon as it can. Teams still left planetside must go to ground and hold out as best they can until they can be picked up. The characters are on their own, and they're by no means safe — after all, there may be other Aberrants out there, and the Chromatics are still in pursuit.

Dead Men Walking

Once clear from the ambush site, the characters have time for Marsden's message to really sink in. They have been left behind. Marsden sounded like he would get the characters off the planet if he had to carry them out of the gravity well on his shoulders, but this isn't a Saturday holoshow. This is war, and the fleet might not make it back in time. Then there is the rumor some of the characters heard on the way to Chrome-Prime. It sounded like typical scuttlebutt and no one expected the rescue missions to fail, but what if the UN commanders really *do* have a plan to nuke the planet if the fleet cannot rescue the Upeo? Would they really do such a thing? Could they afford *not* to? Play up the sense of the characters' isolation and uncertainty, and the sober reality that they may not make it off Chrome-Prime alive. This isn't intended simply to depress the players, but to put the characters in the frame of mind where they must consider what is truly important — waiting like rabbits for the hunters to find them, or sacrificing themselves in a heroic attempt to free the imprisoned Upeo.

The Crash Site

The E-19 slams into the side of a mesa four kilometers northeast of the pickup point at an altitude of less than 15 meters. The cockpit section is crushed on impact, killing the pilot and copilot, but the troop compartment survives largely intact, coming to rest at the base of the mesa. A tendril of greasy, black smoke rises into the sky and marks the crash site for kilometers around. Though the characters initially have no reason to believe that anyone survived the crash and have more than enough problems on their hands as it is, anyone with a compassionate nature (especially vitakinetics) ought to feel compelled to check for survivors. The drop ship's crew risked their lives to try to rescue *them*, after all. At the very least there might be some useful supplies in the wreckage.

There are two survivors in the troop compartment, though both are badly hurt. One is a UN medic, a vitakinetic named Else Boehm. The other is an OBC reporter, Marty Blake, an up-and-coming personality from the news show *HotSpot*. Marty pulled every string he could think of to get press credentials as a war correspondent, and talked the crew of the drop ship into letting him tag along for some footage of the rescue operations. Now he is closer to the war zone than he ever wanted to be. Both Else and Marty have broken bones and contusions (Marty is Crippled, while Else is Incapacitated, all Bashing damage), but there are medical supplies available, including a Wazukana Medsurgeon 11 Portable Medical Kit that can be used to treat their (and the characters') injuries. Else Boehm and Marty Blake are described further in "Dramatis Personae," starting on page 114.

The characters also recover a medical pack containing 10 doses each of CureAlls, stimulants and tranquilizers, a box of anti-infection pads and two bottles of trauma stabilization foam. Four emergency lockers each contain vacuum environment suits.

There is also a weapons rack containing four L-K MAC-803 automatic carbines with two extra clips per weapon. Details on the various tools and weaponry can be found in **Trinity**, pages 262-276.

Marty is barely coherent when the characters arrive, but the minute he sees them he begins babbling effusively about what heroes they are, and how he'll make them the biggest celebrities in the universe if they just get him back to the fleet. He also insists that the team find his biocam (as described in "Technology," page 116), and set it back on his shoulder so he can start getting footage. Once Marty has recovered enough from his injuries to get about without help, he records everything the characters do, likely getting underfoot in the process. But if he manages to make it back to Earth the footage will, indeed, make the characters famous.

If the characters write off the drop ship as destroyed, or are simply too ruthless to worry about any survivors, it's their loss. Else and Marty are helpful but not crucial to the rest of the story. If you still wish for the medic and the media to make an appearance, they can be discovered and captured by Fireclaw and her outcasts and brought to the ruined Hot Sands Holding for study.

Burning Questions

The characters, Greaves and Vermilion make a commando raid, fight a running battle with Chromatics, race across a harsh and dangerous landscape and fight their way out of an Aberrant ambush. They are caked with blood and thick, reddish sand. They are hot, exhausted and likely injured, and there is no way of knowing when their ordeal on Chrome-Prime will end. They must find someplace safe (or at least defensible) where they can regain their strength and figure out what to do next. By this point, the characters might be accustomed enough to Vermilion's help that they simply ask him if he knows a place where they can hide. If not, the Chromatic suggests that he knows of a spot nearby that would make a good hiding place. His colors are muted, neutral, when he says this.

Vermilion has a great deal on his mind.

The battle with the Aberrants brought home to the Chromatic hero just how different the "smooth" corrupters' behavior is from the "bumpy" corrupters'. The Aberrants that Vermilion fought during the Night of Lies cared little for one another's welfare, but at the pickup point the characters put themselves at considerable risk to protect one another — and to even defend Vermilion himself! And the characters fight the other corrupters as fiercely as any Chromatic would. As a race that manipulates illusions as a matter of course, the Chromatics place weight on actions over appearances, and the characters simply haven't *acted* like the evil creatures that Vermilion encountered in the past. The hero trusts his instincts, but he has also heard the Witnesses speak unequivocal truths: smooth-skinned or tentacled, all are corrupt and must be destroyed. The more Vermilion thinks about this, the more questions he has.

The characters should have more than a few questions of their own. Why are the Aberrants on the planet? Clearly the Chromatics hate them, but why do the aliens consider humans and Aberrants to be no different from one another? Obviously Vermilion isn't the savage, unreasoning creature that many on Earth believe the Chromatics to be. The aliens must have compelling reasons for the war they have started, but what are they?

These issues will have to wait for safety to be discussed, but both humans and Chromatic should be interested in a dialogue soon.

The Ruined Keep

Free from pursuit at the moment, Vermilion leads the characters north at a swift pace, drawing ever closer to a small, weathered foothill in the shadow of White Rock Mountain, wreathed in smoke from UN bombing raids and strike teams. From time to time the characters catch sight of the teleport damper as well, a thin, black finger pointing to the sky further off to the northeast.

Vermilion takes the characters to the south face of the foothill, where a narrow cleft climbs a meter-and-a-half up the cliff face. He crouches low, studying the opening carefully, then without a single backward glance, he disappears inside.

The Chromatic does not proceed *in* so much as *down*. The cleft is less than a meter deep, but sinks some 20 meters below the surface. The characters must descend one at a time, and though the cleft offers many hand- and footholds, after five meters the air becomes steamy and the rocks slick. Characters must make a successful **Athletics** roll to safely reach bottom. Failure means the character slips and slides her way down (possibly knocking others loose as well), sustaining one Bashing Health Level in the process. A botch results in a Lethal Health Level and likely a broken bone. If this damage would kill a character, simply have her knocked unconscious for a few hours instead.

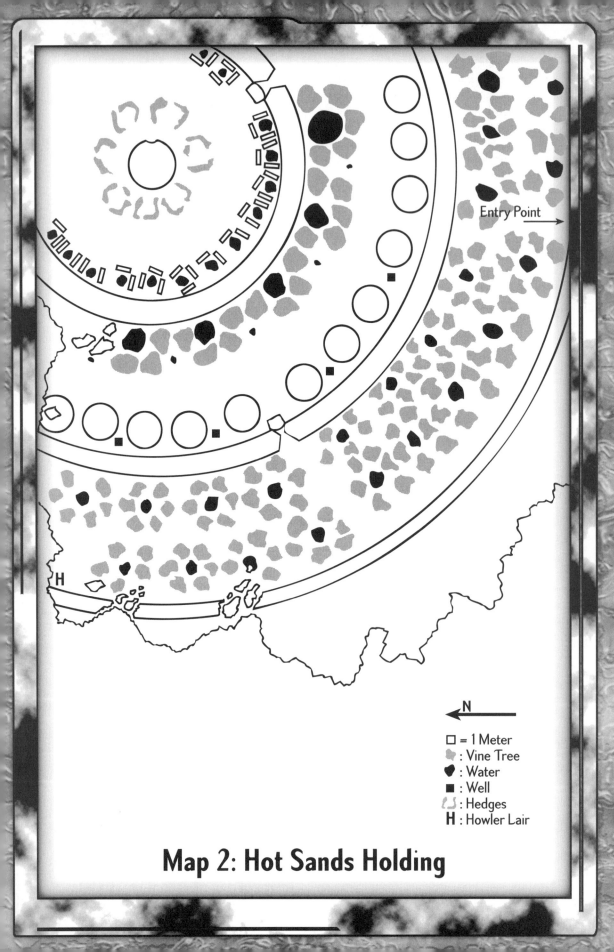

Entry Point →

N ←

☐ = 1 Meter
🔸 : Vine Tree
⬤ : Water
■ : Well
〰 : Hedges
H : Howler Lair

Map 2: Hot Sands Holding

The descent is like something from a children's fable. Entering the cleft from a brutal, desert-like environment, the characters pass bare granite, then steamy, slick rock, then their hands touch thick growths of damp, phosphorescent moss. Ten meters down, the air is noticeably thicker (and more humid), and lush, black-green vines cling to niches in the rock wall. At 15 meters the cleft widens and the characters can make out insect life moving amid dense, leafy growth in the eerie greenish light. At 20 meters the cleft reaches the base of a cavern wall, and the transformation is complete. Tall, thick vines rise like small trees; their runners weave together to form a canopy of sorts five meters high. Smaller, fern-like plants cluster at the bases of the vines, amid carpets of glowing moss and fungus. Somewhere nearby, a trickle of water mutters serenely over bare rock. The characters could be standing in the gloomy depths of a rain forest anywhere on Earth. Vermilion waits for the characters, crouching on his hindquarters in a bed of moss. His body language appears relaxed and assured. The Chromatic hero has returned home.

Inside Hot Sands Holding

The cleft deposits the characters at one end of the holding's outer wall (see map, page 92), and characters with **Science** or **Survival** determine immediately that they are in a partially collapsed cavern whose open area is approximately 30 meters across. Careful characters who study the area further (making a successful **Science** roll) see that the collapse was caused by an earthquake over two decades ago, and subsequent small shocks have brought down smaller parts of the cavern since then. If fact, the whole area is dangerously unstable and could completely cave in should even a minor quake occur. Only the very desperate would stay here for any length of time — making it an ideal refuge for the characters. The ruins of the city-fort have been left to the elements for more than 20 years, but inquisitive characters can still learn much about day-to-day Chromatic life by exploring what remains.

When the holding was inhabited, the area between the outer and middle walls was occupied by young and status-hungry Chromatic warriors in times of trouble, placing them between attacking forces and the rest of the fort's inhabitants. The perimeter of the wall was subdivided into sections with each section assigned to a specific dynasty to maintain and defend. Unlike in the middle and inner walls, no space was made for a gate in the curved, four-meter-high outer wall. Being adept climbers, the Chromatics used braided vine ropes (retracted during conflicts) to enter the holding.

The area between the outer and middle walls was thick with vegetation. Broad, flexible vine-trees were nurtured and braided together to provide sheltered hollows for sleeping at ground level, and platforms were positioned higher off the floor for early warning and general day-to-day activities. These vine-trees remain, clustered in vaguely hexagonal groups around shallow pools carved into the soft rock and filled with water. Each tree-cluster also connected to neighboring clusters by another species of braided vine to allow for swift movement overhead. There are at least 15 to 20 such clusters in the surviving section of the outer wall.

The shallow pools held up to six Chromatics at a time, and provided a source of water as well as a place for a brief social swim. (Chromatics are primarily land-dwellers, but they need at least some regular exposure to water to maintain emotional balance.) When the holding was under siege, the holes were stocked with fish to give the warriors a fresh food supply. Glowing moss, originally cultivated and encouraged by Chromatic gardeners to fill the areas with life-giving light, still grows abundantly in the present. Paths of smooth, white stones, laid years ago across the moss in ribbon-like pathways, still reflect the phosphorescent glow and gleam greenish-white as they meander through the undergrowth.

Four of the ground-level sleeping dens have large, thick-boned skulls hung by the entrance, their brows marked with the stains of a red-dyed petroglyph. They belonged to howlers, and were taken as trophies by the warriors who slew them. The petroglyph, when new, was a multicolored set of dye marks that gave the deed-name of the warrior who made the kill.

The dens themselves were designed to be low-ceilinged but broad, able to hold six to nine Chromatics. They were carpeted with thick, springy mats woven from plant fiber. A large wooden carving of a fierce-looking Chromatic still stands against the curving wall opposite the entrance, its body stained in numerous coats of faded dye. When first made and painted in phosphorescent colors, this "night guardian" stood watch to keep the spirits of darkness away while the warriors slept.

Small shelves in the dens contain clay pots and bowls, expertly glazed in swirls of vivid color. Some contain long-dried dyes; others hold dry leaves or bits of obsidian. Some contain pieces of eggshell.

(Older warriors would eat a piece of Chromatic eggshell before going into battle. They would do this for good luck and because they believed that the eggshell imparted the strength of youth for a short time.) Small globes of volcanic glass are set on shelves spaced evenly around the room; when the den was occupied, large glowworms would swim in the bowls and provide illumination.

Characters curious enough to scale the vine-trees find the platforms stable and more than capable of supporting a human's weight, though they have a disconcerting springiness similar to a hammock. Clay pots and small jars rest on shelves set into the vine-trees' "trunks." One particular egg-shaped bottle contains a thick, sweet-sour liquid: diggerbee honey. Adventurous characters who want a taste find the liquid to be surprisingly fresh and quite tasty — and capable of making the hardiest Legionnaire stupefyingly drunk. Another small jar contains bite-size bits of a reddish-brown bark that, if chewed, tastes extremely bitter and produces a powerful stimulant. Humans can chew the bark and avoid the effects of fatigue for up to 12 hours, though the juices are so acidic that it later causes nausea, stomach cramps and loss of appetite. (Characters have a +1 difficulty to all rolls for 24 hours after the stimulant wears off.)

A Hidden Threat

As the characters make their explorations, however, they are being watched. A pack of howlers equal in number to the entire team (including Greaves, Boehm, Blake and Vermilion) has made one of its rare forays into the upper caverns. This pack established a lair amid the thick vegetation of the holding's outer ring. What is more, two of the howlers are female and have recently laid clutches of eggs in a communal nest that the mothers take turns guarding. Howlers' highly evolved hearing alerts them to the characters as they enter the holding. As the characters work their way through the outer ring, the reptiles stalk them through the dense undergrowth. The howlers move stealthily in four-legged fashion, staying low to the ground and operating as a group. They watch for stragglers or loners in the team and ambush them, attacking in pairs in the hopes of a quick, silent kill.

A howler looks like a large, dark-skinned Chromatic. It takes a closer look (either strong lighting, which howlers don't care for, or two extra successes on a standard **Awareness** roll) to notice that howlers are actually rather different. If fired upon, the howlers retreat deeper into the undergrowth, split into two groups and come at the team from two separate directions. The vegetation provides ample cover for the howlers' movements, allowing them to creep very close to the characters before they attack.

The howlers are formidable hand-to-hand opponents. If the characters are too injured and exhausted to have the upper hand in the fight, you can have Vermilion urge the characters to climb the vine-trees where the howlers have difficulty reaching them. The instant Vermilion sees the howlers he blazes with rage, barking loudly and exhorting the characters to kill the creatures without mercy. The howlers attack fearlessly until all (except the one back with the eggs) are killed. If the characters climb the vine-trees, the howlers don't follow them up, but instead circle through the undergrowth, occasionally howling and uttering complicated series of high, unnerving barks to one another. The characters can snipe at the howlers from the tree platforms or evade them entirely by using the vine-ropes connecting the tree clusters to reach the holding's middle ring. Vermilion does his utmost to persuade the characters to kill the howlers, though. If questioned, he briefly explains the Chromatics' history with howlers and the threat they pose, declaring emphatically, "*black war for the beasts who threaten all people.*"

If the howlers are killed, Vermilion tries to convince the characters to explore the outer ring thoroughly to check for the possibility of a howler nest. The last howler stays with the eggs at all costs and defends them with her life. When she dies, Vermilion personally ensures that all the eggs are destroyed, stomping them to bits with his feet if his hands are still manacled. The brutality of Vermilion's behavior is a stark reminder of the human notion of "vicious Chromatic monsters." If the characters try to stop Vermilion from destroying the eggs, or question his actions, he becomes exasperated. The alien explains that this is a matter of survival; the howlers are beasts that threaten Chromatic safety and, therefore, must be destroyed. It is black war.

Vermilion calms down after he destroys the eggs. But the altercation with the howlers provides him with even more evidence regarding the differences between the behavior of humans and of other "beasts" he has encountered. Vermilion is on the verge of admitting to himself that humans act more like people — like Chromatics — than like beasts.

Further In

The middle wall of the holding has a single, narrow gate, blocked by a large stone that can be rolled aside to allow access deeper into the fort. Moving the huge stone requires a total of seven successes on a **Might** roll — obviously, several characters must employ teamwork to push the rock aside. The area between the middle and inner walls is less overgrown than the warriors' area outside. This allows for the construction of low-ceilinged, circular adobe-style storehouses. Each storehouse is marked with a colorful fiber mat by its entrance, identifying the dynasty that is responsible for its upkeep and the specific Chromatics allowed to take supplies from it. Inside, interior walls are covered in carefully crafted mosaics comprised of volcanic glass and polished stones. These mosaics show hunting scenes of Chromatics stalking and killing sea creatures (clearly relying on photokinetics to stun or blind their prey) and returning home laden with food. The various cool, dark structures hold empty glowworm bowls and rotted baskets containing fish bones.

Interspersed amid the storehouses are four holes, each a meter across, that drop down into darkness and echo with the sounds of rushing water. These wells sink 10 meters down to an underground river and provide the Chromatics access to fish and fresh water, as well as a last-ditch escape route from the holding in the event that the fort is overrun. Ferns have grown up around the wells, making them a hazard for individuals who aren't paying attention to where they're going. A character who's wandering around the immediate area must make an **Awareness** roll at +1 difficulty to see the hole before it's too late. If the roll fails, the character stumbles at the edge of the hole and must make a standard **Athletics** roll to grab onto the edge. It's difficult to climb out, since the ferns offer the only leverage — they're not deeply rooted and pull out of the ground easily. Getting out is an extended **Might** action, requiring three successes. (Other characters may certainly lend a hand.)

A hapless character who fails to grab the edge of the hole falls down a stone shaft. She has one last chance to stop her fall by making a **Might** roll (+1 difficulty) to press against the walls and stop. At this point, another character will have to lower himself into the hole on a rope and grab hold while others pull them both back out. If she fails that **Might** roll, the character is swept away by a swiftly moving river. At this point her fate is in your hands.

Some options in increasing amounts of danger: the character washes up in another cavern and must try to find her way back; she washes out in a rare above-ground pool dangerously close to White Rocks Holding's starport; she comes ashore inside White Rocks Holding where she's promptly jailed with the captive Upeo; she tumbles down a long waterfall into a howler den; she's bashed around in the raging torrent and finally drowns in darkness on an alien world.

After the first well is discovered, characters can sidestep the rest with little trouble. Also, psi techniques may be used to avoid the wells (**Danger Sense**) or to help fellow characters out (**Tow**).

There are more vine-trees growing in clusters against the inner wall and larger communal pools than there were at the outer wall. This part of the holding contained the bulk of the inhabitants: older warriors, elderly noncombatants, craftspeople (weavers, glassblowers, healers) and immature Chromatics not yet ready for battle. Colored mats fringed with long streamers hang from many branches, providing decoration and information about the Chromatics who maintained the area. Smaller pools near the inner wall are covered with a film of algae and contain numerous glowworms. These eel-like creatures are roughly 15 cm long and glow with a bluish-green light from the phosphorous deposits in their skin. There are bowls nearby, used to scoop up the worms and some water in which to keep them safe — a glowworm taken out of the water bursts into flame and burns up as the phosphorous deposits touch the open air. A character handling a worm without protection (vac-suit gloves) takes one Lethal Health Level from burns.

The Treasure of Hot Sands

Beyond this point is the holding's innermost wall. It's five meters high and topped with shards of volcanic glass. A single, narrow gate, similar to the one in the middle wall, is the only means in or out. The center of the holding is the last redoubt, the place where the dynasties would make their last stand, guarding that which is most precious to them — their children.

There is little foliage beyond the inner wall. Instead, the cavern floor is laid with soft, white sand and stone pathways that wind between small, steaming pools of water. These pools, large enough for two Chromatics at a time, fill through simple plumbing techniques from the water table below and are heated geothermally. Edged with square blocks of polished glass that reflect the organic light in warm tones, the pools provide a source of life-sustaining warmth for injured Chromatics. Small stone tables and benches surrounding each pool are for the healers' medicines and poultices. There are numerous jars and bottles set on these benches, along with dried-out leaves and medicinal bark. (Vermilion, if injured, examines these items, looking for useful medicines to treat his wounds. Chromatic physiology does not respond well to human medicine, and vice versa. Vitakinesis may be used to tend the alien's wounds, though.) The entire inside length of the inner wall is worked with intricate, colorful mosaics depicting great deeds of individual Chromatics — hunting scenes, battle scenes, clever thefts and the like.

There is a small amount of vegetation here — lush ferns and thick, hedge-like plants grouped into small, intimate gardens oriented toward the center of the holding. These are the Story Gardens, where Chromatics meet socially and exchange tales. They are also places of instruction, where Chromatic hatchlings are taught by their parents and in time, they are granted their deed-names. Small benches are clustered in a circle around a small pool lit with glowworms in the center of these gardens. Small chunks of what appears to be raw crystal are scattered around the gathering place. These pieces of crystal, if held up to a strong light, contain an iridescent, holographic image (etched into it by a Chromatic laser). These pieces of art depict individual Chromatics, animals — a few even bear the image of an Aberrant. The rocks are used as something like conversation pieces, passed around the pool to stimulate discussion.

At the very center of the holding lies a large, igloo-shaped earthen structure eight meters across, with a single small, tunnel-like entrance. The air inside is warm and dry. There are alcoves at floor level to hold large glowworm bowls. The center of the floor is a patch of fine white sand six meters across, kept at a precise temperature by geothermal heat. This is the hatching ground, a sacred site for the Chromatics, and it is normally watched over by a band of hand-picked warriors. The walls of the hatching ground are covered in intricate mosaics, showing the deeds of some of the greatest Chromatic heroes.

There are numerous places within the holding that would make a good campsite, though any character with **Command** realizes that the area within the inner wall is by far the most secure. While the characters tend to their injuries and rest,

Vermilion settles near one of the healing pools and watches the humans, his head tilted as if in thought.

Dialogue with an Alien

Vermilion has never been talkative, but perceptive characters (call for **Awareness** or **Empathy** rolls or use of **Passive Voice** or **Sense Emotion**) see that the Chromatic is clearly wondering about something. The sights that the characters have seen within the holding should give them plenty to wonder about as well. A successful **Science** roll indicates that the holding is quite old, perhaps a century or so. Many of the items scattered throughout are more recent — as little as 20 years past — but it all depicts a refined, late Stone-Age or early Bronze-Age people. How did the Chromatics go from clay jars to starships in two decades, all seemingly for no other reason than to find and kill humans?

It's important that this conversation, like the interrogation of Vermilion in *Colors of Sacrifice*, should not be a matter of a few dice rolls. This is a pivotal moment not only in the episode, but in the very Trinity Universe. Roleplaying this scene is essential to convey its importance.

The characters have an opportunity to talk with Vermilion now — really *talk*, as opposed to wring-

Truth or Consequences

Chromatic culture has so ingrained the concept of factual statements and honesty as a necessity to survival that the concept of willing deceit is unthinkable, akin to madness or idiocy. When Chromatics communicate, they generate a subtle hue that makes their statements unequivocal. This is akin to a human changing a question into a statement with a slight change of inflection.

When Chromatics use this hue, they are saying that the information being conveyed is utterly true and can be trusted absolutely. This is used as often for trivial statements ("This is absolutely true: I just caught a fish") as it is for important information. If the Chromatic does not use this hue, that means she is unsure about the veracity of the information. ("There were howlers outside the walls.") It is understood that she might be proved incorrect later, but in a way that she won't be accused of spreading deceit.

In short, the hue is not used unless the Chromatic is utterly certain of what she is saying. To use the unequivocal inflection and be proven incorrect later causes a Chromatic to lose respect and status. This instinctive aversion to deceit is why the Chromatic language equates lying with corruption and evil — hence the reason the Aberrants came to be called corrupters.

The translation device the characters use did not previously distinguish this hue inflection. It requires the intense conversation in Hot Sands Holding for the characters to finally understand this added element to Chromatic speech and culture and program it into the translation device accordingly.

ing information. The easiest way to start things off is to begin by asking questions about the holding — describing the functions of the healing pools, interpreting the mosaics and so forth. If the humans move the discussions to one of the Story Gardens, Vermilion is much more at ease. Moving on from more mundane cultural information, Vermilion finally explains about the Aberrants and their treachery in the Night of Lies, the seldom seen Bodiless Ones, the rise of the Witnesses and the capture of the Upeo. ("Behind the Scenes," page 80, contains the relevant information.) While the alien talks, he uses the unequivocal hue to color factual information (see the "Truth or Consequences" sidebar) — "This is the truth: The pools are used to sustain injured Chromatics."

After several sustained uses of this coloration, have the characters make **Awareness** or **Linguistics** rolls to notice the use of the inflection. If the characters question Vermilion about what the unequivocal hue signifies, he is confused at first. Then, as though explaining something to a hatchling, the alien instructs the characters in the need for absolute truth and the social ramifications of equivocal and non-equivocal information. Once the characters grasp this distinction they can program the Orgotek translator to add this hue distinction to its memory.

Some characters may remain suspicious about this and call Vermilion on it. The alien is bemused by such mistrust and calls the character "beast" — but almost in a joking fashion. If pressed, Vermilion grudgingly allows a telepath to sense for the truth regarding the hue inflection in Chromatic speech. Vermilion's mistrust of humans increases a bit due to this, but it does not appreciably hinder further dialogue with him.

This realization, as fundamental as it may be from the Chromatic viewpoint, provides the characters with a potent tool in dealing with Vermilion and learning more about the Chromatic race. Knowing that Vermilion is bound to be utterly honest in his answers should encourage the characters to ask a great number of questions about his people and why they are fighting their holy war. Similarly, if the characters themselves use the translator with the appropriate hue, they can be sure that Vermilion will take their words as truth.

If the characters don't rise to the occasion, the Chromatic himself begins the dialogue with tentative questions. Vermilion wants to know more about his captors, in hopes of answering his own questions about humanity. Steer the course of conversation so that all this information is covered, but don't feel that you must force things along a specific topic.

The Chromatic asks why the humans have returned to his planet, only to fight their fellow corrupters (the battle with Aberrants at the pickup point). The characters can explain to Vermilion the origin of the Aberrants and how they are not the same as humankind. They may well have said all this before, but this is the first time Vermilion has actually listened — well, *seen*, really — and using the hue of honesty provides the weight of truth.

Clever characters can explain the difference between humans and Aberrants by likening it to the difference between Chromatics and howlers. Chromatics and howlers share the same racial heritage, but are still very different beings. This places the distinction in a framework to which Vermilion can easily relate. If the characters are persuasive in their explanations Vermilion is inclined to believe them, though there is still a nagging core of doubt. Vermilion is fighting against generations of cultural heritage here, and he's not going to blithely accept all that the characters say even if they speak in truthful hues. After all, what is a corrupter but one who knowingly deceives others? In the end, Vermilion comes to believe that the Witnesses may simply be mistaken in what the Bodiless Ones told them about humans and corrupters. He's not sure what the message *should* be, but plans on finding out if he ever has a chance to speak with one of the spirit guides.

The more that the characters and Vermilion talk, the more relaxed the alien becomes. He may finally lead the characters around the holding and answers their questions, even letting them examine the hatching ground (though he squawks in alarm if any of the characters go plodding across the sands). One of the mosaics inside shows a Chromatic hatchling rearing out of his egg and attacking a huge howler. If the characters ask who that mural represents, Vermilion puffs out his chest and flashes proudly, *This is the absolute truth: That is me!* He regales the characters about his long and eventful life, finally giving them an idea of the high rank of their prisoner.

The characters can settle in, sharing stories and, perhaps, getting cleaned up in the hot waters of the healing pools. The team can use all the time possible to regain lost energies and recuperate. As isolated as the holding is, it appears that the characters could rest there indefinitely.

They get just eight hours.

The Dispossessed

Since being driven from their dynastic lands, the Chromatic chieftain Fireclaw and her followers (numbering 45 warriors) have lived like the lowest exiles, making quick forays below ground for food and shelter at night and moving across the surface by day. Only the chieftain's oldest enemies acknowledge the black war that the Witnesses have declared against her dynasty, but those are enough to keep Fireclaw and her band constantly on the run.

Prior to the humans' attack, the band of outcasts managed to avoid detection. But now, with hunting parties scouring the land looking for human stragglers, it has taken all of Fireclaw's cunning and illusory skill to avoid capture. A grim plan took hold in the chieftain's mind as she watched Earth bombers sow death and destruction among her people. More than ever, the Chromatic believes that the Witnesses made a mistake, thrusting the people into a war before they were ready. As night draws on, she and her band go to ground at Hot Sands Holding to plan their next move.

The outcasts enter the holding by climbing up the wells located between the middle and inner walls. (Chromatics find it much easier to use the wells for travel than humans would.) If the characters have been prudent and set watches, one moment the middle ground is silent and the next it is crawling with Chromatics flashing and barking at one another.

Fireclaw's band settles down to make camp immediately, not bothering to explore ruins they have visited many times in the past. The characters, behind the inner wall, go unnoticed. If they're wise, they make no threatening moves against so large a force. Vermilion recognizes Fireclaw easily and explains that she is the chieftain of a large and esteemed dynasty.

One disadvantage of a light-based system of communication is that generally one's conversations can be eavesdropped on from a long way away unless those talking intentionally make their speech small and soft. The team's Orgotek translator can convey the gist of what the Chromatics are discussing, but if the characters ask, Vermilion can translate the conversation much more quickly and accurately (keeping his "voice" low for the device to pick up, but so that Fireclaw's band doesn't see Vermilion's speech over the wall).

After sharing a meager store of food, the band gathers around its chieftain, who gives a speech.

The people, Fireclaw says, are in great danger. The corrupters have rained fire all across the land, killing many hundreds of Chromatics. The invasion of Earth failed, and now the enemy has come to wreak vengeance. The band's scouts saw many ships launch during the day to do battle with the invaders. Many hundreds more of their people might die. Fireclaw thinks that the Witnesses moved too quickly, blinded as they were by the brilliance of the Bodiless Ones. The Witnesses forced the Chromatic people into war before they were ready.

Fireclaw observes that Chromatics having to use captured corrupters to travel to the enemy is proof enough. If the Chromatics are meant to cross the "high-far-cold-dark-place," they will find the way within themselves, not by depending on the corrupt. The Witnesses must surrender their power over the people, Fireclaw declares, for their way has only led to defeat and despair. There must be no more invasion fleets, and the key to these fleets is the corrupt "high-far-steppers." Thus, these must be taken out of the equation. Fireclaw isn't foolish enough to think that her band can fight its way through White Rocks Holding, defeat the guard watching the captured teleporters and slay the Upeo. Instead, Fireclaw suggests a way that the high-far-steppers may themselves escape — by destroying the "above-cave," the tower that keeps the Upeo in place.

Fireclaw's speech provides the characters with a number of tantalizing facts: There are divisions within the Chromatic race who oppose the conduct of the war, and there are those who might support peace or at least a cease-fire. It also appears that the Witnesses are ordering a massive counterattack against the fleet, which is dire news indeed for the characters. As powerful as the UN forces are, how would they fare against hundreds of enemy fighters? The fleet could easily be destroyed, or at best forced into retreat. If the UN was going to use nukes, it would have to be soon. But if the characters understand Fireclaw correctly, it appears that the chieftain intends to attack the teleportation damper, shutting it down and allowing the teleporters to escape.

Fireclaw pauses to let her speech sink in, then tells her followers that the "above-cave" is heavily guarded and once the attack began, a large relief force would arrive in minutes. The chieftain as much as says that this is a suicide mission. The only thing the band can hope for is to shut down the system and keep it down long enough for the teleporters to escape. Without the Upeo, the war would be over, and the Witnesses would lose enough of their status to submit to the chieftains.

Several Chromatics glitter with disagreement. Some question the sanity of sacrificing themselves for the sake of corrupters. Others point out that the Chromatics are fighting a war of survival, not a negotiated battle between equals. Fireclaw is proposing a blue war tactic for the sake of beasts! How can they be worthy of such treatment? This sparks a debate that soon flickers throughout the exile band.

Opportunity Knocks

The characters are presented with a series of fateful choices. Fireclaw's plan could free the Upeo and, consequently, allow the characters to escape as well. *If* it works. Vermilion believes that the chieftain's plan is a vain one and tells the characters so. The tower is too well defended and Fireclaw's people are too poorly equipped. They would likely all be killed before they ever made it inside.

The characters themselves could aid the Chromatics, however. The characters' psi abilities, added firepower and technological knowledge might be enough to make the plan work — if they can convince Fireclaw and her band to accept their help.

There lies the challenge. As they overheard (well, over*saw*) the chieftain say, Fireclaw doesn't seem to have a problem with exterminating all corrupters; only in the way that the extermination is being carried out.

Vermilion, however, could go a long way toward persuading her. After all, he's already come to the conclusion that humans are more than beasts that should at least call for a re-evaluation of the conflict's black-war status. Using Vermilion involves another problem, though. As a prisoner to the humans, he is considered a thrall — bereft of status and respect. In fact, Vermilion the hero is *dead* for all practical purposes. Free of the restraint harness, Vermilion regains his status as a well renowned Chromatic hero — able to address Fireclaw as an equal. The characters would have to give Vermilion his freedom for him to speak on their behalf.

Despite everything that has gone between Vermilion and the characters, this should still represent a serious leap of faith. On a deeper level, the act represents a moment of truth for Vermilion as well, for if the characters show the willingness to place their lives in his hands, he is convinced that the Witnesses have made a mistake, and commits himself to ending the war. (If they already gave Vermilion

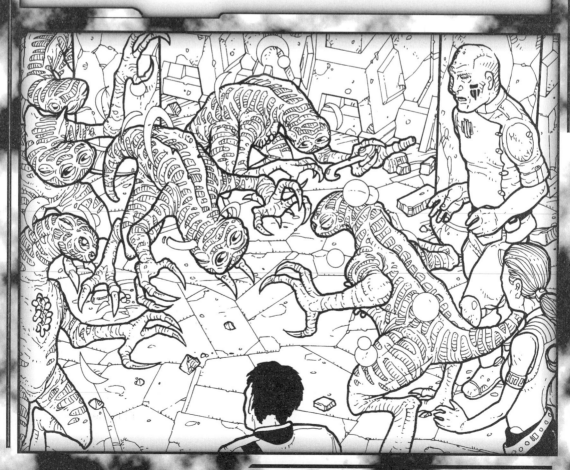

his freedom during the battle with the Seraphim, Vermilion is already at this stage.)

The characters should let Vermilion go, believing that any risk is worth the chance to free the Upeo and ensure the safety of the human race. Don't force them into it, though. If the characters refuse to notice how the relationship has changed with Vermilion and insist on seeing the Chromatics only as evil toadies, that's their choice. You may want to have Greaves or Boehm offer support in favor of the idea as a last ditch effort, though. (Blake thinks they're all mad for even considering it.)

The remainder of this section assumes that the characters free Vermilion. It may still be possible for the characters themselves to meet with Fireclaw without it degenerating into battle. If the characters are clever about it, follow their lead and try to entwine their actions with the information below.

Free of the restraining harness, the Chromatic tells the characters, "*This is the absolute truth: You have given me back my life.*" Then, glowing brightly, he steps through the gate and approaches Fireclaw and her band.

Vermilion's appearance causes pandemonium until Fireclaw recognizes her old ally. She greets Vermilion with obvious surprise, then watches the emerging characters with a mixture of wariness and bewilderment. Many of her band are much more straightforward, snatching up their weapons and glowing angrily. None act without a command from their leader, however.

It was one thing for the characters to convince Vermilion of the nature of humans and Aberrants; now they must win over a hostile chieftain and her followers. It is important to remember that Fireclaw does not have a problem with pursuing black war against humanity; she takes issue with the way that the war is currently being fought. Even with Vermilion on their side, you should push the characters' negotiating skills to their limits, relying primarily on roleplay to make their case before the outlaws. The characters do have two big advantages: Vermilion is putting his towering reputation behind them (which at least makes the outlaws willing to listen); equally important, the characters now have a strong understanding of the Chromatic language and can use the unequivocal inflection to state absolute truth.

Fireclaw is particularly open to the idea that the Witnesses may have made a mistake in interpreting the words of the Bodiless Ones. Many of the Chromatics are opposed to siding with corrupters, but so long as the characters are respectful, non-threatening and rational, they and Vermilion convince Fireclaw and a core group of followers. Once the chieftain and her lieutenants agree to at least include the humans in the attack on the tower, the rest of the band goes along with it — reserving final judgment until the humans follow up their words with concrete action.

Fireclaw says that the attack must occur that night since her scouts have heard large numbers of feet moving through the tunnels near White Rocks Holding. (Fireclaw and members of her band

Desperately Seeking Reinforcements

The characters might feel that even with the addition of Fireclaw's band, they may not have the firepower necessary to take the tower (and survive). One of the team might suggest looking for other ground teams stranded on the planet and enlisting their aid. It's your call whether such efforts are successful, but if you wish to bolster the characters further you can allow for a team of UN troops to go into hiding nearby. These soldiers are monitoring radio transmissions for news and can be contacted relatively quickly. Of course, the Aberrants are also listening in, so linking up with the other team might involve running a gauntlet of small Aberrant and Chromatic patrols unless the characters figure a clever way to communicate (perhaps something as simple as using a foreign language). There can be up to 12 troops in the UN team if you choose. Use the Soldier template in **Trinity**, page 306, for statistics and equipment.

can adjust the temperature enough with basic Pyrokinesis to protect the raiding Chromatics from the worst of the cold.) Chromatic hunting parties will blanket the area after dawn, and there will be no escaping them. No one, human or Chromatic, has more than 12 hours left. After that, they will very likely all be dead.

The Tower Raid

The teleportation damper is a piece of advanced technology provided by the Doyen that disrupts psi energy of the particular wavelength required to perform teleportation. The tower radiates a dampening field over a 1500 kilometer area as part of a relay network with thousands of other towers scattered across the planet. The entire tower is composed of biotech — from the hard carapace protective outer wall to the ribbed stairs — and has its own uniquely designed power plant, sunk 25 meters beneath the surface, which draws on geothermal energy.

Fireclaw knows that there are no living quarters in the tower; in fact, for all its 35 meter height, it has only one room, situated at the top, that contains the field-alignment systems. The tower does not contain the field generator — it *is* the generator. Unlike other Chromatic surface structures, the tower does not have a subterranean entrance; instead, a five-meter-high biotech wall encloses the base of the tower, and its wide gate is secured by a Chromatic retinal-print lock. Inside the walls lie climate-controlled barracks facilities for the tower's garrison and technical staff (see map, page 102). The garrison consists of 60 hand-picked warriors and the technical staff comprises five scientist-priests.

The damper is situated on a flat, alkali plain 10 kilometers from White Rocks Holding. There are no terrain features or cover for two kilometers surrounding the tower and there is a lookout posted on the top, making a stealthy approach extremely difficult.

The characters do not have many options for assaulting the tower. The alarm includes sending up a tremendous flare to which White Rocks responds immediately with its own, signifying a large relief force is on its way. The characters and their newfound allies must reach the damper unseen if they hope to avoid overwhelming odds. The walls are not unlike a bioship hull — smooth as glass and surprisingly slick. Unless there's a member of the team skilled in Telekinesis who can fly up to the lookout post, the characters must bypass the retinal lock to get their force inside. Once in, there's no time to waste. At least half of the garrison should be in their barracks out of the freezing air, so the team must rush past them into the tower, hit the control center, and then hold it for as long as possible until the planetary network overloads and fails.

What neither the characters nor their Chromatic allies know is that the tower has only two entrances — both of which are only accessible through the barracks. The good news, in a way, is that with all the Aberrants running around recently,

the Witnesses ordered the troops to remain on a 24-hour watch, leaving the barracks empty. There are 10 Chromatics at each entrance, 10 Chromatics manning the lookout posts and 10 at each of the three landings within the tower itself. (In each case there's one squad leader in charge of nine warriors.) If the characters can sneak within range, a clairsentient can examine the tower and greatly assist in planning.

However the characters plan the assault, the minute that shooting starts, the lookouts at the top of the tower flash an alarm to White Rocks. The characters then have 15 minutes to fight their way to the control room before the relief force arrives.

The tower assault is grim and bloody. The garrison is determined and loyal and fights to the last Chromatic, making its final stand in the control room itself. Don't pull any punches at this stage — the characters knew they would be facing forbidding odds — but Fireclaw's followers should absorb the lion's share of the damage, dying heroically so that the attackers can drive their way to the control room. Once at the top of the tower, the characters can see a glowing army approaching from the northwest — a thousand Chromatics, grouped by dynasty and blazing with the deed-names of their chieftains, sweeping across the plain at a dead run.

The human Storyteller characters — Clarence Greaves, Else Boehm, Marty Blake — can serve as sacrificial lambs during this scene if need be. Doctor Boehm can suffer a tragic death defending a character from a lethal shot. In a fine cinematic touch, the teleporter Greaves can die heroically in the control room to free the trapped Upeo. Blake, being a reporter, lives a charmed life — at most taking what looks like a mortal wound but carrying on to record the entire climactic scene.

By the time the last of the garrison falls, little more than a third of Fireclaw's followers remain, and many of them are wounded. The relief force from White Rocks is only minutes away. Now the characters have two objectives — shutting down the generator and holding off an overwhelming force of Chromatics.

Shutting Down the System

The generator controls are like nothing the characters have seen before; it is alien technology (Doyen) adapted for use by yet another alien race (Chromatics). Even so, there are some baseline similarities that seem to exist between human- and Chromatic-generated bioware. The hundreds of controls are painstakingly marked with colored petroglyphs, and a re-

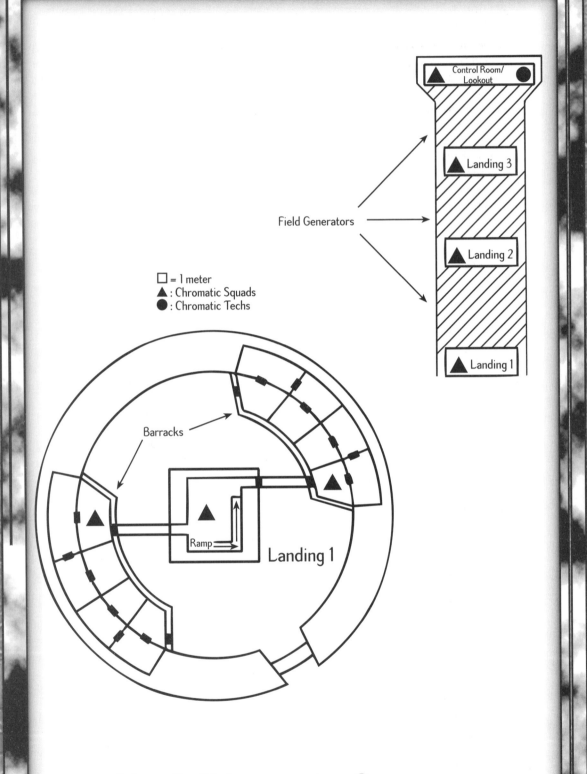

Control Room/
Lookout

Field Generators

Landing 3

Landing 2

Landing 1

□ = 1 meter
▲ : Chromatic Squads
● : Chromatic Techs

Barracks

Ramp

Landing 1

Map 3: Teleportation Dampener

sourceful character employs one of her Chromatic allies (probably Vermilion) to translate the controls while puzzling out their function.

The character must first employ **Science** at +2 difficulty to understand the overall setup. After that, the character must accumulate six successes on **Engineering** at +1 difficulty, making one roll a turn, to determine how to shut it down. Psi can be of tremendous help here. An electrokinetic using **Interface** must defeat an 8 fail-safe to enter the system. But once inside, the protocols are exceedingly simple and the field projection array can be shut down with a standard [**Psi + Engineering**] cross-matched roll.

Of course, a more straightforward character can simply start shooting control panels and ripping out cables. The generator fails after the control room loses 15 Structural Levels, but systems short in the process, giving off bioelectric bursts. Each person in the control room suffers a Severe level electrical shock in the process (see "Electrocution" in **Trinity**, page 254).

Once the damper is shut down, the rest of the planetary network overloads and fails. It takes an indeterminate time before the subquantum interference subsides enough to allow for teleportation. The characters must keep the Chromatics out of the tower long enough for this to occur, no matter the cost. Even if they wanted to, escaping from the tower isn't a feasible option at this point. The Chromatic army has arrived.

Defending the tower from them isn't quite as impossible as it seems. The main gate can be closed and the lock destroyed, buying the characters time while the aliens burn down the gate. Even after a hole is blown through, only two Chromatics can enter abreast, creating a choke point where a few defenders can hold out for quite some time. The Chromatic attackers don't have the luxury to come up with cunning strategies — they simply hurl themselves at the breach, attempting to force their way through with sheer numbers.

Play this battle for maximum drama, stretching the characters to the breaking point. The defenders wreak a terrible slaughter at the gate, but for every enemy that falls, another takes its place. One by one, Fireclaw's people fall until barely a handful are left and the characters are almost out of ammunition and psi energy. The Chromatic attackers pull back to regroup for the final push at an appropriately dramatic moment, giving the characters the chance to make their farewells to one another.

Give this a real Alamo feel. The characters have had a helluva ride, but it looks like this is it.

Then the shooting resumes — only this time it's coming from *outside* the walls. Bolts of plasma detonate within the Chromatic ranks. Soon, bioguns bark in reply. The Seraphim have launched their own attack. It is undoubtedly the first time that the characters are actually *grateful* to see a horde of Aberrants appear.

Unholy War

The Seraphim took full advantage of the chaos generated by the UN attack, staging several hit-and-run raids on Chromatic holdings and wiping out a number of isolated human assault teams. Years of cowering in the mountains and dreaming of vengeance has come to a head, and no matter how much damage is inflicted against them, it only whets the Aberrants' maddened appetites further.

The Seraphim grow ever bolder, a group of 50 Aberrants finally gather for a surprise attack on White Rocks Holding. Moving through the foothills in the pre-dawn, the corrupters come across the Chromatic army attacking the damper. The Aberrants conclude that the large alien force undoubtedly comprises much of the defending troops left in the area. If these Chromatics were destroyed, White Rocks would be all but defenseless. The Seraphim change course, attacking the Chromatics from the rear. Bolts of plasma wreak terrible damage in the aliens' tightly packed ranks. Other Aberrants rush into hand-to-hand range.

The Chromatic relief force suddenly finds itself pinned between the wall of the tower and the largest force of Aberrants encountered since the Night of Lies. Over a hundred Chromatics die in the first Aberrant volley, but the aliens stand their ground and turn to face the corrupters.

The characters can see little from their positions at the gate, only that their foes have suddenly lost interest in them. A standard **Attunement** roll easily registers the presence of a strong taint source some distance beyond the wall.

Anyone who makes their way up to the top of the tower has a panoramic view of the battle below. Half of the Aberrant force is holding back, hurling plasma into the Chromatics' rear ranks, while the other half attacks in hand-to-hand. Vermilion and the survivors of Fireclaw's band flare in anger and outrage at the appearance of their black-war foes. Where moments before the Chromatics from White Rocks had been bitter enemies, now the outlaws beg their leaders to join the fight against the corrupters.

This puts the characters into a curious position. The Chromatic army is fighting valiantly, but is suffering terrible losses. The Aberrants are the real enemy, the menace that threatens all life. Are the characters not obligated to fight that menace wherever it appears, regardless of circumstances? Vermilion tells the characters unequivocally that if the humans speak the truth about their hatred of the corrupters, then honor demands that they help in the battle.

Yet another surprise occurs at this point as the characters' radios crackle to life. Robert Linsey Marsden's voice calls out to the team's leader, asking for their situation. Marsden explains that the fleet is under heavy attack, but thanks to humanity's higher level of experience in space combat the Earth fleet has the upper hand. Despite serious damage, a group of frigates has fought its way into orbit and a drop ship with fighter escort is ready to pick up the characters. The cavalry has arrived!

The alkali plain provides more open terrain than the characters had in the first pickup attempt, so the ships can come right to them. The characters must simply relay their coordinates and four E-15s will pin the enemy down with strafing runs until the team can escape the tower and make it to the drop ship. The nightmare will be over soon.

Another Option Presents Itself

The characters have a chance to escape, but the incoming fighters provide a golden opportunity to change the way the Chromatics view humanity. If the characters fail to grasp the significance of what is happening, you can point out to characters with **Command** that the incoming fighters will bomb everything in sight if they're not given specific targets — Chromatics and Aberrants alike. It should be painfully obvious to the characters at this point that the Chromatics aren't the enemy, and blasting the battlefield out there is tantamount to slaughter. Not to mention that this could easily break the fragile alliance the characters have with Fireclaw.

Again, don't force the characters' decision, but make sure it's clear that the truly humane choice is to direct the fighters to target the Aberrants. From their vantage point atop the tower, the characters can call down pinpoint strikes against the Aberrants attacking at a distance, allowing the remainder of the Chromatic army to focus on the handful of corrupters fighting them up close.

If the characters go with this course of action (and those who don't should seriously re-evaluate where their loyalties lie), they must first convince Marsden of their plan. (Once again, let the characters argue their case; don't simply leave it to a die roll.) Marsden is willing to go with the characters on this, but they must sound sure of the progress they've made with Vermilion and his fellow aliens. Once Marsden gives the go-ahead, a character must stay in close contact with the fighters to provide appropriate coordinates to strike the Aberrants (via a standard **Command** roll).

In glorious, poetic fashion, the sleek E-15s streak into sight as dawn breaks over the scene. The ships reach the battle zone in seconds and fire smart missiles among the Aberrants. The explosions toss misshapen bodies about like rag dolls. A few of the Seraphim take to the air, but the spacecraft are quite maneuverable. One of the fighters is destroyed in the brief dogfight, and the others strike the Aberrant ground forces again.

The Chromatics, their backs to the wall (literally), keep their wits and pounce on their surprised opponents. In a heartbeat, the tide of battle turns. Soon, the remaining Seraphim flee into the

They Have Chosen... Poorly

If the characters, against all reason, elect to call down fighter attacks against both the Chromatics and the Aberrants outside the tower, the ramifications go far beyond merely blowing an indiscriminate hole for the team to escape through. Vermilion, Fireclaw and the surviving outlaws see the act as a betrayal. Worse, it reveals a willing deception on the characters' part. What happened to all the bold talk of uniting against the real corrupters plaguing both races?

Vermilion, Fireclaw, and the rest attack the characters without hesitation. Worse, if any of the Chromatics survive, word of the betrayal makes its way back to White Rocks Holding, and the Witnesses use it to cement their hold over the race. Any hope of further negotiations between humans and Chromatics is irreparably lost as the Witnesses now have conclusive proof that humanity is just another face of corruption.

foothills. The warriors watch in disbelief and consternation, many sinking onto their haunches to recover their breath or tend to comrades' wounds.

After the Battle

The E-19 lands on the alkali plain 500 meters north of the tower. Hundreds of bodies, Chromatic and Aberrant, litter the battlefield. Smoke rises from craters gouged into the earth by plasma and missile fire. An eerie silence hangs over the scene as the characters emerge from the tower alongside Vermilion, Fireclaw and a bare handful of the 45 Chromatics who fought with them.

A small group of Chromatics rises from the relief force and approaches the characters. They are stumbling and radiate confusion. They address Vermilion and Fireclaw, demanding to know what's going on. Their fellow Chromatics are baffled, not only that the two Chromatic heroes are in the company of so-called corrupters, but that the aliens just witnessed corrupters fighting corrupters. *"What does it mean?"* the translator interprets one Chromatic's plea to Vermilion.

The Chromatic hero looks at the characters, then turns to face his fellow Chromatics. Vermilion says simply, *"This is the absolute truth: The people have made a terrible mistake."*

The surprises aren't over yet, though. A burst of light explodes over the battlefield, followed by a noetic wave (have characters roll **Attunement** against backlash). A voice thunders in the heads of everyone present, human and alien alike: *BEWARE THE DECEIVERS! REMEMBER THE NIGHT OF LIES! DESTROY THE CORRUPT ONES!*

Flashes of terror and surprise glow from the Chromatics as they react to the appearance of a god.

The Bodiless One

The being hovers a few meters over the field, a seething two-meter-diameter sphere of plasma sheathed in telekinetic force. If the characters participated in the events of **Ascent into Light**, they immediately recognize it as the same kind of entity that possessed Robert Wei, the Ministry telepath — the Chromatics' god is really one of the Doyen! Its energies flare and seethe more powerfully than the one that controlled Wei, though. Tendrils of incandescent plasma leap and arc across its surface like solar flares, crackling like miniature thunder and filling the characters' nostrils with the reek of ozone.

The Chromatics are transfixed by the entity; even Fireclaw and Vermilion are stunned by the

sight. *THEY ARE CREATURES OF DECEIT, MY CHILDREN*, the Doyen telepathically declares, the mental word-pictures clearly indicating the characters themselves. *SEE HOW THEY HAVE CONTAMINATED YOUR GREAT HEROES? FEAR THEIR POWER. DESTROY THEM BEFORE IT IS TOO LATE.*

The situation teeters on a razor's edge. None of the Chromatics are willing to confront the Doyen, but the characters know the entity better. They can challenge the "god," arguing its assertions. ("We saved these people when we could have let them die! Explain that! We hate the corrupters as much as the Chromatics do! If you were really a god you would know that!")

The Doyen race operates with a different perception of time from such short-lived beings as humans (and Chromatics); they're much more deliberate, long-term thinkers. One of the ways this becomes apparent is in this Doyen's reaction to rapid-fire questions. The alien avoids the questions as best it can with more bluster and shouted commands. It becomes apparent to clever characters (**Rapport** rolls at +1 difficulty) that the Doyen has trouble adjusting to the fast pace, something that can be used to the characters' advantage.

Also, bear in mind that the translator device automatically relates the characters' spoken words in the Chromatics' light-speech. Not only does this enable the Chromatics to follow the dialogue, but it could be used to bolster the characters' side. The characters, supposed enemies of Chromatics, speak in the aliens' own fashion — why doesn't the Bodiless One, a spirit supposedly dedicated to aiding Chromatics, do the same?

Vermilion asks that very question (or supports one of the characters if she proposes it first). *Why is it that our "enemies" have taken the time to learn our language, but our gods speak with mind-shouts?* the Chromatic hero queries. *This is the absolute truth: These humans have saved my life many times. That is not the way of the corrupters. This is the absolute truth: They saved this army from the first corrupters. The Witnesses say that these newcomers are the same as the first corrupters, but they do not act the same. Why?* Vermilion does not glow angrily, but asks out of a sincere and obvious desire to understand the confusing events that have overtaken him. On the one hand, he has seen with his own eyes that humans and Aberrants are different, but on the other hand he is also witnessing the appearance of a *god*. He desperately wants to believe *something*, but is not sure what.

The Chromatics listen to their hero speak, then turn expectant eyes to their god. Be sure to convey the mood here. The Doyen faction influencing the Chromatics is so superior in its self-view that it assumes other beings must also recognize this superiority or be taught the error of presumption. Chromatics believe that their spirits of light are enlightened advisors and guides, not omnipotent rulers. Vermilion's status as a dynastic leader and proven hero gives his comments tremendous weight. His fellow Chromatics consider his questions valid and worthy of response from their god. Vermilion and the Doyen are considered by the Chromatics to be influential figures who should treat one another with deference. It is what leaders do.

You can have the characters make standard **Command** or **Rapport** rolls, or use **Mind's Eye** or **Sense Emotion** to perceive that the Chromatics only need another nudge to turn doubt into full-blown defiance against the Doyen. Bold characters can keep up the pressure on the entity, confronting it with questions about its conduct. This is the characters' only real chance for success, but it will likely end in the death of a key figure. Already thrown off-balance by the fast-paced events, the Doyen panics in its own alien fashion, focusing upon the individual that will make the best object lesson — the argumentative Vermilion. *YOU DARE TO DEFY YOUR GODS!? THE SERVANT THAT REBELS AGAINST ITS MASTER IS DESTROYED.*

With that, the Doyen unleashes a powerful cryokinetic strike on Vermilion. The proud Chromatic is mortally wounded, dying tragically at the "hands" of a Bodiless One in full view of many Chromatics. Each human character within two meters of Vermilion also feels the killing chill (taking one Bashing Health Level unless the character has appropriate psionic defense from cold), as does any Chromatic within four meters (taking one Lethal Health Level due to a cold-blooded physiology).

A perceptive character may try to save Vermilion before he's blasted. The most obvious way is to take the shot instead — active **Danger Sense** or an **Awareness** roll at +4 difficulty can pick up the impending attack in time to perform a single action. While it's clear that the Doyen is about to assault Vermilion, the individual has no idea what form the attack will take. There's no time to think, only to *act* — leaping in front of the Chromatic hero, shoving him forcefully out of the way. The

Telling it Like it is

It is crucial for the characters to be active participants in this scene. They should not sit back and let Vermilion ask all the hard questions. Emphasize roleplay and make the characters think on their feet. (They have the advantage of numbers against the menacing Doyen; the characters can take turns lobbing arguments while the rest think furiously.)

Vermilion cannot keep the Doyen off-balance on his own, and is soon drowned out by the being's telepathic tirade. The Doyen controls the exchange, quickly labeling Vermilion as mad, a pawn of the corrupters. The other Chromatics are certainly terrified when the Doyen strikes Vermilion down, but the aliens remain unconvinced that humans are any different than Aberrants. The words of one Chromatic are not enough to throw off the shackles of their gods, at least not at that moment. Once Vermilion falls, all the characters can do is run like hell for the drop ship in the few moments of confusion.

Things don't go nearly as well if the characters attack the Doyen when it appears. The being holds great influence over the Chromatics until it strikes down Vermilion; *then* the characters can gain a lot out of blasting away at the false god. Prior to that point, violence against the "Bodiless One" brings the wrath of the assembled Chromatics down upon the characters.

In the end, if the characters don't step in, there's no real hope for reconciliation. UN command decides that the aliens are intractable and the appearance of Aberrants requires decisive action. Nukes fall on Chrome-Prime (as alluded to previously). Millions of innocent Chromatics die, and the possibility of peace between humans and Chromatics is effectively lost.

On the up side, some of the Upeo do manage to escape, jumping out-system as soon as they gather the energy.

character then suffers Vermilion's fate (including the possibility of being saved by any docs on-hand as noted below), but the event shatters the Doyen's hold on the Chromatics. There's no explaining away what was obviously a selfless act on the part of the Chromatics' supposed enemy.

A vitakinetic character (or Else Boehm if you choose to apply Storyteller *fiat*) may try to save Vermilion by healing three Lethal Health Levels that same turn. This leaves Vermilion at Incapacitated, but alive. More that just saving the characters' newfound friend, this gesture goes a tremendous way toward enlightening the other Chromatics. Even if the characters cannot save Vermilion, showing obvious concern and remorse for the hero's death provides a similar impact. The supposed "corrupters" have saved, or tried to save, the life of a Chromatic who was struck down by one of the aliens' own "gods." Not only does this show that humans seem to be as Vermilion says, but also that the Doyen is not a benevolent spirit guide.

The being senses the empathic backlash from the surrounding Chromatics as their emotions turn from doubt to shock, dismay and anger. Although the Doyen has trouble adjusting to the fast pace of short-lived mortals, it isn't stupid. The alien realizes it's made a serious tactical error. Rather than compound it further, the Doyen decides that retreat is the best option.

The false god flares brightly, its telepathic shout drowning out all other thoughts. *WRETCHED CREATURES!* the Doyen proclaims as noetic energies coalesce around it. *YOU OPPOSE OUR WISHES AT YOUR OWN PERIL. YOUR DEFIANCE CORRUPTS YOU ALL. EVEN NOW, THE SEEDS OF YOUR DESTRUCTION ARE BEING SOWN. I HAVE NO PITY LEFT FOR YOU.*

There is a rippling flash as the Doyen vanishes, teleporting away. (This also shows that the teleportation damper has finally dispersed.) One by one, the Chromatics from White Rocks look to each other, then drop their bioguns and other equipment provided through the "wisdom" of the Bodiless Ones. The Chromatics gather around the fallen Vermilion, looking at the characters questioningly. The characters sense no hint of threat from the aliens, but instead feel tremendous doubt, shame, curiosity and loss.

This dramatic moment is rendered with cinematic precision as the sun finishes its climb over the eastern mountains. Brilliant light illuminates the scene — a gathering of races amidst the ruins of battle, a new beginning in the aftermath of tragedy.

Conclusion

A handful of heroic and dedicated humans have stood together against an entire world and triumphed. The Upeo are freed, teleporting from their prisons to places of safety, and the course of the Chromatic War has been profoundly affected.

The Doyens' scheme for controlling the Chromatics has been hindered greatly. Enough Chromatics observed the climactic confrontation between the "god" and Vermilion (and the characters) that the Witnesses' hold over the people is shattered. The Chromatics now have the opportunity to make their own decisions concerning the worth of humanity.

Hurried signals from the tower to White Rocks Holding spread the news of the battle and the confrontation with the Bodiless One. Other chieftains, hearing Fireclaw's testimony (and Vermilion's fate) speak out openly against the Witnesses. Over the holy seekers' objections, most of the Chromatic forces engaging the humans in space withdraw to Chrome-Prime. Not all of the dynasties are convinced, however, and the Witnesses remain committed to their black war. Accusations of corruption and treason fly throughout the Chromatic ranks, and political upheaval spreads across the planet as each side builds support for its cause.

Those Chromatics on the battlefield have no immediate interest in the characters, and Marsden commands that the team get out of there before the mood shifts yet again. The humans aren't stopped from boarding the E-19 and speeding off to *Chicago*. The characters have little time to rest, as they're pulled in to undergo debriefing. Marsden coordinates a teleconference among the fleet commanders where the characters' escapades on-planet are dissected to get key data.

After the characters receive any necessary medical treatment and eight hours of rest, they're at it again. Further debriefings, both verbal and telepathic, go on for hours to glean everything the characters have learned about the Chromatics. This is all passed on to the small core of scientists and scholars who accompanied the fleet, as well as to an *ad hoc* ambassadorial team led by Admiral Mkumba.

Aftermath

Once the characters have recuperated they're transferred to *Europa* to assist the UN commanders in establishing relations with the Chromatics. The characters are now the resident experts on Chromatics, after all.

Two-thirds of the fleet return to Earth with the wounded, and to spread the news of victory. Clairsentient scans have registered almost a dozen confirmed noetic fluctuations from within White Rock Holding — subquantum fluctuations consistent with teleportation. No Upeo have appeared to the fleet, but that's not surprising since the teleporters haven't gotten good enough looks at the ships to jump there. The clears think it's quite likely that the captive Upeo leapt in small groups, helping those without the energy or concentration to teleport. The projected numbers — based on these scans and input from Clarence Greaves — suggest that between 20 and 30 Upeo escaped Chrome-Prime. This accounts for about one-quarter of the entire Upeo wa Macho Order.

The characters have managed to reap some amount of personal status with the aliens (especially if Vermilion survived his injuries), and their recommendations to the Chromatics go a long way toward "handing off" human-Chromatic relations to diplomats. Finally, a month after the raid an official UN delegation arrives to relieve *Europa*'s exhausted crew, and the jump ship returns home to a heroes' welcome. The characters are celebrities throughout human space (especially if Marty Blake was rescued from the crash — he is true to his word, his exclusive footage making the characters household names for the moment). The UN honors the characters with the United Nations Freedom Medal at a gala ceremony held at Olympus.

It's not all victory celebrations and talk-show appearances, however. The characters have proven themselves to be among the most capable, resourceful individuals in all of humanity. The Æon Trinity, the United Nations, psi orders, governments and private-interest groups are sure to come forward with enticing offers.

These days, Earth needs heroes more than ever before.

Other Endings

Much of *Vermilion Falling* relies on characters making spur-of-the-moment decisions that decide the course of human history (no pressure!). The course of the war could take any number of alternate courses based on what the characters choose, and their future roles are inevitably shaped by those decisions. You can also alter events in such a way as to better suit your series.

• **The shell game:** Instead of being tied together in a mutually dependent network, you may assume that the dampening towers covering

Character Development

A player may spend experience points on his character to signify permanent benefits from recent efforts. Any Attributes, Abilities or Aptitude Modes that were used are obvious choices for development.

The Allies, Contacts and Status Backgrounds may also be purchased to indicate the results of intense involvement with the United Nations — or possibly even with the Chromatics, depending on how events unfolded.

The characters' public visibility is close to that of people like the proxies, the Pope or major media personalities. You may grant each character Influence 3 — if the character is already at that level, bump it up an additional dot. Conversely, a character who made a point of avoiding the limelight (even to the extent of "encouraging" Marty Blake to edit out that character's involvement) does not receive this Influence reward.

Subsequent episodes may result in the characters being approached for endorsements or other lucrative endeavors. This can enable a player to increase his character's Resources Background as well.

Chrome-Prime are discrete generators with interlocking fields of interference. This means that the dampener that the characters shut down only affects their immediate area, freeing a few Upeo held locally, but leaving others scattered around the planet. The characters and newfound Chromatic allies must launch a campaign to locate the other Upeo and assault the specific dampers restraining them. This sets up an extended military scenario that is also a battle of wits, as forces loyal to the Witnesses can keep the prisoners on the move in a cat-and-mouse tactic to foil rescue attempts.

• **The characters as ambassadors:** The tide of war has changed dramatically, but the leadership of the Chromatic people is still divided (and there are still Chromatic troops fighting the Karrooans in the Crab Nebula!). Tensions are headed for civil war, and humanity must take steps to create a political situation on Chrome-Prime that is favorable to Earth. The characters can remain behind on Chrome-Prime and work with Vermilion (if he lives) and Fireclaw's faction of chieftains to win other dynasties away from the Witnesses and end the war once and for all. Alternatively, the characters can return to Earth with Vermilion or Fireclaw and become embroiled in human politics.

• **Aberrants in the hills:** UN forces, augmented later by elements of the Seventh Legion, are charged with conducting seek-and-destroy missions against survivors of the Seraphim still lurking in the mountains of Chrome-Prime. The humans must work closely with Fireclaw's Chromatics to support their diplomatic efforts and not run afoul of dynasties still supporting the Witnesses. The characters can join the hunt for the Aberrants, perhaps with the goal of learning why they came to be on Chrome-Prime in the first place.

• **On the trail of the Norça:** You may assume that Luis Ulloa, the Norça extremist who had Vermilion kidnapped in *Colors of Sacrifice*, was not acting alone. The characters return to Earth and attempt to gather information on the Norça faction and its agenda.

• **Tracking down Upeo:** None of the teleporters fleeing Chrome-Prime appear on ships in the invasion fleet, since they haven't seen the craft well enough to jump there. Instead, the Upeo arrive at places where they have strong psionic impressions — their homes, special bolt-holes, the closed-down Upeo headquarters. The characters are assigned to recover these scattered teleporters so that humanity can learn more about the Chromatics and so that the Upeo can help in further causes. It's not easy to track down someone who can relocate at will, though, and it's quite likely that some of the Upeo don't want to be found.

Dramatis Personae

The following are general profiles for extras (e.g., Chromatic squad leaders, Fireclaw and her outcasts, the Seraphim, flora and fauna of Chrome-Prime) and detailed templates for important characters who appear during the course of *Vermilion Falling*.

Chrome-Prime Native Life

This section provides detailed information and statistics for some of the animals and plants that the characters might encounter on the surface of Chrome-Prime.

• **Rock devils:** These predatory reptiles hunt in packs of four to six and can be found both on the surface and below ground. They are large, monitor-like lizards, three meters from nose to tail, with long, curved talons and a narrow mouth full of teeth. Upon sighting prey, rock devils spread out and circle it, hissing threateningly. The reptiles pick the physically smallest target and attack it *en masse* from different directions. Their reddish-colored skin blends with the landscape and allows them to lie in wait for unsuspecting prey (**Awareness** rolls are at +2 difficulty to spot rock devils).

Relevant Traits: Strength 3, Dexterity 4, Stamina 3. A rock devil's tough hide provides [2/1, 0] armor. It has 4 Health Levels, and its claws inflict Strength + 1d10 L.

• **Sandeaters:** A huge, bizarre creature, the sandeater is egg-shaped and brown in color, reaching nearly eight meters in height and six meters in diameter at its broad base. Four thick, elephant-like legs sprout at equidistant points around the base of the sandeater's body and propel it along at a tortoise-like pace. The creature has no apparent sensory organs, though its tapering upper half is dotted with dozens of sphincter-like orifices. A single round mouth two meters across opens and closes like an iris at the creature's nether end, between its four legs.

The sandeater survives by drawing huge amounts of sand through its mouth, "eating" its way as deep as three meters into the earth. Then a complex set of sifting organs inside the mouth separates precious moisture and organic matter for digestion. The mouthful of sand then passes through the body, worked into small balls by means of a sticky, saliva-like paste, then ejected through the orifices at the upper part of the body. This also provides the creature with a natural defense mechanism against predators, firing these sticky, eight-centimeter "spitwads" at any creature that comes too close.

Sandeaters travel in herds of four to eight, frequenting the shady gullies near subterranean water sources. Any animal (or hapless character) who draws within two meters of a sandeater is pelted by sandballs.

Relevant Traits: Strength 5, Dexterity 1, Stamina 5. A sandeater's thick skin provides [4/3, 0] armor. The creature has a formidable 12 Health Levels, and its rapid-fire sandballs act at Accuracy 4 and inflict 4d10 B (an individual sandball simply stings, but dozens shot in a few seconds can easily inflict bruises). The sticky, sandy paste that covers the hapless target may cause discomfort and possibly harm her equipment, at the Storyteller's discretion.

• **Diggerbee:** This deadly insect is four centimeters long and vaguely resembles a wasp. It has an iridescent, almost metallic-looking carapace and a powerful set of complex, serrated mandibles. A diggerbee produces a metabolic byproduct from its abdomen — a sticky, reddish-amber resin with a bittersweet taste that acts as an intoxicant. Chro-matics consider it a great delicacy.

The diggerbee is nocturnal and nomadic, sheltering in dark rocky clefts or caves during the day — or in a victim's carcass. The insect is attracted to even the slightest scent of moisture. A diggerbee does not sting, but attacks its prey with its saw-like mandibles, burrowing as deeply as possible into the prey and feeding on the fluids within.

An individual diggerbee is killed easily with one Health Level of damage (Bashing or Lethal). The insect can fly up to 15 meters each turn and swarms in groups of 100 or more. The swarm has an effective **Awareness** 8 to sense moisture (from a natural spring to human bodily fluids) up to 1000 meters distant.

Roll 1d10 L per turn for each victim caught within a swarm. This damage ignores any defense and represents five to eight diggerbees that have burrowed deep into the victim's body — where they remain until removed surgically (or until the victim runs out of fluid).

The only way to repulse a swarm is to use attacks that diffuse through the air — mundane effects like sonics or flamethrowers or psi techniques such as **Hypothermic Blast**, **Heatburn** or **Static Burst**. These effects can also kill diggerbees inside a victim (although the subject also takes that damage). The swarm disperses once eight Health Levels of damage are inflicted.

• **Tangleweed:** This small carnivorous plant (two to four centimeters at its base with tendrils six centimeters long) wedges itself deeply into narrow crevices or holes, then spreads its powerful tendrils like a net. Small creatures that try to shelter inside the hole are enveloped and suffocated, then the plant draws nourishment from its prey's decaying tissues. Creatures too large to be killed outright are simply held in an iron grip until they succumb to dehydration. The plant favors narrow spaces to limit the size of the creatures it encounters, and to make the plant itself very hard to reach.

A tangleweed taking two Health Levels (Bashing or Lethal) releases its prey, although it's hard to damage the plant without also injuring the trapped victim (+2 difficulty to accuracy). Simply pulling the tangleweed free from its roots is surprisingly difficult, requiring a **Might** roll at +2 difficulty.

• **Desert belladonna:** This small, dark-green plant is similar to a cactus and grows in patches of 15-20 along the edges of gully floors, sinking taproots deep into the soil to hoard precious moisture. The plant combines water and sunlight to grow, not unlike photosynthesis, but the plant's metabolism creates an alkaloid by-product that if ingested dramatically affects the victim's brain functions.

An hour after ingesting water or plant material from desert belladonna, the victim feels highly alert and clear-headed, with improved recall and creativity (add two dice to all Mental Trait rolls). The feelings continue over a half-hour, then segue into vivid hallucinations and feelings of psychotic paranoia. (The added dice are lost and the subject receives +3 difficulty to all Mental Trait rolls, in addition to suffering whatever mental instability the Storyteller wishes to inflict.) The after-effects last up to 12 hours, but each hour a **Resistance** roll may be made at +2 difficulty to throw off the drug's effects. A botch can leave the character with a permanent derangement, at the Storyteller's discretion. Ironically, if the alkaloid were properly synthesized, it could be used to treat everything from senility to recovery from brain damage.

The Seraphim

The Aberrant cult that called itself the Seraphim traveled to Chrome-Prime after its leader, Uriel, claimed to have a vision from God that showed the way to "a new Canaan." The Aberrants found a harsh, rocky planet with a subterranean paradise — populated by packs of savage reptiles. Uriel told his people that the Godless creatures must be destroyed, and the Seraphim employed two tactics that had served them well on Earth: treachery and mind-numbing brutality. Twelve thousand Chromatics died in a single night, wiping out entire dynasties in the blink of an eye, but the savages refused to submit to their new masters. The Chromatics closed ranks and turned on the Aberrants with something akin to righteous fury. Sheer numbers, coupled with potent photokinetic abilities that the Aberrants had never encountered, allowed the Chromatics to kill more than a third of the Seraphim, including their egomaniacal patriarch, and drive the rest into hiding. Since that time, the Seraphim have lurked in the inhospitable mountains of Chrome-Prime, nursing their hatred and alert for any opportunity to strike back.

By the time of the UN assault, only four truly powerful Aberrants remain on Chrome-Prime. The remaining 200 Seraphim find their powers stunted by the taint that overwhelmed them. Storytellers should make the ranking Aberrants as powerful as they feel is suitable; the remainder can be built referring to the Aberrant template in **Trinity**, page 303.

Holy Fire: A small number of Seraphim have developed the ability to hurl what they call "holy fire." This manifests either as a focused laser (5d10 L), or bolts of hellish plasma (8d10 L, with a grenade-like blast effect).

Fireclaw

Fireclaw is a highly influential and hidebound chieftain known as much for her outspoken nature as for her ferocity in battle. Like Vermilion, Fireclaw earned her deed-name and status during the darkest part of the Howler War, fighting back the hordes of savage invaders.

Fireclaw initially welcomed the Witnesses and their gifts from the Bodiless Ones. She supported the holy war wholeheartedly against the hated corrupters. But as the war dragged on and Chromatic losses mounted, Fireclaw noticed that the Witnesses would not listen to the chieftains' advice. It became apparent to her that the priests were less interested in winning the war than they were in maintaining their own vast influence. When Fireclaw spoke out against the Witnesses and the way they were conducting the war, the outraged holy seekers declared black war on her. Since then Fireclaw and a core group of loyal followers have lived like exiles, while she looks for a means to break the Witnesses' hold on her people.

Image: Fireclaw is an older Chromatic, her powerful body is covered in old scars and shows the ravages of six months' existence on the surface of her world.

Roleplaying Hints: You have led your dynasty through the darkest times of Chromatic history, having proven your worth in battle more times than you can count. The corrupters must be rooted out and destroyed — there is no denying this — but the Witnesses' way is too hasty, too haphazard. The war must be fought by chieftains, and you will do whatever it takes to make that possible.

Nature: Judge

Allegiance: Chromatics

Physical Attributes	Abilities
Strength (Rugged) 4	Brawl 5, Might 3
Dexterity (Nimble) 5	Athletics 4, Firearms 3, Melee 2, Stealth 4
Stamina (Resilient) 4	Endurance 4

Mental Attributes	Abilities
Perception 3	Awareness 5
Intelligence 3	Bureaucracy 2, Engineering 1, Medicine 1, Survival 4
Wits (Level-headed) 4	Meditation 2, Rapport 1

Social Attributes	Abilities
Appearance 2	Intimidation 5
Manipulation (Imperious) 4	Command 4, Subterfuge 4
Charisma (Arresting) 4	

Aptitude: [Electrokinesis] Electromanipulation 2, Photokinesis 5; [additional Mode] Pyrokinesis 2

Backgrounds: Influence 5, Status 5

Willpower: 9

Psi: 8

Gear: Biogun (statistics are equivalent to L-K Vindicator 11 laser carbine), hunting knife, weapon harness

Special Abilities: Every Chromatic has the ability to generate lasers and disperse energy attacks. Used properly, the Photokinesis and Pyrokinesis powers described in **Trinity** are sufficient to create those effects. Below are two additional powers that every Chromatic has.

Thermal Sensing: A Chromatic uses the "eye spots" on its body to sense light and heat emissions, even those from another living creature. It's virtually impossible to sneak up on one of the aliens (think of the being in the movie *Predator*, except with 360° perception). A Chromatic is allowed an **Awareness** roll no matter from what direction a target approaches. If successful, the alien perceives the thermal signature and may react appropriately. Heat suppressants (such as flame-retardant foam) apply a +3 difficulty to **Awareness** rolls.

Blending: As part of its photokinetic mastery, a Chromatic can manipulate light to become virtually invisible. Spend a **Psi** point and roll **Psi**; each success equals a difficulty added to all **Awareness** rolls made to perceive the Chromatic. Blending lasts for a number of minutes equal to the successes rolled.

Chromatic Warriors

Warriors are split in a five-to-one ratio between troopers and squad commanders. Use the Chromatic template in **Trinity**, page 306, for the troopers. Squad leaders' statistics are generally superior to that template, but do not attain the level listed here for Fireclaw or for Vermilion (see page 53). The main distinction between troopers and commanders is that the latter demonstrate the proper combination of innovative thinking, solid tactical planning and unswerving loyalty to superiors.

Howlers

In the early days of Chromatic evolution, not long after the species developed from deep-sea predators to amphibians, a series of geological upheavals isolated one of the race's burgeoning species. The small underground sea that had sustained them was rendered uninhabitable, but instead of slowly dying out, these beings managed to adapt to their new environment, becoming strictly land-dwelling reptiles. The howlers evolved parallel to the Chromatics, existing in deep tunnels that kept them separate from their cousins for millennia. The demands of their new existence favored physical power over intelligence, retarding their noetic development and stimulating echolocation abilities and verbal rather than visual communication.

After the Howler War, the Chromatics used the weapons provided by the Witnesses to drive the howlers to near-extinction. The few that remain linger in the deepest tunnels of Chrome-Prime, but packs make rare forays into the upper caverns to kill and eat their cousins.

Image: Howlers look similar to Chromatics, though the former are uniformly larger and more heavily muscled. Howlers' fore and hind limbs are equal in proportion and allow for two- or four-legged movement, and their extremities are tipped with thick, curved claws. The beings have also retained a full, thick-bodied tail, adding balance for running and leaping. Their hide still glows occasionally in mottled shapes, but has thickened to provide extra protection from other predators. Howlers are excellent runners but poor climbers, unlike their cousins. They are entirely carnivorous, and their furious metabolism drives the creatures to hunt and feed four to six times a day. They are especially attracted to the flesh of Chromatics.

Roleplaying Hints: Howlers have little more than rudimentary intelligence but they possess great animal cunning. They don't know anything about the war between humanity and Chromatic, and wouldn't care if it was explained to them. Indeed, howlers would much rather chew on the instructor's meaty thigh than listen.

Nature: Bravo

Allegiance: The pack

Physical Attributes	Abilities
Strength (Powerful) 4	Brawl 3, Might 2
Dexterity (Quick) 4	Athletics 3, Stealth 4
Stamina (Tenacious) 5	Endurance 2

Mental Attributes	Abilities
Perception 3	Awareness 3
Intelligence 1	Survival 4
Wits 2	

Social Attributes	Abilities
Appearance 1	Intimidation 5
Manipulation 2	
Charisma 1	

Aptitude: Howlers are psionically latent, but do not manifest any Aptitudes. A rare few might manifest one or two dots in Photokinesis.

Backgrounds: None of note

Willpower: 4

Psi: 2

Gear: None

Special Abilities: Howlers have sharp claws that inflict Strength + 3d10 L damage. Their naturally thick hide provides [2/2, 0] armor. Further, howlers have developed a highly sensitive echolocation ability. For the purposes of this episode, consider them to have the **Sense Mastery** and **Danger Sense** psi powers (see **Trinity**, page 206-207). The howlers don't use Psi to power them, though; instead, they sustain a continual series of hypersonic chirps, not unlike a bat does.

The "Bodiless One" (a.k.a. Doyen)

A Doyen's personality is utterly inhuman. It is part of a nigh-immortal race that measures time and reality in a very different fashion from humanity. Although a master of viewing every angle of a situation and subsequently planning for a desired course of action, a Doyen is not naturally inclined to react swiftly to things. Instead, it prefers to ponder every element first. As a result, a Doyen does not care to present itself to other races. It is much better off staying behind the scenes, nudging the other races through subtlety and finesse.

Image: A two-meter diameter sphere of telekinetic force containing a kind of plasmic gel. The Doyen seems to be a kind of smoky, viscous cloud that crackles with bioelectrical energy. All in all, the sight is quite alien and rather disturbing.

Roleplaying Hints: You have lived far longer than these upstart races. You are confident that the goal your faction strives for — total eradication of the taint and all those who carry it — is for the good of the universe. It is galling when your pawns, these lesser races, presume to question the wisdom of your actions. They know nothing of the greater events taking place in the universe — their minds are too puny to comprehend it all. It is in their best interests for you to guide their future course, whether they know it or not.

Nature: Alien

Allegiance: Doyen

Physical Attributes	Abilities
Strength (Powerful) 4	Brawl 4, Might 3
Dexterity (Fast) 5	Athletics 4, Legerdemain 3, Stealth 4, Survival 5
Stamina (Resilient) 5	Endurance 4, Resistance 4

Mental Attributes	Abilities
Perception (Observant) 5	Awareness 5, Investigation 1
Intelligence (Rational) 5	Academics 3, Bureaucracy 4, Engineering 5, Intrusion 3, Medicine 4, Science 5
Wits (Cunning) 4	Meditation 5, Rapport 3

Social Attributes	Abilities
Appearance (Disturbing) 4	Intimidation 5
Manipulation (Arrogant) 4	Command 5, Subterfuge 4
Charisma 3	Etiquette 3, Perform 2

Willpower: 9

Psi: 9

Backgrounds: Allies 5, Cipher 5, Contacts 3, Followers (Chromatics) 5, Influence (Chromatics) 5, Status (Doyen) 3

Equipment: None

Special Abilities: The Doyen manifests its Physical Attributes as focused Telekinesis.

Psi Mastery: Doyen have powerful natural psionic abilities. Consider that the creature has each Telepathy Mode at 5; each Biokinesis, Psychokinesis and Vitakinesis Mode at 4; and each Clairsentience and Electrokinesis Mode at 3.

Reduced Damage: All mundane attacks (Bashing *and* Lethal) inflict half damage after soak (round down). Psionic attacks are applied normally.

Psi Pool: As Doyen are composed of concentrated psi energy, the alien has a significant amount of subquantum power to throw around. The Doyen starts with 25 current Psi to spend, and can make a Psi-recovery roll once every 15 minutes.

Else Boehm

Else is a 27-year-old Æsculapian serving out a four-year hitch as a combat medic in the UN military. As a first-year medical student in Heidelberg, her latent psionic ability was detected by a visiting member of the Vitakinesis Order. Boehm took the opportunity to undergo the Prometheus Effect without hesitation. Upon graduating from training at Montressor, the German-born vitakinetic opted for military duty over a clinic residency because she wanted the challenge of treating patients in the most difficult of situations. Operating as an in-flight medic on a UN drop ship, the raid on Chrome-Prime is Boehm's first exposure to the pressures of a war zone.

Image: Else Boehm is square-shouldered and fit, with strong-boned features that are more handsome than beautiful. Her vivid blue eyes and natural poise convey an aura of self-assurance and professionalism, and her tall, lithe physique has the grace of a dedicated athlete. Else's manner is generally direct and businesslike, accented with brutal honesty and a sharp wit. With patients, however, she is warm and compassionate, comforting the injured with good humor and natural charm.

Roleplaying Hints: You are a highly capable psion and a skilled medic, and enjoy situations that challenge your abilities. You are eager and enthusiastic, facing difficult situations with good humor

and unflagging determination. Conversely, your intense and caring nature has no patience for foolishness or vanity, and self-centered or pretentious individuals become quick targets for scathing sarcasm. Colleagues have branded you a thrill-seeker or an adrenaline junkie because of your drive to hone your skills under the most difficult of conditions. The way you see it, if you can save lives hanging upside-down on a sheer cliff face in a raging storm, it means that you can make a difference for people anytime, anywhere.

Nature: Caregiver
Allegiance: Æsculapian

Physical Attributes	Abilities
Strength 3	Might 1
Dexterity 3	Athletics 2, Drive 1, Firearms 2
Stamina (Unflagging) 4	Endurance 1
Mental Attributes	**Abilities**
Perception 2	Awareness 1
Intelligence (Sharp) 4	Academics 3, Bureaucracy 1, Linguistics (French, English) 2, Medicine 3, Science 2
Wits 3	Meditation 2, Rapport 2
Social Attributes	**Abilities**
Appearance (Striking) 4	
Manipulation 2	Command 2
Charisma 3	

Aptitude: [Vitakinesis] Iatrosis 3, Mentatis 2
Backgrounds: Contacts 2, Resources 3, Status (Æsculapians) 2
Willpower: 6
Psi: 5
Gear: L-K Avenger 11mm heavy autopistol, medkit, hunting knife, vac suit

Marty Blake

Marty Blake is a popular talking head on the "hard-hitting, issues-oriented" media hype holoshow called *HotSpot*. Intense and slightly manic (think Quentin Tarantino gone Establishment), Blake saw the UN mission to Chrome-Prime as his ticket to stardom. With the networks keeping valuable commodities like Cori Heisler back on Earth and out of harm's way, Blake obtained permission to travel with the fleet — ostensibly to interview the UN high command. Once on board he managed to bribe his way into a jump seat on one of the combat drop ships so he could be closer to the action.

Image: Marty is young and whipcord-thin, with a slightly receding hairline and no concept of personal space. His movements are jerky and energetic,

and when he isn't conducting interviews he chatters about everything and everyone around him.

Roleplaying Hints: You are the next Cori Heisler. You are the future of holonews, and once you get back to Earth with your exclusive report you're going to take OBC by storm! Can you say corner office?

Nature: Conniver
Allegiance: OBC

Physical Attributes	Abilities
Strength 2	
Dexterity 3	Athletics 1, Drive 2, Legerdemain 3, Pilot 1
Stamina 2	

Mental Attributes	Abilities
Perception 3	Awareness 2, Investigation 4
Intelligence 2	Academics 2, Bureaucracy 2, Engineering 3, Intrusion 2
Wits (Shrewd) 4	Rapport 3

Social Attributes	Abilities
Appearance 3	Style 2
Manipulation 3	Interrogation 4, Subterfuge 2
Charisma (Charming) 4	Etiquette 2, Perform 3, Savvy 3

Backgrounds: Contacts 4, Resources 3, Status (OBC) 3
Willpower: 6
Psi: 1
Gear: Biocam, vac suit, vocoder (Chinese, French, German, Portuguese, Swahili)

Technology

- **Zip-Strip:** This is the Post-It note of the future, a simple re-usable polymer strip with embedded circuitry. Each Zip-Strip is 5 cm x 10 cm and can be folded as easily as a piece of paper. It can be run through a minicomp printer, the computer triggering the basic circuits to "print" a new message each time. Each Zip-Strip is good for dozens of messages before the circuitry degrades. (It could likely be made even more durable, but then the Zip-Strip people wouldn't get enough repeat sales to stay in business.)

Tech: Ω, Mass: Negligible, Cost: • (packet of 50)

- **RATRI (Sedative for Chromatics):** This is the most recent version of a Chromatic sedative developed by human science. (The name is an acronym for the chemical formula.) One dose renders a Chromatic immobile for eight hours. (If you want a little added complexity, roll Stamina for a dosed alien. Duration is then nine hours minus the successes rolled. On a botch, the Chromatic reacts badly, dying on a failed second Stamina roll.) RATRI may be fired in dart form instead of being applied through an injector; dart-shells, compatible with the Stavros .00 Shotgun, are available (each shot delivers one dose). Operation Safeguard has an effectively unlimited supply of RATRI, including dart-shells and shotguns. The Norça-hired mercs' doses must be administered via hypodermic.

Tech: Ω, Mass: Negligible, Cost: Not available commercially

- **Chromatic Restraint Harness, Mark II:** This is an updated version of the harness first seen in **Ascent into Light**. It is a much less invasive and onerous device than the original, simply leeching off the energies a Chromatic needs to gather in order to activate his powers. It does not have the hood or the random light-effects of the original. It locks around a Chromatic's torso via three small bands and can only be unlocked with the correct key. The lock is positioned in the small of the back, unreachable by the Chromatic wearing it. Operation Safeguard has one for Vermilion, and one backup.

Tech: Ψ, Mass: 3, Tolerance: n/a, Cost: Not available commercially

- **Biocam:** The biocamera is a favorite of action photographers and news-hounds who value the freedom of movement the camera provides and the sensitive biological interface that allows precise tuning of camera angle and focus with nothing more than a twitch of the eye muscles. The unit weighs 1.5 kilograms and is form-fitted to ride on the user's shoulder. A small control lead adheres to the temple and picks up neural impulses that direct eye movement. The holographic camera, mounted on a biomechanical gimbal, follows the owner's eye movements, providing close ups in response to a slight squint, etc. The biocam's memory can execute a routine of up to 24 preprogrammed visual effects, and has an onboard storage of 12 hours' holographic footage.

The device must receive a nutrient injection every two days to sustain internal power. If it goes three days without an injection, the biocam shuts down into self-imposed stasis.

If formatted to the user, the biocam can be directed to orient and focus independent of the direction the user faces. The user must concentrate to keep this up (+1 difficulty to other actions).

Tech: Ψ, Mass: 1.5 kg, Tolerance: •, Cost: •••

- **Bakuhatsu E-19 Stealth Drop Ship:** The E-19 is a specialized hybrid craft designed for the rapid deployment of personnel from orbit to ground targets. It is fast and hard to detect, but poorly armed and armored. It can carry up to 10 people with typical field equipment, including vac suits if necessary. Sensor detection is extremely difficult, requiring two extra successes. Since it is a delicate vehicle, all repair times on the E-19 are tripled.

VT: Hybrid
Tech: Ω

CS: Mach 2.3
TS: Mach 4
VS: 4
Handling: +3
Mass: 25
Cost: Not available commercially
Armor: 2 [5]
Weapons: Front-mounted light laser cannon (Accuracy +2, Damage: 5d10 [5] L); two smart missiles (Accuracy: +3, Damage: 10d10 [15] L)

ALIEN ENCOUNTER™
INVASION

Credits

Writers: Jonathan Woodward (*Colors of Sacrifice*) and Michael Lee (*Vermilion Falling*)
Developer: Andrew Bates
Editor: Cary Goff
Vice President in charge of Production: Richard Thomas
Art Director: Aileen E. Miles
Cover Art: David Seeley
Front & Back Cover Design: Aileen E. Miles
Layout and typesetting: Aileen E. Miles
Artists: Robert Dixon, Langdon Foss, Jeff Holt, Matthew Milberger, Steven Otte, Jeff Rebner

Author Dedications

Jonathan Woodward: To my father, who first introduced me to science fiction.

Michael Lee: To Janet, for inspiration, love, and patience.

735 PARK NORTH BLVD.
SUITE 128
CLARKSTON, GA 30021
USA

CURRENT TITLES AVAILABLE FOR TRINITY.

TRINITY ($29.95) — Your adventures in the 22nd century begin here.

HIDDEN AGENDAS ($14.95) — Storyteller screen and supplement.

TRINITY TECHNOLOGY MANUAL ($15.95) — This book is more than just a list of cool gadgets, powerful weapons and amazing vehicles. The **Technology Manual** also shows how all these wondrous inventions and innovations have changed life in the 22nd century.

PSI ORDER/REGION BOOKS — A sourcebook series that explores the various psion groups and the region each influences.

TRINITY: LUNA RISING ($17.95) — **Luna Rising** covers the enigmatic clairsentients of ISRA and the many colonies of the Moon.

TRINITY: AMERICA OFFLINE ($17.95) — Takes a look at the electrokinetics of Orgotek and their dealings with the fascist Federated States of America.

TRINITY: SHATTERED EUROPE ($19.95) — Details both the Æsculapian psi order and the war-torn continent of Europe. December 1999.

FIELD REPORTS — "Minibooks" or short, full-color sourcebooks that fill in critical corners of the Trinity Universe.

FIELD REPORT: EXTRASOLAR COLONIES ($4.95) —The current condition of the orphaned space colonies.

FIELD REPORT: ALIEN RACES ($4.95) — Information on the Chromatics, the Qin and the Coalition races.

THE **DARKNESS REVEALED** TRILOGY — This series of adventure books reveals the answers to some of the greatest mysteries in the Trinity Universe.

1. DARKNESS REVEALED: DESCENT INTO DARKNESS ($15.95) — Your characters investigate rumors of disappearances and bizarre experiments. The truth is more shocking than anyone could imagine.

2. DARKNESS REVEALED: PASSAGE THROUGH SHADOW ($15.95) — Pursuing rogue psions, the characters are swept up in affairs that threaten to tear apart human society!

3. DARKNESS REVEALED: ASCENT INTO LIGHT ($15.95) The characters are center-stage, venturing into deep space in search of the final truth to the many mysteries and conflicts that stagger humanity.